MW00710847

The Conveyance

By

Brian W. Matthews

JournalStone
San Francisco

JOURNALSTONE
YOUR LINK TO ARTISTIC TALENT

Copyright © 2016 by Brian W. Matthews

All rights reserved. No part of this book may be used or reproduced by any means, graphic, electronic, or mechanical, including photocopying, recording, taping or by any information storage retrieval system without the written permission of the publisher except in the case of brief quotations embodied in critical articles and reviews.

This is a work of fiction. All of the characters, names, incidents, organizations, and dialogue in this novel are either the products of the author's imagination or are used fictitiously.

JournalStone books may be ordered through booksellers or by contacting:

JournalStone
www.journalstone.com
The views expressed in this work are solely those of the authors and do not necessarily reflect the views of the publisher, and the publisher hereby disclaims any responsibility for them.

ISBN: 978-1-945373-00-8   (sc)
ISBN: 978-1-942712-81-7   (ebook)

JournalStone rev. date: June 17, 2016

Library of Congress Control Number: 2016939785

Printed in the United States of America

Cover Art & Design: Chuck Killorin
Images: A derivative of a photo by Ales Krivec, unsplash.com - A derivative of a photo by Christopher Campbell, unsplash.com - A derivative of a photo by Wil Stewart. CC0, unsplash.com

Edited by: Aaron J. French

The Conveyance

For my mom, whose years of unwavering support and love have helped make me the man I am today.

Chapter One

"I can't imagine how difficult your life's been," I said to the rail-thin boy slouched in the chair opposite mine. At twelve, he wore the characteristic sneer of a child who knew little about the world but hadn't failed enough times to realize it.

Doug Belle didn't respond, not that I expected him to. The question had been a trial balloon, my way of gauging his willingness to converse. It worked about half the time. This wasn't one of them.

"Fighting," I said. "Not listening to your teachers. At risk for failing classes. Quite a change for you, if I'm not mistaken."

I paused, letting the message sink in: I already knew something about you, we didn't have to start from scratch. I left out that I also knew about his other, more serious issues: tendencies towards self-abusive behavior, occasional property destruction, two episodes of running away. Important as they were, they would have to wait. I needed to build a rapport first.

So I waited.

Silence burned the long minutes to ash.

I let the disquiet to play out. From an early age, parental interactions and social norms conditioned us to converse, to follow the ritual back-and-forth pattern of communication, and long periods of silence tended to make us anxious. That, in turn, prompted us to say something—anything—to fill the void.

Another trick, if you will. A way of encouraging patients to open up.

It also failed.

Time to change tactics, see if a little empathy would help.

"A lot's changed. New home, new school. Forced to make new friends while leaving the old ones behind. Nobody likes having to do that."

Doug sat, head down, arms clenched over his chest. One leg kicked back and forth, the heel of his sneaker smacking against the sofa.

Bang bang bang

Neither of us spoke, conscripted soldiers in a wordless war. But like a man defending his native country, I had an advantage: I knew the terrain. I knew every treacherous drop-off, every false turn, every dead end. Eventually, I would win. Not that victory would come easily. A fourteen-year-old girl I'd treated for an eating disorder sat through six sessions before uttering her first word. She was a tough nut. I liked her.

I was beginning to like Doug, too.

That didn't mean I wanted to spend the next few sessions playing Easter Island with him, staring at one another like great stone statues. I reached into my desk, withdrew a handful of small, squarish objects wrapped in white wax paper and covered with blue and red lettering. I unwrapped one and popped the pink tablet into my mouth.

Bubble gum, and not just any kind of bubble gum.

Bazooka bubble gum.

I chewed loudly, waiting.

Bang bang bang

The cloying smell of sugar filled my office. Some in my field might have called this tactic immature, or even unfair. Perhaps they were right. But to me it was more about encouraging kids to open up than quibbling about the method used. It was, after all, only bubble gum. And sometimes a cigar really was just a cigar.

Bang bang bang

Bang bang

Bang

Doug's defiance wound down like a pendulum running out of time, until his jean-clad leg hung motionless over the edge of the sofa. He fidgeted a little—reluctant to give up the fight, no doubt. His shoulders gradually unclenched. His hands, which had been tight balls of anger, opened, and he wiped his sweaty palms on his shirt.

That was all he would allow. His head remained firmly down, his eyes averted.

I held out my hand. "Care for one?"

No response—then, a slight nod of his head.

"Do you have braces?"

He mumbled something unintelligible.

"I didn't catch that."

"No."

"Sorry, champ. You'll have to prove it. I don't want any trouble with your mom."

Another pause, longer this time. I began to worry that I hadn't won him over.

Before I could withdraw the treats, he lifted his head. Strands of fine ginger hair covered the upper half of his face. He brushed them aside to reveal brilliant green eyes.

His lips parted into a reluctant smile.

He had told the truth: no braces.

"Here you go." I dumped the gum into his hand. "The rest are for later."

He unwrapped one and began chewing.

"What do you prefer to be called?" I said. "Dougie, or Doug?"

"Doug. I hate Dougie." He paused. "What am I supposed to call you?"

"Well, my name is Doctor Bradley Jordan, but that's a mouthful. Most kids stick with Doctor Brad."

* * *

Doug unwrapped another piece of gum and stuffed it into his mouth. His jaws worked like a wood chipper trying to grind a forest into sawdust.

For the first ten minutes we chatted about this and that, skirting the more emotionally charged issues. Eventually, we arrived at the difficulties of being "the new kid."

"Johnny Richardson's pretty cool," Doug said. "He's got one of those funny divots here." He jabbed a finger at the middle of his upper lip. "What do you call those?"

"Harelip?"

"Yeah, that's it. A harelip. Anyway, his ain't so bad. Johnny says there's lots worse. Still, he's gotta have surgery. I feel bad for him. He gets picked on a lot."

"It's never easy being different."

"That's why Johnny and me, we stick together. We're pals. He's got my back, and I got his."

"He's lucky to have a friend like you." I paused. "Is Johnny one of the reasons you're getting into fights?"

Doug made a sour face. "He don't know how to defend himself. He stands there like an idiot, arms hanging at his sides. He don't know nothin' about fighting. Never hits back, just stands there, eyes big and shiny. I'm surprised he hasn't pissed himself." He looked at me with hard, unforgiving eyes. "That's the worst part, you know— letting them see you're scared, showing them you're weak. You might as well wear a shirt that says 'fuck with me' across the front. I tried to tell him, tried to get him to man up, but he don't listen. He never listens."

"You associate fear with weakness."

"You mean you don't?"

"I'm more interested in what you think."

"Nobody cares what I think." He picked up a stuffed animal, a fuzzy orangutan I occasionally used during play therapy with my younger patients, and began tossing it in the air. "I'm just a kid."

"That doesn't make you unimportant."

"If you say so."

"Somebody's told you different?"

"Kids are kids," Doug said glumly. "They're meant to be seen and not heard." He caught the orangutan in his fists and stared at it. "Why do you have a toy monkey in your office?"

He was stalling, changing the subject. Fine, at least he was still talking.

"I sometimes use them in my work." I pointed to a large plastic container in the corner of my office. It was filled to the top with dolls, hand puppets, Matchbox cars, and games like Connect Four and Trouble and Uno.

"People pay you to play games?"

"Among other things."

"Did you have to go to school for this job?"

"College, eight years. It was a long time."

Doug snorted. "All that, just to play fucking games?"

His words hung in the air. More time passed. Therapy was often a waiting game.

"That's twice I dropped the f-bomb," he said finally, "and you didn't say anything. How come?"

"It's one of the rules. You can say what you want in here, within reason, and you don't have to worry about being judged. Another rule: our talks are confidential. No one will know what you've said. Only under certain circumstances will I break that confidence."

Doug's eyes narrowed. "What circumstances?"

"If you say you're going to hurt yourself or someone else, I will tell your mother, possibly the school authorities, maybe even the police. I won't allow anyone to get hurt. And if I receive a court order for your records, I'll have to turn them over. That's usually not an issue, but you have a right to know."

"Whatevs." He held out his hand. "You got a tissue or something?"

I handed him the box of Kleenex. I had nineteen more in the closet next to the door. I ran through them like they were...well, like they were tissue paper. I should own stock in Kimberly-Clark.

Snatching a tissue, Doug hawked the wad of gum into it, wrapped it into a lumpy, gooey ball, and lobbed it at my trash can. The pinkish-white monstrosity bounced off the rim and tumbled to the floor.

"No worries," I said, picking up the sticky mess and dropping it into the can. "Three-point range. Not an easy shot."

He looked around the room. "Why am I here? What am I supposed to do?"

"What you've been doing. Talk, ask questions, think."

"Sounds like a waste of time."

"It could be, if you let it. Therapy is like any other activity—the more you put into it, the more you get out. Work hard enough and you might be surprised at what you could accomplish." I paused. "Tell you what, you agree to work hard, and I promise to work just as hard. What do you say, do we have a deal?"

He stared at me, his expression tight. "What do I have to talk about?"

"Whatever you want. It's your time."

My answer must have pleased him. His face relaxed, and he lost some of his adolescent guardedness. For a moment, I caught a glimpse of what he would look like as an adult: strong, bold, yet at the same time, sensitive. A rare mix in a world where role models were spoiled pop stars and unapologetic, multimillionaire athletes.

Doug Belle was a good kid.

He was also a troubled kid.

"I know there have been problems," I said. "You're not here as a punishment. My only concern is for you and how you're feeling. I'd like to help, but in the end, it'll be up to you. No one can force you to talk."

More silence, longer this time. The overpowering smell of bubble gum had thinned to a nauseating wrinkle in the air. Outside my office, a door opened, followed by heavy footsteps as someone lumbered toward the waiting room.

I resisted glancing at my watch. Never let someone think your time was more important than his. George H. W. Bush made that mistake and it had cost him the trust of the American people.

Doug held the orangutan, his thumb caressing its tattered cheek. He blinked, three times in rapid succession. A tear spilled from the corner of his eye and traced a path down his cheek. He wiped at it with an angry hand.

Was he thinking of his father, or his mother, now a widow?

Was he thinking of himself?

Would he see his tears as a sign of weakness and shut down?

I didn't know. I could only wait, so I did.

Doug finally let out a long, slow sigh and tossed the doll aside. "Do I have to talk about my dad?"

"Only if you want to."

"And if I don't?"

I spread my hands. "Like I said, it's your time."

"You always this easygoing?"

"Mostly."

He eyed the container of toys. "I'm pretty good at Connect Four."

I felt comfortable checking the time. "Maybe a game or two."

Doug reached for the container. There was a hint of a grin on his freckled face.

Yeah, he was one of the good ones.

* * *

Doug hadn't lied. He was killer at Connect Four, beating me

three games straight. I frequently let patients win, but by the last match, I was putting my full effort into the game. He still trounced me, blocking my pieces time and again.

I congratulated him, told him it was time to go, and packed up the game.

We found his mother in the waiting room, sitting alone and leafing through an old edition of Entertainment Weekly. Desiree Belle was in her mid-thirties, but grief had eroded her youthfulness and left behind a woman who looked much older. She had limp, languid hair parted down the middle, haunted eyes, and she wore a dark jacket that hung like a sack over her thin frame. Her socks didn't even match.

Doug wasn't the only one in trouble.

Desiree Belle noticed us standing in the doorway. A smile erased some of the years. She rose and held out her arms. "How'd it go, honey?"

Doug slipped into her embrace. The hug didn't last long. "Pretty good. He wants me to come back next week."

"If that's okay with you," I said.

"I'll do whatever he needs." Her smile faded; the years returned. "Do you think you can help him?"

"He's bright. As long as he keeps working, I think we can do some good."

Desiree touched Doug's shoulder. "He's the man of the house now. We need him to straighten up."

Oops, there went my red flags. "Can we talk for a moment, Mrs. Belle?" I pointed to the hallway. "In private."

"Sure, I guess." She turned to Doug. "Go have a seat, honey. I'll be right back."

I led her down the hallway, far enough from the waiting room so Doug couldn't hear us. Cheery watercolor prints hung on the walls. I doubted they would soften the blow of what I was about to say.

"Mrs. Belle—"

"Call me Dee Dee. Everyone does."

"All right. Dee Dee, please keep in mind your son is only twelve. That's a difficult age. Couple it with the loss of his father and you can see what happens." I paused. "He's trying to cope with a lot right now. Too much, really, for him to process effectively. That's why he's here."

"I know all this," she said stiffly. "It's why I'm getting him help."

"I think his school suggested the therapy, but that's beside the point. What concerns me is your 'man of the house' statement. It puts unintended pressure on Doug. He'll want to please you; to prove he can live up to your expectations. The trouble is, he can't. He can't be a man when he's still a boy, and he needs to be a boy for a little while longer. You need to *let* him be a boy."

"Are you saying this is my fault? He's behaving like this because of me?"

"No, of course not. I just want you to understand that words carry power, and with them, consequences. Doug loves you very much. He'll want to make you happy. But for now he needs to focus on himself. Making him responsible for the family, even if it's just an off-hand comment, won't help."

Dee Dee Belle snugged her jacket more tightly over her shoulders, as if it were a shield against my words. A classic defensive gesture.

"I'm doing the best I can," she said. "I hadn't planned on being a single mother."

"None of this is meant as an accusation. I'm simply looking out for your son's best interests."

"Fine, I'll watch what I say."

"Another thing." I lowered my voice. "I know this has been tough on everyone. If you don't mind, I'd like to give you the name of a colleague, a woman who specializes in grief counseling. I think she might be able to help you, and in the process, help you help Doug."

Her expression grew hard. I'd seen the same look on her son, not an hour ago. "You think I'm the one who needs a shrink."

"Everyone needs help from time to time. It's not a sign of weakness."

"I appreciate your concern, but I coping well enough. I don't need to talk to someone."

Then she glanced at her watch, and I knew I'd lost her.

I stifled a sigh. Doug was my patient, not her, and I knew better than to push. I led her back to the waiting room.

"Will next week at the same time work for you?" I asked.

"I'll let you know." She grabbed her son by the arm and practically dragged him out of the waiting room.

Doug glanced over his shoulder and waved goodbye.

Chapter Two

Back in my office, I dictated an intake note for Doug, returned phone calls, and checked next week's schedule. I'd forgotten to put my new patient into the Friday afternoon slot and entered his name in the planner. Whether his mom brought him or not was another matter.

Satisfied, I slipped on my jacket and made my way to the parking lot.

I drove a used Malibu I'd bought after completing my post-grad training. That was seven years ago (ten since the Chevy rolled off the assembly line in Kansas City) and the car had started showing its age. I'd kept up with the maintenance—changed the oil and rotated the tires every five thousand miles, washed and waxed it regularly—but the odometer had recently ventured into six-figure territory, and the battle for its longevity would soon become too difficult and too expensive. Still, I was determined to squeak at least another year out of the old girl. With the ongoing cuts in insurance reimbursements eroding my earnings and Lansing's endless desire to slash teachers' salaries capping my wife's wages, Toni and I could ill afford adding a large car payment to our already tight budget.

Such was life in the service of America's youth.

Rolling out of the parking lot, I headed north to the interstate and eased onto the ramp heading west.

A few minutes later, I arrived at my exit. I hit the turn signal, wedged my way in front of a big twelve-wheeler, the cab decorated with a pattern of stars falling across a midnight sky, and happily left the congestion of city life behind me.

I drove south along Highway 40 toward Rock Mills. This part of Michigan was farm country, wide open and flatter than the Lions' defense. Crops consisted mostly of soybeans and hay, potatoes, wheat. And corn. Lots and lots of corn. Vast fields of it grew on either side of the road in the endless, uniform rows that stretched, uninterrupted, all the way to the horizon. During the summer months, when the heat of the sun beat down on you like a blacksmith's hammer, you would often see giant watering apparatuses, long and low to the ground, spraying life-giving nutrition over the valuable green stalks. Now, with the crops harvested, they sat idle, their steel frames looking like evil alien machines from an H. G. Wells novel, long ago abandoned by their owners and left to rot among the desiccated, yellowing husks of their victims.

A flash of light on the road pulled me out of my daydreaming. Debris was strewn across both lanes of the highway, about a dozen yards in front of me. I jerked the wheel and smashed the brake pedal against the floorboard. The Malibu fishtailed, the rear end skidding in fitful jerks and starts, the tires wailing as they shed inches of black skin onto the tarmac. I heard a loud pop like a gun going off and the car lurched to one side. The airbag exploded, shoving me back into the seat, followed by the tortured squeal of metal grinding against concrete. I kept my hands on the wheel as the car's back swung around. The bouncing continued until my poor, dependable Malibu shuddered to a stop in the northbound lane.

My heart thudded hard against my ribs. I blinked sweat from my eyes. The sudden quiet was unsettling, much like I imagined it would be after a tornado ripped apart your house.

Then I remembered I was sitting in the wrong lane and my eyes darted to the rearview mirror.

A long-hauler barreled down the highway toward me, its lights flashing wildly, no doubt signaling for me to get the hell out of the way.

My hand shot to the door handle. Sweat made my fingers slick and they slipped. I tried again, managed to hook two under the latch, and pulled. The door popped open.

I threw my body sideways but only moved a few inches before the heavy nylon straps across my shoulder and waist jerked me to a stop.

I looked down in horror. The damn seatbelt!

The long-hauler's horn gave a frightful scream, over and over, as it thundered toward me like a runaway freight train. The massive front grill grew bigger and bigger in the unforgiving surface of the mirror.

I jabbed at the seatbelt release and yanked on the strap across my chest. Nothing. Yanked again, harder. Nothing. The belt refused to give.

With an ear-splitting screech, the long-hauler's brakes locked and the rig began to shudder violently against the inertia it had built. It didn't take a mathematician to see that it wouldn't stop in time.

Muttering a quick prayer, I hunched over the seatbelt release and thumbed the button repeatedly.

"COME ON, YOU ROTTEN MOTHER'S WHORE!"

I hit the button as hard as I could and felt my thumbnail tear on the hard plastic casing. Fiery pain shot up my arm. Still, I managed to the push button a fraction of an inch more.

I jerked on the belt and it came free. Diving out the door I landed on my belly and crawled like a madman to get away from the car.

I'd barely rolled onto the embankment when the long-hauler smashed into the Malibu, lifting it off the ground and flipping it over. It seemed to sail through the air in slow motion, like a crappy shot in a bad action movie, and landed, its frame bent and twisted. Windows exploded in grainy clouds of safety glass.

The impact had torn the car nearly in half.

I tasted the bitter burn of gasoline. Jerking to my feet, I stumbled toward the long-hauler. It had come to a stop about twenty yards up the road.

The driver dropped from the cab, her face pasty white.

"Jesus, mister. You okay?" Her voice was breathy from her own exertions.

I waved away her concern. "We need to get away from—"

The Malibu detonated into a ball of flame and black smoke. Something exploded out of the burning mass, screamed through the air, and punched a hole into the long hauler's cargo trailer mere inches above the driver's head. It ricocheted off something inside and shot out the top, trailing smoke. The firefighters found it later, deep in a corn field. It was the Malibu's right, front strut.

"Holy fuck!" the woman cried.

I fumbled for my cell phone. "Yeah, holy fuck."

* * *

Colored lights flashed with surreal urgency, the alternating pulses of red and blue taking on an odd, Doppler-like quality. They momentarily jerked the rescue vehicles—the fire truck, the police cars, the ambulance—into stark focus, only to have them recede to shadowy, indistinct blobs.

*Forward and back, forward and back...*over and over. Watching it reminded me of a scene from an old Vincent Price movie, *House of Wax*, where a slick-talking carnie playing paddle ball smacked the red rubber orb directly at the audience, over and over. Back then, the effect had been unsettling. Nothing had changed. I started to feel nauseous.

An EMT knelt before me. "Sir, you really should be checked out by a doctor. Airbag deployments can be nasty." He was young, perhaps mid-twenties, and had the kind of bad boy looks you rarely see outside of a movie theater. He brought up a penlight, flashed the beam into one eye and then the other. I tried not to wince. Lowering the penlight, he adopted an expression so sincere Jared Leto would have wept with envy. "You sure you won't reconsider?"

I started to shake my head and thought better of it. Everything from the waist up ached, as if glass rods had been driven up my spine and then shattered. Instead, I pointed to the Malibu's charred corpse.

"If that didn't kill me, I doubt a little dizziness will."

"You're feeling dizzy?" the EMT said with dramatic perfection. "Like, concussion dizzy?"

"No." I was unwilling to admit he might be right. "More like fortunate dizzy. You saw the wreck—I could have been inside when it happened. A little dizziness is a small price to pay for keeping my insides on the inside." A midnight blue Dodge Charger rolled to a stop behind the ambulance, the grill's emergency flashers working overtime. "Don't worry about me, I'll be fine. Besides, there's my ride."

A man stepped out of the Charger. Frank Swinicki wore a brown suit that looked like it had come straight-off-the-rack at Kohl's, a paisley tie, and slip-on loafers. Running a hand through his thick hair, he sized up the scene with a cop's practiced efficiency, his eyes darting from the police cruisers to the ambulance and, finally, to the blackened remains of the Malibu. He winced. Frank had liked the car as much as I did.

I waved. He didn't return it. That didn't bode well.

He stomped toward the ambulance. I was surprised the concrete didn't crack with each step.

"You okay, Paco?" he asked me. Not bothering to wait for a reply, he turned to the EMT. "Yo, pretty boy. Is he gonna be okay?"

If the EMT took offense, he didn't show it. Slipping the penlight into his shirt pocket, he said, "That's what the man's telling me, but I'm not convinced. See the abrasions on his face? They were caused by the airbag. He must've slammed into it pretty hard. I'm worried about cervical muscle strain, a torn ligament or two, possibly a concussion or a traumatic brain injury. He needs to be checked out by a doctor."

Frank hesitated. A cigarette pack stuck out of his shirt pocket. He carried them as a reminder of why he'd stopped smoking. His parents, both long-time tobacco junkies, had died from aggressive forms of lung cancer before the age of sixty. Their deaths had shaken him, and he'd ended his own habit soon afterward. To help keep him honest, he thought of carrying around the memorial cards from their funerals. I suggested the cigarettes. They didn't need to be looked at for them to be effective: a simple touch would do the trick. Besides, tangible worked better than visual in these cases.

He reached up and caressed the pack with his thumb. He did the cigarette thing when he felt nervous or concerned. The EMT's words were weighing on him, and if he believed our future Oscar contender, I'd be stuck with an unwanted trip to the hospital.

I caught his eye and shook my head, ignoring the pain the movement caused. I'd made my mind up. I was going home.

One side of his mouth pulled down in a look of disapproval.

I stared blandly back at him.

Frank grunted. Turning to the EMT, he said, "If Paco here says he's all right, he's all right. I'll take him home. His wife can look after him. Shit, maybe I'll come by and hold his hand while he sleeps. It'll be special."

The EMT rolled his baby blues, reached into the back of the

ambulance, and pulled out a clipboard full of forms. Finding the correct one, he handed it to me, along with a ballpoint. "Sign here, please. Refusal of medical assistance."

I scrawled my name across the bottom and handed it back. "Thanks, I appreciate your help."

"Any signs of nausea, any vomiting or blurred or double vision, and you get to an ER. Understand?"

"Perfectly."

"And follow up with your family doctor." The EMT turned to go, stopped, and looked at Frank. "Why do you call him 'Paco'? He doesn't look Hispanic."

"Because it'd sound dumb if I called him 'Taco.'" Frank's grin was all teeth and biting sarcasm.

My own lips twitched into a smile. It was an old joke between Frank and me, one that never seemed to grow old, even as we did.

The EMT wasn't amused. Stuffing the form into his pocket, he said, "You gentlemen have a good day." He walked away, his stride red-carpet perfect.

Frank shook his head. "Fucking hose hauler. Bet his dick gets hard every time he wraps his hands around one of those canvas monsters."

"You're biased," I said. "Besides, I think he was a paramedic."

"There's a difference? Come on, I wanna pay my respects to the old shit-kicker."

We approached the smoldering husk of twisted metal. The death stench of burned rubber and melted plastic assaulted our senses. We stopped at a safe distance.

"Thanks for coming," I said.

"Tell me you kept the comprehensive."

"Dropped it last year. Just PLPD."

"That sucks."

"Undoubtedly."

Frank kicked at a piece of debris and sent it tumbling across the tarmac. "We had a lot of fun in that car."

"Remember the time we got tossed out of Soaring Eagle?"

Frank snorted. "That was your fault. I claim no responsibility."

I'd arranged for a guys' weekend at the casino in Mount Pleasant. Figured we could benefit from a little downtime. Frank had been embroiled in a nasty manslaughter case involving a powerful state senator intent on keeping her involvement out of the papers and out of the courtroom. She brought to bear her considerable influence to hinder the investigation. But Frank was Frank and, despite almost losing his job, he'd followed the investigation to its conclusion. The senator was currently on probation and working as a consultant to a K Street lobbying firm. Not quite justice for the man she'd killed, but the world wasn't always fair.

As for me, I had been recovering from a gunshot wound I'd received from an angry parent opposed to my involvement in his child's custody case. After nearly two days of testimony, where I had outlined the various horrors the man had inflicted on his eight-year-old son and the ramifications of such abuse, the court recessed for lunch. The man, Jerome Bailey Hutchinson, out on bail for domestic violence, cornered me outside the courthouse, pulled a small caliber pistol he'd retrieved from his car, and shot me. I felt a pinching in my thigh, like a bee sting, which quickly grew to a burning pain, which then became a throbbing ache that brought me to my knees. Hutchinson pulled the trigger three more times before a bystander tackled him. Luckily those shots went wild. Today, Jerome Hutchinson wore a blue jumpsuit and wandered the grounds of the prison facility in Standish.

Hence, the downtime.

After checking into the hotel, we started drinking. I fed Frank whiskey sours to match my beers, the alcohol flowing as easy as the indignities we had suffered at the hands of John Q. Public. Later that night Frank began arguing with the pit boss running a craps table. Claimed he'd rolled a Little Joe—double twos—on his pass line bet and wanted his point. The pit boss reviewed the video and politely corrected him. Slurring his words like a man having a stroke, Frank insisted he receive his *fushin point!* Things deteriorated quickly, with Frank shambling about, yelling for his *fushin point* among the flashing lights and ringing bells of the nearby slots, and generally scaring the hell out of everybody.

The pit boss whispered a few words into his sleeve. Three big men wearing suits and no-nonsense expressions converged on us. Frank tried to badge them, but his alcohol infused body seemed to have malfunctioned. He couldn't pull out his shield.

Security hustled us, gently but firmly, out of the casino, and we spent an uncomfortable night in the Malibu, sleeping it off. I had booked a room for the weekend at the casino's hotel but felt too embarrassed to go in and ask for a refund.

"You called Toni?" Frank asked as we stared at our dead friend.

"First one I made. No answer, which worries me a little. She should be home by now."

"I checked with Kerry after you called. She said they left work together." He shuffled back and forth from one foot to the other. That's what I liked about Frank: get him away from the Job and he wasn't so almighty tough.

"Call her again?" he said.

I pulled out my cell and hit my wife's speed dial. I knew by the third ring she wasn't going to answer. I was officially overdue, and Toni would either have called me or would be waiting anxiously for me to call her. No way her phone would have rung more than three times before she pounced on it.

I waited for her voicemail. "Hey, hon. Call me when you get this. Love you."

I disconnected and slipped the phone back into my pocket.

The fire truck rumbled to life, followed by the ambulance. Both left; the cops stayed. This side of the road remained closed as the police waited for the tow truck that would haul away the wreckage.

Finally, Frank asked, "Want me to have Kerry go check on her?"

He made it sound as if he were offering to expunge a sin.

"She's not with him," I said, more to myself than to him. "She made a promise, and I trust her to keep it. Sending Kerry would—"

"Send the wrong message. Yeah, I know, and I agree. She'll be true to her word. But what if she's hurt? You know, slipped and fell or something. She might need help."

Turning away from the Malibu, I said, "Let's go find out."

Chapter Three

The Charger's grill lights flashed hot and the traffic melted away.

Frank had his cell glued to the side of his face as he yammered with the State Police about the accident. I slouched in the seat next to him, keeping as still as possible and staring out the window. My neck pain had migrated to my entire body, every nerve and fiber aflame and protesting the abuse I had put them through. My right thumb felt as if someone had flayed the skin off with a razor and dipped it in battery acid. And if that weren't enough, a dull ache had lodged itself behind my eyes. It beat a painful tympani against my retinas.

I was all messed up.

After grunting his goodbye, Frank tossed the phone onto the dashboard. "Goddamn idiots," he said. "They have no idea where the debris on the road came from. Said maybe there was an unreported accident earlier. Oh, gee, what a stunning example of investigative police work."

"Knowing the cause isn't going to change the outcome."

"That's no excuse for laziness."

"Maybe it's more a matter of priority than apathy."

"Kill the reasonableness, Paco. You're harshing my angst."

I stared at Frank's cell. "Should I think about getting a lawyer?"

"What would they charge you with? Reckless saving-your-ass-from-certain-death?"

"Malicious destruction of a Chevy. That's a felony in some states."

"Others might consider it a blessing."

"Unlike your cooking. Now there's a crime."

"Funny guy." His eyes cut over to mine. "Look, let's scratch tonight's card game. I doubt you're gonna feel up to it. Another time, maybe?"

I frowned. Card game?

Oh, right. Our once-a-month gathering—me and Toni, Frank and Kerry, food, drink, camaraderie, and euchre.

"Let's see what's up with Toni first," I said. "She looks forward to these nights, and I don't want to disappoint her. I can always take a couple Advil when I get home. I'm sure it'll be fine."

"So says the man who can barely sit up straight."

"Keep driving."

"As you wish." He blew me a kiss.

"Now look who's being funny."

He grinned and pressed on the accelerator.

I pulled out my cell and checked the display. The call log was as empty as my sense of security.

Where was she? Why hadn't she called?

We reached Rock Mills as the setting sun threw purple bruises across the Midwestern sky. The city was located forty miles outside Kalamazoo, far enough to escape the status of suburb, yet close enough you could drive there without having to pack a lunch. I liked Rock Mills for its small town feel. No Wal-Mart or Home Depot. No Costco. Just places with names like Grigg's IGA and Duke's Sporting Goods and Westphal Pharmacy. Real stores owned by real people and not stockholders. Toni liked it because it was far removed from the inner-city holocaust teachers endured in places like Detroit or Pontiac. In Rock Mills, kids got to know their teachers, saw them outside the classroom, and seemed to develop a measure of respect students in the larger districts lacked. Plus, when parents shopped at the same stores and prayed in the same churches and cheered at the same Friday night football games and really got to know the men and women responsible for educating their children, blaming the teachers out-of-hand for dismal test performances became more difficult.

Knowledge might breed contempt, but community bred cohesion: we knew we were in the same boat, and we would all drown if it suddenly sprang a leak.

Frank killed the Charger's flashers, hung a left on Camilla, raced past Brenner, and turned right onto North Waltz. My house was halfway down the street.

He pulled up to the curb. "Want me to come with?"

I shook my head. "I'll call you about the card game."

Frank put a hand on my arm. He had that hound-dog look he gets when he's about to enter a crime scene. "You sure? I can go in and look around, make sure everything's okay."

"And scare the hell out of Toni while you're at it?" I opened the door and stepped gingerly onto the driveway. A streetlamp spilled light the color of week-old custard onto the ground. "The place looks quiet. There's no sign of trouble. I'm telling you, go home. Give Kerry a hug. I'll call as soon as I know something."

"All right, but call Kerry. The battery on my cell just died."

Frank needed a new phone but stubbornly refused to give up his Blackberry. "They make car chargers, you know."

"Just another waste of my money." Frank leaned across the center console. "At least let me wait until I know you're both okay."

"Go home, Frank." I shut the car door.

He stared at me through the Charger's tinted glass.

I waved. He flipped me off, and drove away.

Such was our friendship, long may it last.

I turned to face my house, a sagging, post-war rambler that was one-part charm and three-parts home maintenance nightmare. There was a light on in the living room. Toni's 4Runner sat in the driveway, pulled far enough up to give me room to park.

I started up the walk to the front door. A few late-season crickets chirped noisily nearby. I strained to hear past them, to detect any sounds coming from inside the house.

Everything was still. No blare of the television, no clatter of pots and pans as snacks were prepared for tonight's euchre game.

I began to wonder if she was home.

No, that's not true. I began to worry that she wasn't alone.

I placed my hand on the doorknob. The metal felt warm, slick.

Locked.

Like a jackass, I pressed my ear to the door. It was my house—I had a key, for Christ's sake—yet I listened like some creepy voyeur, a repressed Peeping Tom getting his rocks off by spying on people.

I heard something—the strains of a melody, playing faintly from inside and, even fainter, the sound of running water.

Toni was home.

I let myself in. The music and the running water came from the back of the house.

"Hey, honey!" I called out. "It's me. Sorry I'm late."

I wandered down the hallway to the bathroom. The door was shut and locked, the shower inside running.

I knocked. "Honey, you okay?"

When she didn't answer, I called out, "Toni, are you all right?"

No reply.

The music I'd heard was coming from our bedroom. Toni liked to listen to the radio while correcting papers.

I poked my head inside and saw her school bag on the bed, the top open and a sheaf of papers sticking out like a fan of feathers. A barely-touched glass of water sat on the nightstand next to the radio.

My skin began to crawl. Turning back to the bathroom door, I pounded with the flat of my hand.

"Toni!"

We kept the key to the door on the narrow overhang created by the molding. I snatched the thin piece of brass and shoved it into the doorknob. The lock released and I threw open the door.

Steam billowed out, white and swirling. I waded into the mist. Moisture clung to my face, my shirt. Crossing the room, I drew aside the shower curtain, terrified I would find my wife lying in the tub, unconscious, water splashing down on her pale body as she bled out from a nasty head wound.

Toni sat fully clothed, knees drawn up to her chin, arms wrapped around her legs, her forehead pressed into her thighs.

She was crying.

I noticed something clutched in her hand—a plastic stick about the size of a toothbrush with a window in the middle that displayed a single, vertical blue line—and my heart sank.

She had taken a home pregnancy test.

It was negative.

I'd been worried about her cheating on me. Instead, she'd been devastated by another setback in our efforts to become parents. Jesus, I could be such an idiot.

Knees popping painfully, I squatted. Water ran over my hand as I placed it on the back of her head. "Sweetheart?"

She stiffened under my touch, and I thought she might scream.

"It's okay," I said. "It's me."

Her sobs dwindled to a series of hitching sniffles. "You were running late," she said, her head still down. "I wanted to wait for you, have us to do this together." She waved the test stick in a feeble arc. "I was too excited. Six days late, Brad. Six goddamn days. I thought we'd did it this time. I thought we were finally going to have a baby."

I moved my hand to her shoulder, gave it a reassuring squeeze. "It'll happen one day. You'll see."

"I was so sure. That was my mistake. I got my hopes up." She hugged herself tighter. "I should've known better."

"I'm sorry, baby. I know you're disappointed. So am I." I squeezed her shoulder again. "Don't beat yourself up. It's not your fault."

She sat in the tub, water spraying, not saying a word. Her body trembled beneath my hand.

"We'll get this done," I continued. "You're a wonderful, amazing, beautiful woman, and when you set your mind to something, you rarely fail. That's what drew me to you in the first place. It's one of the many reasons I love you so much."

Her trembling grew to a shaking. She was crying again. Watching her suffer broke my heart.

"Here, move over." I climbed into the tub and sat behind her, where we could both fit. Soon my clothes were as soaked as hers. I put my arms around her and hugged her. "Go ahead and cry."

Toni wept, ridding herself of a pain she couldn't put into words.

The water cooled, and her crying subsided. She hadn't lifted her head.

"Your clothes are wet," she said.

"Small price to pay if it helps you feel better."

"I didn't want you to see me like this."

"Is that why you locked the door?"

She nodded, her forehead rubbing against her thighs.

I hugged her tighter. "It's okay to feel upset. There's nothing wrong with that."

Toni lifted her head. She turned to give me a kiss and halted when she saw my face.

"Good Lord, Brad! What happened?"

I kissed her, a small peck on the cheek. It was all I could muster without crying out in pain. "This is about you, not me."

"But—"

"Hush," I said. "Just let me hold you for a little while longer."

She stared at me, her fingers coming up to touch my injuries.

"Are you going to argue with me?" I asked, smiling.

"Wouldn't dream of it," she said, and nuzzled against me.

I closed my eyes. Sometimes I needed to remember that, as an adult, you care for others as much as you care for yourself.

And you trust them with your heart, if not your life.

* * *

Less than two hours later we walked out the front door, dried off and wearing a change of clothes.

The euchre game was on.

"Buckle up," she said, taking the wheel. "I got this."

I set the cold cuts, crackers, and a six pack of beer in the back of the 4Runner and climbed in. I hadn't confessed my misplaced—*selfish,* the little voice in my head whispered—concern over old wounds that should have long since healed. I wanted to tell her, she deserved honesty from me as much as I deserved it from her, but the pregnancy test had wounded her spirit. I didn't want to cause more pain. Better I learned from my mistake and kept her out of it.

Which was a roundabout way of saying, I was too much of a coward to come clean.

Ten minutes later, Toni pulled the car into the Swinicki's driveway and killed the headlights. I felt more than saw her reach out and grip my hand. "Kerry had her gallbladder out last year. Maybe she has something a little stronger than ibuprofen left over from the surgery. Want me to ask?"

I rubbed at an especially painful knot in the big muscle of my thigh. It was amazing how every part of your body ached after a car accident. "I'd rather not. I've seen too many unintended addicts created that way."

Her grip on my hand tightened. "You look awful, honey. Your thumb is swollen. The skin on your face is scraped raw. Your chest has a bruise the size of Texas spreading across it. I know you didn't break anything, but it's clear you're hurting. You need a painkiller with some teeth."

"It's sore muscles and stiff joints. Nothing a few beers and a hand or three of cards won't fix."

"And if they don't?"

"Give me an hour. If I don't feel better, you can ask Kerry what she's got lying around. Okay?"

She stared at me through the darkness. "Is that a promise?"

I traced an **X** over my chest. "Cross my heart and hope to die."

"It'd better not come to that." She gave my hand a final squeeze. "Let's go. We look like a couple of fools sitting out here in the dark."

"What about you?" I said. "Are you sure *you* want to do this? No one would blame you if you passed on tonight."

"I'm not letting this ruin our evening. We'll have our baby one day. This was a speed bump, nothing more. Now, come on before they start wondering what we're doing."

"Maybe they'll think we're working on that baby."

She laughed and opened her door. "I think you've had enough car action for one day."

I followed her to the front door. She rang the bell, and I took advantage of the wait to steal a kiss.

She was returning my kiss when the door opened. Frank's large frame filled the opening.

"What is it about a near death experience that kicks the libido into overdrive?"

Our lips parted. Toni handed the platter of cold cuts to Frank. "Nothing wrong with a healthy display of affection, especially after you realize what you might have lost. Give this to Kerry. I'll settle our daredevil here into his chair with a cold beer."

Frank hesitated, not for long, just a beat or two, and stepped aside. I removed my jacket and hung it in the closet. Toni did the same. Frank lumbered down the hallway toward the kitchen.

"We're in the dining room," he said. "I already set out plates and glasses. Kerry picked up some tzatziki and hummus from that Greek place downtown. We got kabobs, too. Real lamb. Gonna grill them later. Ooh-la-la, ain't we fancy."

I nuzzled up close to Toni's ear. "Think he'll shout *opa!* for us?"

"If you weren't so sore, you might've been the one shouting. Later tonight, after we've crawled into bed."

"Ooh la la," I said as we headed down the hallway.

The Swinicki house smelled of cucumber and chickpeas and sweaty teenagers. In the living room, the twins, Dave and Danny, sat hunched on the couch, their hands clamped onto the controls of their gaming system. Danny leaned left, his arms wrenching the controller around like a drunken NASCAR driver as he tried to evade death at the hands of his brother. But he had miscalculated: either he'd overestimated his ability to keep his balance, or he hadn't accounted for the added mass of his broadening shoulders. Regardless of the reason, he leaned too far and, like a god cast from Olympus, slid off the couch. His hip knocked over a bowl on the floor and sent corn chips sailing through the air. The controller flew out of his hand and bounced on the carpet.

Cackling, Dave thumbed a button repeatedly. On the television, a machine gun burped round after round in rapid succession. The screen exploded in streams of pixelated blood.

"Godammit," Danny shouted. "Why do you have to kill me every single time?"

Dave grinned. "Why do you have to make it so easy?"

"*LANGUAGE!*" Kerry called out from the kitchen.

"Hey guys," I said. The twins looked up, and for a moment I saw two identical people staring back at me, separated by a foot or two of distance. The vision had a kind of weird, dizzying effect. The room seemed to tilt. I closed my eyes until the sensation passed. I'd known the twins since birth, and I'd never had this kind of reaction to seeing them.

"Holy crap, Uncle Brad. What happened to you?" It was Danny.

"Yeah," Dave said. "You look like something out of *The Walking Dead*."

"Your parents don't let you watch that show," Toni said. "It's disgusting."

"Kids stream it on their phones," Dave said. "We watch it during lunch."

I noticed a doll sitting on a small wood chair in the corner of the living room. Made of cloth, it was fashioned in the image of a little girl, with a cotton print dress, yarn for hair, and a mouth made of stitched Xs. Except it didn't look quite right. The arms were too long, making it look as if it would lope around on all fours, and it had different sized buttons for eyes. The flat plastic discs gave the doll an eerie, startled look.

I thrust my chin at the doll. "That's new, isn't it?"

Danny climbed back onto the couch, while Dave glanced

nervously at the doll. "Mom and dad bought it few weeks ago," Dave said. "They found it at some store that sells antiques and stuff."

"She told me about the trip," Toni said. "Didn't know they'd bought anything." She frowned at the doll. "Creepy little thing, isn't it?"

Dave nodded. "Yeah, we don't like it. Nate doesn't either."

"Your brother's smart," I said. Nathan, oldest of the three Swinicki boys, often spent his evenings with friends. Given he had twin younger brothers, I couldn't blame him. "You guys go ahead with your game. We've got cards to play."

"Have fun," Dave said, and grabbed a controller.

"Hope you feel better," added Danny as he hit the start button.

The action on the television resumed. Gyrations commenced. Death was sure to follow.

Toni and I moved into the kitchen. The room was small and crammed with essentials: blender, mixer, Dutch oven sitting on a gas range, spice rack, and a pink salt pig on the counter. There were a few family heirlooms. On one wall hung a black metal crucifix, which had belonged to Kerry's maternal grandfather and had purportedly been blessed by Pope John Paul II. Shelving ran along the top edge of two walls, on which sat Frank's mother's collection of wood butter molds. There were shapes for sheep and chicks and the traditional Christmas and Easter squares. While I doubt Frank or Kerry had ever utilized them, Frank's mother had, and the oils had stained the wood a dark almond color.

The kitchen had the busy, lived-in look that we lacked in our own house. Kerry called it "homey." Frank called it "functional Polish."

Kerry stood at the sink, her hands under running water. Frank leaned against the counter, liberally sprinkling spices onto the kabobs. I smelled oregano, mint, and basil.

"Where do you want this?" Toni lifted the six pack.

"Dining room," Frank said, not looking up from his work. "We'll drink that first, and save the stuff in the fridge for later."

She handed me the beer. "Pour the drinks. I'll see what I can do to help." She kissed my cheek, "Remember to take it easy. You're officially on the injured reserve list."

Kerry turned. "That's right. Frank told me about—" She froze, her mouth gaping open. "You look horrible."

"Your boys think I look like a zombie."

"Not quite that bad," Frank said. "But not far from it."

"You poor dear." Kerry wiped her hands on a towel and took the six-pack from me. "Go sit down. Have you taken something for the pain? I've got stuff that would knock a toothache out of a hippo."

The den mother of the group, Kerry was warmth and nurturing wrapped in a pink cardigan, which pretty much made her the polar opposite of her husband. Where Frank would approach a problem armed with facts and logic and to hell with the consequences, Kerry would bake it in an apple pie, serve it with ice cream, top it with nuts and a cherry.

"I'm tougher than I look." I puffed out my chest, a frivolous act which did nothing more than make it ache like a motherfucker.

"You need an infusion of narcotics." Kerry turned me around and pushed me toward the dining room. "Preferably by needle, with a continuous feed."

I stumbled forward. It was going to be a long night.

What I didn't know was how long.

* * *

In the dining room, I stole a cushion from an extra chair and tossed it onto mine. The table was already set with glasses, small plates, and napkins. There were two stoneware bowls, one filled with pita slices, the other with hummus. The third was empty. I slathered a piece of bread with ground chickpeas and stuffed it into my mouth. I hadn't eaten much since the accident, and the snack made me want more.

Toni walked in carrying the beer and a bag of chips. She set the beer next to me, ripped open the shiny Mylar bag, and dumped the chips into the empty bowl. She popped one into her mouth.

"How are you holding up?" she asked.

"The food helped." I grabbed another piece of bread. "How about you? Think you can do this?"

She eased into the chair next to me and smiled, but the joy never touched her eyes. They looked haunted, much the same way they had earlier, and I felt a stab of guilt over my selfishness. While her indiscretion had taken place more than six years ago, I'd never been good at letting go of the past. Odd, given I spent most of my work day encouraging people to do just that.

Physician, heal thyself.

What a joke.

"Afraid we'll kick your butt again?" she asked playfully.

"I'm serious, Toni."

She stopped smiling. "This was a setback, but it won't derail our lives. We want a child, and by damned, we'll have one. Just not today."

She spoke plainly, with the matter-of-fact quality of a teacher explaining a lesson plan. By the time she'd finished, though, her eyes were moist with tears.

"I couldn't agree more." I took her hand. I'm a tactile person and find special comfort in physical contact. "We keep trying. No one could fault us for that. Besides"—I gave her my best lecherous grin—"I'm willing to try as often as you are."

She handed me the bottle opener. "The only way you're getting lucky tonight is if you win a hand or two, which pretty much rules out sex."

I popped open a beer, emptied the contents into a glass, and handed it to her. "Keep dreaming. Frank and I are determined to break your winning streak."

She stared at her beer. "Did you notice the funny look Frank gave us when we walked in?"

"I did. Think he and Kerry are having a disagreement?"

"They seemed pretty cozy in the kitchen."

I opened another beer. "Sometimes he gets like that when he's working a difficult case. Remember a few years back, when heroin started showing up in the high school? He was consumed with finding the guy who was pushing the stuff. Lost sleep, dropped weight, had the same look on his face." I poured the rest of the beers. "Could be something as simple as that."

"As simple as what?" Frank strode into the room, his bulk momentarily blocking the light from the kitchen. He skirted two chairs and sat opposite me. Our games were men against women. "What are you two going on about?"

"Life, the universe, and everything," I said.

"Ah, I get it. Forty-two. As in the number of State Troopers it takes to count to three, or to figure out why there was debris on the road."

I picked up the cards and began removing the unnecessary ones. "Did you hear anything more?"

"Of course not. Trying to get a Troop to do anything is like trying to chase a fart through a keg of nails. Damn near impossible."

"Are they really that bad?" Toni said. "Won't they at least try to find out what happened?"

"To answer your first question, hell yes, they're that bad. Troops are elitists. They lord over common cops like they own the state. To answer your second question, I don't think they'll put much time into it. To be fair, what good would it do? I just happen to hate loose ends, especially when they almost take out my best friend." He washed down his food with a swig of beer and called over his shoulder, "Kerry! Let's go!"

"I'll only be a minute," she said from the kitchen. "Just finishing up the snacks."

I separated out the fives, gave two to Toni, and kept the others for myself. They were our point markers. Next, I flipped cards so they landed face up, one for each player, going around the circuit, until the Jack of Clubs landed in front of Frank. Looked like the big guy would deal first.

"Yeah, baby. This is gonna be fun." Frank swept up the cards. "No mercy tonight, ladies. No mercy at all. You'll be mewling like a couple of clubbed seals before we're through with you."

Toni shot me a pained glance. "We've already got tenderized Paco on the menu."

Kerry entered carrying a container full of dip and a plate of veggie slices. "Leave my boy alone. Picking on the weak and infirm is against the American way." She set the plate on the table. "Better we trounce him with our card playing and rapier-sharp wit and send him staggering home to lick his wounds. Or even better, have him stagger home to lick Toni." She broke out in muffled laughter.

"Jesus, Kerry," Frank said. "What if the kids heard that?"

Spots of crimson glowed like banked coals high on Kerry's cheeks, and she fanned herself with a napkin. "Trust me, it sounded funnier in my head." She used the napkin to pat her cheeks. "Does it feel warm in here to you? Frank, could you get me a glass of water, please?"

Wordlessly, Frank rose and stormed out of the room. My eyes found Toni's. She bit her lower lip, and I nodded.

Maybe there was trouble in paradise.

Toni hurried around the table and wrapped an arm around her friend. "Honey, are you okay?"

"Don't worry about me. I'll be fine," Kerry said, melting into the embrace. "Sorry about my little joke. It was totally inappropriate. Can't blame Frank for being upset. The last few weeks have been stressful."

That sealed it. There was definitely trouble in paradise.

"Anything we can do to help?" I asked.

Kerry shook her head. "No, but thanks for offering."

"We're here for you," Toni said. "All you have to do is ask."

"I know. You guys are the best."

Kerry sounded almost resigned, as if she didn't expect her situation to improve. I played out several scenarios in rapid order: financial problems, illness, trouble with one or more of the kids. Divorce.

My mind settled on the last one. Could I have missed something, an unraveling of their relationship severe enough to threaten their marriage? I thought back to the last time we were together. Nothing unusual stood out. Their interactions had been normal, caring.

Yet Kerry was upset.

Perhaps divide and conquer might work. Leaving Toni with Kerry, I headed for the kitchen.

I found Frank standing at the sink, the tap running. He held a water glass but wasn't filling it. He stared blankly at the glass, as if he had forgotten why he was holding it. I watched him, my sense of alarm growing.

He didn't move. He didn't seem to be breathing.

I couldn't take any more. Crossing the room, I placed a hand on his shoulder. "Hey, you want to tell me what's going on?"

My touch jolted Frank out of his reverie. He jerked upright. The glass slipped from his fingers and shattered in the sink.

"Huh? Wha—?"

"Relax. It's only me."

"Brad?" Toni called out from the dining room. "Is everything okay in there?"

"We're good. Frank dropped a glass. Give us a minute to clean up." Lowering my voice, I said to Frank, "Okay, time to come clean. Is there something going on I should know about?"

Frank reached into a cabinet below the sink and pulled out a paper bag, the kind you put your groceries in at the IGA. He dropped shards of broken glass into it. "Could you grab me another glass?"

Frank was like that. He'd break through a brick wall to help you, but when it came to his own issues, he'd rather play hermit crab, retreating into his shell and shutting you out. It was one of his more frustrating habits, one I typically ignored.

Not today.

I handed him the glass. "You don't want to talk, fine. I'll respect your privacy. Let me know if there's anything I can do."

I limped back toward the dining room.

"Come on, Paco. Don't be like that."

I kept limping.

"Brad. Seriously, wait a second."

Frank rarely used my given name. I turned to face him.

"What?"

Frank drew in a heavy sigh. His finger caressed the cigarette packet in his shirt pocket. "I promise I'm not shutting you out. It's just—the whole damn thing is complicated."

My stance softened. "That's all you had to say. I understand complicated, I deal with it every day. But we're friends, and I'm always willing to listen. Keep that in mind, *amigo*."

I didn't know what had gotten into me. Maybe it was the accident, the shock of knowing I could have died in a massive Malibu fireball. Maybe it was the pain wracking my body. Whatever the reason, I didn't want to deal with Frank or his evasiveness.

I left before he could say anything.

* * *

Toni and Kerry had reached some sort of neutral ground. They remained huddled, foreheads almost touching as they whispered back and forth. When I walked in, Toni looked up without moving her head, the question plain on her face.

Did you learn anything?

I gave her a curt shake of my head. She rolled her eyes. Apparently, she hadn't been successful either.

"Water's on the way," I said. "Everything okay in here?"

"I think so." Toni pushed away from her Kerry. Tears had

dampened the other woman's face. Toni brushed a strand of hair from Kerry's forehead. "What about you, sweetie? You sure you're all right?"

Kerry's cheeks were blotchy, the flesh around her eyes puffy. Her breath hitched, as if she had been crying for hours and not minutes. She grabbed another napkin and blew her nose. "Sorry for acting like a ninny. I'm not used to being this emotional."

"Stress affects us all in different ways," I said as I took my chair. "No need to apologize for being human."

Kerry stuffed the napkin into her pocket. "Thank you. Sometimes I need reminding."

Frank returned with the glass of water and set it in front of his wife. He paused, his eyes traveling from face to face to face; the veteran cop assessing the scene of the crime. "Everything good? We can go back to playing cards?"

I caught another look from Toni. He hadn't asked how his wife was.

"Sure," I said. "Have a seat. It's your deal."

Forty minutes later, the women won. Frank and I had made it close. We'd only lost by two points.

Kerry called for a bathroom break and left. Toni took the snack bowls into the kitchen to refill them.

That left Frank and me: Paco and the Man.

Frank's fingers drummed the tabletop like a piano player with a grudge against the music. I watched, not responding, and let his uneasiness play out to its natural conclusion.

It didn't take long.

"Ah, shit," he said. "I didn't want this to be so complicated. God knows neither of us needs more chaos in our lives." He dropped his head in his hands. "How did life get so screwed up?"

I wasn't sure what he was talking about, so I waited for him to continue.

He finally looked at me. I was shocked at the anguish in his eyes.

"Kerry's pregnant," he said. "About six weeks. We found out last week."

The news stunned me. I had expected a lot of things, but not this. "You're not happy?"

"I already got three kids, and they all play hockey. You know how expensive that sport is? Over a grand a month in ice time alone.

Then it'll be college. Figure a hundred grand per kid and my debts add up fast. Now I'm gonna have another one. More cost, more time. My retirement gets pushed back another decade, not to mention I'm older and changing diapers no longer appeals to me. I tell you, Paco, this is not where I planned to be at this point in my life. It's some fucked up shit."

"Kerry knows how you feel?"

"Oh, yeah. We've had hours of discussion."

His tone told me those hours hadn't been pleasant. "Go on."

"She gets why I'm mad, but she doesn't care. She's a mothering type. Having another kid around feels natural to her. The costs are secondary."

"They're also real. So is the effect it's having on your relationship."

"That part will pass."

Maybe, or maybe not. I'd seen plenty of marriages splinter because of financial stresses. It was the number one cause of divorce, ahead of adultery and spousal abuse. No need to tell him, though. He already felt bad enough.

"Have you told the boys?" I said.

"We're gonna wait until after the first trimester. In case, you know, something happens."

"And ending the pregnancy isn't an option?"

"Come on, Paco. We're talking about a life here."

"It was only a question. I didn't mean to offend."

His eyes cut away from mine. "I'll be honest, I've thought about it, but I can't. It's not how my parents raised me."

"Okay, so that option is off the table." There was one beer left. I filled Frank's glass. "Aside from the obvious, how did this happen? I thought she was on birth control pills."

"She was." He grabbed the beer and downed half of it. "I did some research. Even on the pill, there's a one-tenth of one percent chance a woman could get pregnant. Just my luck, huh? Instead of winning the lottery and retiring to a beach in Hawaii, I get another mouth to feed."

"That explains her being emotional," I said. "For now, try not to worry. Give yourself time. You need to wrap your head around the idea of being a new dad."

"There's more, and this one involves you."

"Oh?"

"Toni. Remember what happened today. How's she gonna react when she hears her best friend is having her fourth kid?"

My mouth suddenly went dry. Images of Toni sitting in the shower, clutching the test stick and crying so hard her shoulders shook, returned with the force of an avalanche. I took a swig of beer and said, "You think she told her?"

"She's trying to find the right time."

"There might not be a right time."

I heard a noise behind me. Kerry rounded the corner from the living room. Her cheeks were rosy and she smelled of soap. We must have looked suspicious, because she pulled up short of her chair and placed her hands on her ample hips.

"You two are up to something. You both look—" The blood drained from her face. She turned to Frank. "You told him, didn't you?"

Frank nodded, but otherwise kept silent.

Kerry shifted her attention to me. "Does Toni know?"

"Not yet."

"How do you think she'll react? Do you think she'll get mad?"

There was an excellent chance of that, but I didn't want to alarm her. Instead, I said, "She's your friend. Trust her as you would trust yourself."

"In other words, I'm on my own."

I shrugged. Sometimes the truth isn't what we wanted to hear.

Toni entered from the kitchen, a snack bowl in each hand, her dark hair swept back from her forehead. She set the bowls on the table and took her seat.

"Okay, whose deal is it? Has to be me or Kerry. Frank started last game."

"Toni, honey—" I began.

"No fair trying to steal the deal, mister," Toni said, then noticed our expressions and frowned. "What's the matter?"

I took her hand. "Kerry has something to tell you."

"What?" She turned to her friend. "Tell me what?"

Kerry tried to smile. It didn't work, and she gave up. "I've been to the doctor."

Toni's face paled. "Is it something serious? Oh my god, it is. Please tell me it isn't cancer." Her hand clutched painfully at mine. "It is, it's cancer. I think I'm going to throw up."

"I don't have cancer."

Toni looked doubtful. "Really?"

"Really, I'm not sick."

"What is it then? What's the matter?"

Kerry gnawed on her lower lip. "I'm not sure how to tell you."

"Tell me *what*?"

"I'm pregnant," Kerry said. "I'm going to have a baby."

There was a moment of hesitation, then Toni jumped out of her chair, rushed over, threw her arms around Kerry, and hugged her.

"Why wouldn't you want to tell me?" Toni said. "This is wonderful news. I'm so happy for you."

Frank slumped in relief, and Kerry happily returned Toni's embrace.

I seemed to be the only one who noticed Toni wasn't smiling.

"I was worried you might be upset," Kerry said. "I know how much you and Brad want to have a baby, and here I am, knocked up for the fourth time. It doesn't seem fair. Then there was Brad's accident. You could have lost your husband." She hugged Toni tighter. "I want you to have a baby too."

"Oh sweetie, don't worry about me. Everything will work out. Brad and I will have our baby, you'll see."

"I know, but telling you felt like rubbing salt in a wound. I hated it. I hated it down to my bones. I would never want to hurt you."

"Your happiness could never hurt me." Toni kissed Kerry on the cheek and slipped out of her embrace. "How far along are you?"

"Six weeks, give or take. We'll know more when we get the ultrasound." Her hands knotted together. "This is going to be hard on everyone. It's not like we planned on another child."

Toni suddenly glared at Frank. "Is this why you were being such a jerk earlier?"

I felt my stomach clench—here we go.

Frank's expression grew frosty. "It's more complicated than that."

"What's complicated about supporting your wife? Your *pregnant* wife?"

"Toni—" I wanted to get her attention, to warn her.

"What?" she said, her eyes bright with anger.

I was right. The news had upset her. "It's not our place to get involved. This is between them and should be left that way."

"Why, so he can take his frustrations out on her? Fat chance of that!"

Frank bristled at her words. Kerry looked helplessly between me and Toni. Both now sensed the coming storm, and neither knew how to prevent it.

"I doubt it's that bad," I told her calmly. "We both know Frank. He's a better man than that."

"He practically took her head off earlier."

"That's an exaggeration, and more than a little unfair."

"You're deliberately ignoring the way he treated her."

"I'm trying to see both sides."

"Sides?" Toni said. "She's pregnant, and he's being an ass. What else is there to see?"

I took a breath. This wasn't going well. "Can we get back to playing euchre?"

"I'm sorry," Kerry said. "I didn't mean to start a fight."

"Don't apologize for being a woman," Toni said. "Motherhood is a wonderful, natural thing. These two don't have a clue what you're going through, especially him." She shot another angry look at Frank. "If he did, he wouldn't be acting like this."

Frank rose from his chair. "That's it, I've taken enough shit for one night. Kerry, I'll see you upstairs."

Kerry grabbed his arm. "Don't go." She turned to Toni. "You've gone too far. You have no right to talk to him like that."

"Let him go," Toni said, her mouth twisting. "Let them both go. They're useless. Frank gets you pregnant and can't handle it. As for Brad—well, he can't seem to get the job done."

Kerry gasped. Frank looked stunned. They'd never heard Toni speak so cruelly.

Neither had I.

"I think it's time you stopped," I said. "This isn't about Kerry. It's about you. It's about the fact she's expecting and you're not. I know it sucks, but it's also life. Deal with it. Don't take it out on Frank and don't take it out on me. It's not fair, and it won't make the pain go away. It'll only make it worse."

"You don't understand—"

I raised my voice. "I understand you're embarrassing yourself. I understand it's the pain talking and not you. And I understand you owe Kerry and Frank an apology. That's what I understand."

Her face darkened. It now resembled the deepest, hottest embers of humiliation. "You don't understand a thing! Not a goddamn thing!"

Then she grabbed a glass and threw beer in my face.

"Mom? Dad?"

The twins stood in the doorway. Each held a game controller, and both looked scared.

"Is Mrs. Jordan okay?" David asked, his adolescent voice cracking.

I picked up a napkin and wiped my face. "No, but she will be."

"Let's get this mess cleaned up," Frank said, gathering up the bowls. "Looks like we're done playing cards for tonight."

I tossed the napkin onto the table. "Gee, you think?"

* * *

Toni and I rode home in silence.

I drove. In her current emotional state, I didn't trust her behind the wheel. She didn't argue, which told me how horrible she felt.

I swung into our driveway. She didn't immediately get out. I glanced over but couldn't see her clearly in the darkness. I could, though, hear her sniffling.

She kept a small package of tissues in the center console. I pulled one out and handed it to her. She took it. She didn't thank me.

A minute passed, two minutes. I listened to the engine tick as it cooled.

Finally, she said, "I was pretty awful tonight."

"Yes, you were."

"I don't know what to say, other than I'm sorry. I didn't mean the things I said. You're not the reason we're childless."

"Neither are you, but I get the feeling you blame yourself."

She stared into the darkness and whispered, "I do."

The engine stopped ticking. With the heat off, the interior quickly grew chilly and I shivered. It might not have been entirely from the cold.

"You're my wife," I said. "You're my partner and my best friend. We live this life together. What we accomplish, we accomplish together. Same goes for the opposite. We share in everything, the good and the bad. When we hit a speed bump, we help each other."

Earlier she had used the same phrase—speed bump—to describe the failure at not being pregnant. I wanted to let her know that I had been listening, and that I remembered. "Blame makes it easy to focus on the past, when we should be looking toward the future."

Toni grabbed another tissue and blew her nose.

"Are you going to be okay?" I asked.

"I don't know. I said some pretty horrible things." She shifted in her seat. I sensed she was facing me. "Do we have a future?"

"Of course we do. I'm not going to throw away the best thing in my life because of a few harsh words and a wet face." I shivered again, this time strong enough to hurt. The Advil had worn off, and my body ached. "Can we go inside? It's cold, and I need another painkiller."

"That's right, I forgot." Toni cracked open the door. The dome light winked on. She removed an amber-colored vial from her purse and shook out a pill. "Vicodin. Kerry gave them to me."

"I'll stick with ibuprofen."

"Don't be stubborn. You're hurting."

"It's not bad. I'll be fine."

She lifted my shirt, exposing the ugly bruise on my chest. "Not bad?"

"So I'm a little sore."

"More than a little, mister." With a cat-like grin, she slipped the pill in her mouth, leaned across the center console, and kissed me. I felt her tongue push the pill into my mouth. I tried to pull away, but she grabbed my head and held it in place. Her tongue pushed farther into my mouth, forcing the pill into the back of my throat. I had no choice but to swallow.

She kissed me in earnest before pulling away.

"Thank you for understanding," she said. "You're the most amazing man. I'm lucky to have you."

"The feeling goes both ways."

We got out of the car. The night was clear, moonless and vast, with stars shining like silver sequins.

"Let's get you tucked in," Toni said. "It's past your bedtime, and you need your rest."

"But I thought we would fool around."

"Not tonight, mister. It's sleepy time for you."

As if on cue, I yawned. My jaw creaked painfully. Was there any part of my body that didn't hurt?

"You win," I said, and followed her into the house.

She glanced over her shoulder. "Was there any doubt?"

* * *

I fell asleep quickly, so quickly I barely remembered crawling into bed, and dreamed my dreams. About what, I didn't recall. But I did know one thing.

I didn't like them.

Chapter Four

I woke the next morning groggy from the narcotics and in a lot of pain. My muscles ached, my joints felt stiff. And whoever had taken the baseball bat to the back of my neck was going to suffer big time.

With considerable effort, I shrugged off the covers and stood.

Disorientation swept over me. An image surfaced in my mind, greasy, like oil on the skin of a bubble.

Stars falling.

That was it—no sky, no earth, no nothing. Just stars falling.

The bubble burst.

The image was unsettling, like watching a Stanley Kubrick film on mushrooms.

I limped into the bathroom to brush my teeth.

The day had only started, and already I didn't like it.

* * *

I found Toni in the kitchen, sitting at the table and reading the morning paper.

"Good morning, sleepy head. How are you feeling?"

"Every part of me hurts." I shuffled over to the coffee pot. "You want a refill?"

"I'm good, thanks."

I poured a cup, opened the cabinet that held our cold medicine, and found the Advil. I shook out a tablet, thought about it, and added a second. I popped them into my mouth, followed by a coffee chaser. The whole mess burned going down.

"You look terrible," she said. "Didn't you sleep well?"

"Right through to morning."

"Me, too. I don't think I dreamed."

"I did. Bunch of weird ones. I bet they had something to do with the pill you gave me."

She went to the sink and rinsed her coffee cup. When she was done, she turned and crossed her arms under her breasts.

"I'm not going to apologize. You needed the sleep, and you weren't going to get any if you ached all night."

"Your concern is duly noted."

"I did what I thought was best. Tell me you wouldn't have done the same had the situation been reversed."

"I might have, but not the same way you did."

The corners of her mouth turned up. "It was kind of sneaky."

"Yes, it was."

"You want some eggs? Taking ibuprofen on an empty stomach isn't good."

"Sure, thanks."

She opened the refrigerator door and reached inside. "Over easy, scrambled, or an omelet?"

"Surprise me," I said, picking up the newspaper. "But no mushrooms. I'm not in the mood today."

* * *

By the time we'd finished breakfast, I felt well enough to help with the dishes.

Toni stood at the sink, her hands in warm, soapy water as she scrubbed the skillet clean. I stood beside her, dish towel in hand.

"How's your thumb?"

I glanced at my bandaged hand. "I cleaned it this morning and didn't see any redness or swelling, nothing to indicate an infection. I'll keep checking it for the next few days. I think the nail's a goner, though."

"Small price to pay for keeping your life." She handed me the skillet. I dried it and put it away.

"Have you thought about what you want to do today?" I folded the towel and laid it on the counter. "Yard work is off my list for now, so we've got some free time."

"I'll cut the grass. You go lay down. Your body needs to heal."

"How about we go lay down together? I'm too sore for romance, but we could cuddle. I know that'd help me feel better."

"But the grass—"

"—will be there next week."

The sounds of children playing outside drew her attention, and her gaze drifted to the kitchen window. She watched them: the childless mother.

"Hey," I said, and touched her shoulder. "What're you thinking?"

She didn't look away from the children. "I was awful last night. I need to make up for it."

"What's say we forget about last night. Neither of us was at our best."

"You didn't do anything wrong."

"I didn't do anything right, either."

"You ended up with beer on your face."

"And we both had our say about it. We told each other how we felt. There's nothing else to cover. It's time to move on."

"Is that what you tell your patients—pretend it never happened?"

"You're twisting my words around. Last night happened, and we addressed it. It's over. What good would it do to dwell on it?"

Still gazing out the window, Toni said, "I can't put it aside as easily as you can. I don't have your capacity for forgiveness."

"You see misbehavior every day at work. Do you hold grudges against your students?"

"Of course not. They're only kids."

"You forgive them."

She hesitated. "I suppose."

"Then forgive yourself. You're as deserving as they are."

I wanted to add "it's as easy as that" but didn't. Nothing about self-esteem and change was easy: ask any homeless person in a shelter, any drug addict in rehab, any criminal in a jail cell. If it were easy, we would all live in a perfect world.

"You're asking too much," she said. "I don't have enough room. My heart is too constricted."

"There's always room for forgiveness."

"Perhaps not for me."

I considered what she was asking. "You really want to do this?"

She nodded. "I think I have to."

"And cutting the grass will be enough? We won't have the same discussion later?"

She finally turned to face me. There was a hint of relief in her eyes, and no small amount of gratitude. "Promise."

"Fair enough. I only ask that we do it together. I'll trim and edge, you push the mower. Deal?"

"Deal." She gave me a hug. "I love you."

"Love you, too."

* * *

It took us two hours to finish the lawn. Toni smiled the entire time.

I struggled with the trimmer. It was gas powered and required a pull on a starter cord to fire it up. With my wounded thumb, I couldn't grip the handle properly. Each time I gave it a yank, it would slip through my fingers. I tried pulling left-handed. It was still painful, not to mention awkward, but finally the trimmer whirred to life. I was in business.

We ended our respective jobs at nearly the same time, though I should have finished long before her. Toni put the lawn mower in the garage. I set the trimmer next to it.

"Time to hit the showers, mister," she said.

"Sounds like a plan."

In the bathroom, I shed my soiled, sweaty clothes. I saw in the mirror that the bruise on my chest had spread to my back, and the color had deepened to a brutal purple-black. No wonder my body ached.

Toni entered the bathroom and saw the bruise. Her expression darkened. "Why didn't you tell me?"

"You wouldn't have let me help if I had."

"This looks bad." She lightly ran her hands over my chest. "You want another Advil, or something stronger? I still have Kerry's Vicodin."

"Maybe later," I said, and turned the shower to hot. "Is there something you wanted to do this afternoon?"

"What I want is for you to stay in bed and heal."

I grabbed a towel. "I'd rather go somewhere. You know, get out of the house. Yesterday was a bitch. Let's make today better."

She stepped closer. Her hand gently traced the scrapes on my face, the bruise on my chest. Then, smiling, she slipped her hand around my penis and gave it a squeeze.

I felt myself stiffen. "Care to join me?" I said, nodding at the shower.

She began to unbutton her shirt. "I thought you'd never ask."

* * *

I slept after the shower.

When I woke, I found a glass of water and two Vicodin sitting on the nightstand. There was a note stuck to the glass.

EAT ME

I wasn't sure if it was a reference to Lewis Carroll's timeless story or a reminder of our adventures during the shower.

Maybe it was both.

Given how terrible I felt, I swallowed both and went in search of my wife.

I found her sitting in front of the computer, reading glasses perched on her nose. The screen displayed a map with directions listed along one side.

I kissed her on the cheek. "What're you doing?"

"Looking up the town Kerry and Frank visited when they went antiquing."

I leaned in. "Emersville?"

"Not as big as Shipshewana, but cute. Kerry liked it."

Shipshewana was one of Toni's favorite places to visit, a sprawling Indiana town near Michigan's border where you could buy all kinds of craft items, most of questionable usefulness or value. It was an easy way to waste several hours, especially if the weather was clear and cool.

"Why not just go to Shipshewana?" I asked. "You know what to expect there."

"It's closer. You shouldn't be gone for hours."

I scanned the directions. Emersville was less than an hour's drive. "You think it's worth the trip?"

"Kerry keeps bugging Frank to go back."

"Why doesn't he?"

"You seriously have to ask?"

Frank was a homicide detective. He sweated macho. To take him antiquing was akin to driving bamboo shoots under his fingernails.

"You sure you want to go there?"

"Yes."

"Let me grab a jacket."

Chapter Five

The drive to Emersville passed pleasantly enough. Traffic on Interstate 131 was light despite the clear sky and crisp, invigorating air. Autumn was special in Michigan, a time where the land grew into its own. Apple orchards drew visitors by the thousands for cider and donuts and hayrides. Families spent afternoons together scouring pumpkin patches for the perfect Halloween jack-o-lantern. Couples walked hand-in-hand along the trails that wound through the state's many parks.

The real treat, though, was the fall colors. Whole forests blazed with reds and yellows and oranges, a canopy of beauty unparalleled in the Midwest. Visitors flocked to the state from Ohio and Indiana and Wisconsin and even Canada to drive our highways and marvel at a land alive with breathtaking vistas.

We drove through this explosion of beauty until we reached the exit for Emersville.

"Do you know anything about this town?" I asked Toni, who had once again insisted on driving.

"Only what Kerry told me. It's full of little shops and restaurants. A bed and breakfast. A motel. It even has a cafe that serves high end coffees. Not the fake 'gourmet' stuff you find at grocery stores. We're talking top shelf stuff—Stumptown, Java Master, Monkey and Sons. Sounds like big business, too. Kerry and Frank had to wait fifteen minutes for their drinks."

The average price for quality coffees ran north of sixteen dollars a pound. What kind of population, both in size and household income, would the town need to support a product that expensive?

"How big did you say this place is?"

"I don't know. Can't be too big, not out here."

"Must have one hell of a tourist trade to support an expensive coffee shop."

We approached an intersection. The light turned red, and Toni stopped.

I fidgeted with my shoulder harness. It was digging into my sore chest. "Are you looking for anything specific on this excursion?"

"Christmas gifts, mostly, for my sisters and yours. I doubt Steve would be interested in anything we find there."

"Not unless it was made of microcircuits." My brother was a professor of electrical engineering at the University of Michigan and had little interest in anything bigger than an electron. "You're right about the girls. They love artsy-craftsy stuff."

"We also need something for my parents." She hesitated. "Any chance we'll hear from Doc Vader?"

Toni's parents, Ezra and Della, lived outside Gaylord in a house with lakefront footage and a covered pontoon boat Ezra used for fishing. Both had retired years ago, Ezra from teaching and Della from accounting, where she'd skillfully managed the family's finances into a tidy nest egg. I loved them both dearly.

My father, Ray (or as the family called him, Doc Vader), was another story. He and my mother attended medical school together. Dad specialized in vascular surgery. Mom's calling was internal medicine. Despite her passion for general practice, Dad felt she was wasting her talents on "people who didn't know better and couldn't have cared less." He urged her to specialize in something he felt was challenging enough, whether or not she had an interest in it. Mom flat-out refused and opened an office in one of the poorer suburbs of Grand Rapids, treating anyone who walked through her door, most on a paying basis, some not.

Dad hated the clinic. He told her the work was beneath them, when, in fact, he meant it was beneath *him*. He had chosen his career for the prestige. Seeing his wife find joy in being a simple family doctor vexed and perplexed him.

Theirs wasn't a happy marriage, for obvious reasons. I was surprised they'd gotten together long enough to have five kids.

Their dispute came to a head when Mom was diagnosed with ovarian cancer. Dad's unwavering faith in specialists was put to the test, and the specialists were found lacking.

He took her death hard. Not simply because she was gone, but because everything he had worked for, everything he had believed in, had failed him. He became angry and sullen and, finally, depressed. In the weeks following Mom's death, his depression worsened. All we could do was watch helplessly from the sidelines. Doc Vader would never tolerate interference from his children.

The hospital's chief of surgery urged him to take a bereavement leave, to get away from the stresses of the operating room. Dad flat-out refused. He equated taking the leave with a public display of failure, an indication that he wasn't coping, that he wasn't perfect. In his stubbornness, he failed to see the leave as an integral part of the coping process.

Then one day, not too long after the funeral, he was the surgeon on-call when rescue workers rushed a young boy into the ER. The kid had been involved in a head-on collision, a nasty accident that killed his parents. The force of the impact had caused a tear in his aorta—a small wound, barely a pinprick, but it would kill him if it wasn't immediately repaired.

Dad performed the surgery, an operation he should've been able to do in his sleep. Midway through the procedure, though, he started arguing with the nurse anesthetist. It was a minor thing, something to do with a fluctuation in the boy's blood pressure. When the nurse questioned him about it, Doc Vader lost it—he began yelling at the man, calling him a "dumb son of a bitch" who should "let those who know better run the goddamned operating room." In the middle of his rant, Dad jerked his head up, probably intent on further reprimanding the nurse, and when he did, his hand—the one holding the scalpel—moved. Not much, but enough. The blade sliced open the boy's aorta and he bled out in less than a minute.

Dad shouldn't have been working. He was still grieving. The review board came to the same conclusion and found him guilty of negligence by not taking the necessary leave.

Fines and a suspension followed, as did a civil suit.

Last I heard, Dad was living somewhere in California with a woman half his age. He no longer practiced medicine.

The light changed and Toni hit the gas.

We crossed a bridge, a narrow two-laner with steel guardrails. There was a blue SUV parked off to one side. A man leaned into the rear hatch. When he emerged, he was holding a fishing rod, a creel, and a pair of neoprene waders. He was older with gray hair and tanned skin. He waved as we passed.

I returned his wave. "The natives seem friendly enough."

"You were expecting cannibals?"

"It's a thing with small towns. Isolation makes them suspicious of strangers."

"It's a tourist town. They thrive on strangers. Besides, we're ten miles outside of town. The guy was probably from Battle Creek or Portage."

"Did you see the decals on the window?"

"I was too busy driving."

"There were two. One was a POAM sticker, the other a black badge with EPD written across in yellow." Frank had a POAM sticker on his car. It stood for Police Officers Association of Michigan. "I bet EPD stands for Emersville Police Department."

Toni eased up on the accelerator. "Was I speeding?"

"I think he was more interested in the trout than you. He's probably waist deep in that stream by now and praying the brownies bite."

She looked sheepishly at me. "Pretty silly, huh?"

"Yeah, pretty silly."

We traveled the rest of the way in silence.

Eventually I saw a tall, broad sign next to the road. As we drew near, the words on it became clear.

WELCOME TO EMERSVILLE
LITTLE CITY OF WONDERS!

"You found it," I said.

"Was there ever a doubt?"

Toni slowed the car as the speed limit plunged. We passed a newer-looking gas station. A Ford pickup sat at one of the pumps with a burly man in jeans filling the tank. His dark eyes followed us as we drove, his expression as muddy as his pickup.

"That's more like it," I said. "He could give Clint Eastwood squinting lessons."

"Maybe we made his day."

"Funny. Real funny."

"You should see me when I'm on a roll."

"Croissant or bagel?"

She laughed. "Stick with the shrink stuff, mister. Adam Sandler you ain't."

"Thank God."

The city of Emersville fleshed out. Retail stores populated the outer edges—two car dealerships (one Chevy, one Ford), a pharmacy, a grocer, bait and tackle shops (a requisite for every small town north and west of Detroit), a dry cleaner, and several other necessary but thoroughly mundane businesses.

I made a clucking noise with my tongue. "I don't see anything special. Certainly nothing that stands out from any other town."

"Wait until we get to the city center. Kerry said all the cool stuff was there."

Not likely, I thought.

The residential district was more upscale. Nice, in fact, with well-maintained homes and, in a few cases, white picket fences. Two women in light jackets walked a Yorkshire Terrier and chatted animatedly. Another woman jogged past them, headed in the other direction, her ponytail bouncing with each step. They nodded to one another as they passed.

"What do you think now?" Toni said.

"Okay, the homes are nice. But I still don't understand the allure of this place."

She turned a corner, we hit the central part of Emersville, and I had to eat my words.

The town opened up. Businesses loomed on larger parcels of land, giving the impression that the city had somehow grown, that it occupied more space than it actually did. Gone were the utilitarian stores of the suburbs. Here the shops (some would call them boutiques) appeared more inviting, the buildings rendered in warmer shades of brown and green. The old-time quaint vibe was so strong I found myself searching for a wooden Indian standing in front of a five-and-dime.

What shocked me most, though, was how new everything looked, as if this part of town had sprung up overnight. Buildings had fresh coats of paint. Sidewalks and roads seemed freshly poured.

There was no wear or tear, no graffiti, no litter.

"This looks a little too perfect," I said.

Toni pointed. "See, there's the coffee shop."

The place was called *Black and Brewed*, and it was massive. Two stories tall with an open roof where patrons could sit under wide umbrellas and sip espresso, the brick and steel edifice took up most of a city block. Heavy metal guardrails ran the length of the roof line. Tinted windows like great dark eyes glared out from beneath scalloped awnings.

The word *formidable* sprang to mind: Fort Knox for Generation C. Why any business would want to project that kind of image baffled me.

A line of customers trailed out the door.

I checked my watch. "It's four in the afternoon."

"Coffee's big business here." Toni pulled into an open spot near the far end of the street.

I climbed out of the 4Runner, my muscles stiff and sore, my knees popping like firecrackers. I stepped onto the sidewalk. Toni met me there. Her hand slipped into mine.

"Where do you want to start?" she asked, dashing any hope I had that this would be a quick, get-in-and-get-out operation.

"Well, we've got the coffee shop. There's a *Dairy Queen* and a restaurant, if you're hungry. Something called *Lost Desires*." I checked out the other direction. "Not much this way. Mostly a bed and breakfast and a—"

I stopped, the rest of the words stuck in the back of my throat, choking me. The hairs on my arms rose in a terrified wave.

My dream from last night, it returned with a crash, threatening to overwhelm me. Vague images of something sickly green and glowing. Mist hanging low on a lake. Water. Suffocating water. And...and....

I began to tremble.

"Brad, are you okay?" Toni's voice sounded distant, as if it had travelled from a distant place and time. She shook my shoulder. "Hey, say something. You're scaring me."

"I—oh, Jesus—look at that." I pointed over her shoulder.

She turned to look. "You mean the motel?"

"Yes, the motel."

"What about it?"

"Look at the sign."

"I don't get it. What's wrong with the sign?"

I glanced fearfully over her shoulder. The motel stood two blocks away, an old fashioned, one story structure stretching from a corner office to the end of the block. Each room had a brass number on its door. A large marquee loomed over the office, midnight blue with bright white lights spelling out its name.

Star Fall Motel.

To complete the picture, the sign had several shooting stars streaking across the background, their long comas trailing behind them like fiery tongues.

My dream. Stars falling. *Stars falling.*

I swallowed. My spit burned like acid going down.

Toni moved to block my view, her face etched with concern. "Brad, honey. You're freaking me out."

"I had a dream last night," I said. "Several, really, but I don't remember much about the others. The one that stood out involved stars...stars falling through a night sky. They fell and fell, and I fell with them. I fell for what seemed like years." My eyes found hers. "I cried out for you. I remember screaming your name, over and over, but I couldn't hear my voice. I couldn't hear anything. There was nothing. I think that frightened me the most. I was completely alone."

As I talked, a car rolled slowly by—the pickup we'd seen earlier at the gas station. The driver stared at us, his eyes now hidden behind a pair of sunglasses. When he saw me staring back, he quickly accelerated and was gone.

I returned my attention to Toni. "Pretty stupid, huh. Letting a dream bother me that much."

"Everyone's entitled to a nightmare now and then." She cocked her head to one side. "Why didn't you tell me about it?"

"It was silly, a fragment of an image. I didn't fully remember it until I saw the sign."

"Let's forget the motel for now," Toni said. "How about we get a cup of coffee?"

"Sure, sounds great."

We walked toward the coffee shop. For some reason, I felt an urge to glance over my shoulder. It was strong, powerful: a pressure, like someone poking a finger into the back of my brain. It was so compelling I almost stopped and turned. But I resisted. I kept my face forward. I didn't want to see the sign again, stupid as it sounded.

The sun had fallen, lengthening the shadows. Cool air swept in, carrying the clean smell of pine and water. There was probably a lake nearby. No surprise. Michigan was full of them.

We came to an intersection, waited patiently for a car to pass, and crossed.

The stores here had a definite touristy feel. We passed a bakery called Patty's Pastries, the display window filled with an assortment of decadent confections. Next was the five-and-dime I'd looked for earlier, sans the wooden Indian. It did, however, have a penny press in front—an old fashioned, crank-style machine where you put in a penny and it pressed the coin into a smooth oval. Pretty stupid, if you asked me.

We ignored the penny press, not sparing it a second look, and arrived at the trinket store, *Lost Desires*.

The building had perfect cedar siding and a wood awning stained dark walnut. Iron coat hooks were nailed to the support poles. A water barrel sat at the far end with a downspout ending just above its surface. There was even a horseshoe nailed above the door; like everything else here, it looked brand new. All the place needed was a wagon wheel bolted to the storefront to complete the western theme.

Toni stopped. "This place looks cute."

"Absolutely," I said, straight-faced. "As adorable as it gets."

"Sorry, I know you don't like this kind of thing."

Her admonition, however gently delivered, stung. We were here because of me, though I had insisted we go more for her sake than anything else. Now I was acting smug and trite. Talk about being off your game.

"Want to take a look inside?"

"Would you mind?"

"Of course not." I opened the door. "Ladies first."

"Why, thank you, sir," she said, and scooted inside.

As expected, the typical tourist trinkets filled the first few shelves. To my surprise, I also saw a section of pottery pieces, most of which looked Native American, and hammered copper sculptures, tall and graceful and sweeping. As we wandered through the store, we found shelves of hand-painted ornaments, laminated jewelry boxes, hand-blown glass baubles, and other collectibles. Surprisingly, one section contained an assortment of toys, dolls, and games that would make a child quake with excitement. I picked up a *Monopoly* box, the surface worn smooth by years of handling, and lifted the lid.

"Damn," I said softly.

Toni stepped closer. "What is it?"

"The game. See the black border on the box? And there are two patents listed, with no copyright. It's a Black Box Number Five edition, released in 1935. Very rare. Looks like it has all the pieces too."

"You're the game junkie, not me. Is it worth much?"

I turned the game over and showed her the price tag.

"You're kidding," she said. "Who'd pay that much for a game?"

A woman stepped around the end of the aisle. She was slender as a willow, her silver hair done up in a bun, and wore clothes nearly as old as the *Monopoly* game. "Not as many as I would like, I'm afraid."

"Are you the owner?" Toni asked.

The woman nodded. "Annabelle St. Crux."

"Pleased to meet you. I'm Toni Jordan, and this is my husband, Brad."

I held out the game. "Where did you find this?"

Annabelle's smile widened, revealing small teeth stained a dingy brown. "Garage sale, if you can believe it. The owner practically gave it away."

"Nice find." I eyed the box a final time and set it back on the shelf. "Quite a collection you have here."

"The toy section is my favorite."

"Is there a demand for high end toys?" I asked.

Annabelle caressed the *Monopoly* game with a thin, shaking finger. "Like I said, not much. I sell maybe a piece or two a month. People mostly go for the everyday trinkets near the front. Tourists are all the same." She took in the bruises on my face. "You look awful. Are you all right?"

I smiled. "A little sore, but I'll live."

"I thought this town was some sort of antiquing mecca," Toni said.

"There are enough shops to keep you busy," Annabelle said, "but we only recently started building our antiquing reputation. I suspect Shipshewana still gets a majority of the hardcore collectors."

"Have you been here long?" I asked.

"Two years this November," she said with a sigh. "They haven't been easy years either. Starting a new venture like this never is. I hope to turn a profit with the fall shopping season. My seed money is dwindling rapidly."

"We're hoping to find gifts for our family," Toni said. "Christmas presents and such. Our friends were here a few weeks ago. They bought a doll, possibly from you. Yarn for hair, white button eyes. Blue dress."

Annabelle nodded. "I remember them. A pleasant woman. Her husband was big, kind of direct."

"Kerry and Frank," Toni said. "Kerry suggested we visit. She loved this town."

"A charming woman. I hope she's enjoying the doll. It's very special."

"Special?" I said. "In what way?"

"I'm sorry, I meant the doll is special to me. I make them myself and consider them all special." Stepping over to the collection, Annabelle picked one up, a classic Raggedy Ann, and hugged it to her chest. "I love my dolls. I name each one, you know. This is Thumbkin. She's one of my favorites."

"Thumbkin," said Toni. "As in the nursery rhyme?"

Annabelle yawned, her jaw stretching to the point where the joints popped. "Pardon me. I haven't gotten much sleep lately. Where was I? Oh, yes. Thumbkin. When I first held her, the name popped into my head. It's been that way for each member of my little family." She returned Thumbkin to her spot. "Were you looking for anything particular?"

"I'm a child psychologist. Dolls are part of my therapy routine. How would you like to see one of your family help a troubled child?" I picked up Thumbkin. "This one, perhaps. If you don't mind parting with her?"

"I wouldn't have her out if I didn't want to sell her." Annabelle took the doll from me. To Toni, she said, "And what about you? Were you looking for something specific? Perhaps a gift for a son or daughter? We have an assortment of toys. I wouldn't recommend the *Monopoly* game, of course. That's more for a collector, not a—" She frowned at Toni. "Is there something wrong, dear? You've gone pale."

Toni had indeed turned pale, and her lower lip began to quiver.

"Why don't you go look for something for your parents?" I gave her shoulder a reassuring squeeze. "I'll join you in a moment."

"Excuse me," she said to Annabelle and hurried off.

Annabelle watched her go. "What did I say?"

"It's not you. We've been trying to start a family, without much success. Your comment about children struck a nerve. She'll be fine in a few minutes."

"Poor dear. I didn't mean to upset her."

"It's not your fault. You didn't know." I gestured to the toy collection. "You seem fond of toys. Do you have children?"

A sadness came over her, and she shook her head. "Kids never worked out for me. I never married, so I never had the opportunity. I guess that's why I enjoy my dolls. They're surrogates. I care about them as much as I would my own children." She held up Thumbkin. "Thank you for giving her a home."

"More office than home, but at least she'll be with kids."

"Better than spending your life on a store shelf." She made a dismissive gesture. "I've taken up enough of your time. You're here to shop, not gab with an old biddy. Let's go see if your wife found anything."

It turned out she had. We met at the counter near the cash register.

"I can't believe this place," Toni said, handing her credit card to Annabelle. "Look at all this. I've finished a lot of my holiday shopping."

I smiled at her happiness. Retail therapy at its finest.

"Here," I said, setting Thumbkin on the counter. "Don't forget her."

Annabelle rang up the purchases and handed Toni the receipt. "I want to apologize for upsetting you. I hope it didn't turn you off to the town."

"Nonsense," Toni said. "I found you and your store charming. I'll be sure to tell my friends. Maybe drum up some business."

"You are a dear." Annabelle yawned again, her hand covering her mouth. "I think I need more coffee." Her expression brightened. "Wait here, I'll be right back. I want to do something special for you." She hurried off.

"What was that about?" Toni asked me.

"Beats me. Guess we'll find out."

Annabelle returned carrying a bar of soap wrapped in clear cellophane and tied with a lavender bow. She handed it to Toni. "You've heard about aromatherapy? Well, this is our most fragrant soap. Smells like pine and fertile earth. Hold it up to your nose."

Toni inhaled. "Wow. I've never smelled anything like this in a soap."

She held it to my nose. "That is different," I said.

"Take it," Annabelle said. "Use it. I guarantee it'll help."

"Help with what?" Toni said.

"Everything," Annabelle said excitedly. "It's good for everything."

"Okay," I said, not understanding the woman's excitement. It was only soap. "Thanks, I guess."

Toni gave me a sharp look. "Don't be rude."

"It's okay, dear," Annabelle said. "He's a man, and men don't understand these things. Use the soap. Nighttime is best. It'll help you relax."

Toni dropped the bar into her purse. "I will. Thank you so much."

Annabelle yawned a third time, the widest yet. Her hand came up to cover her mouth, except this time it slid part way *into* her mouth. Then, to my dismay, she bit down, her teeth pressing into the flesh until I thought she would draw blood.

"Ms. St. Crux?" I said, alarmed by the sudden bizarre behavior.

Annabelle bit down harder. A drop of blood rolled down the back of her hand. She turned her head toward the doll collection, and when she did, her eyes jerked back and forth, as if someone were tugging on them with an invisible string. This eerie tremor continued until she turned back to face us.

Alarm changed to concern. The jerky eye movement was called nystagmus, an involuntary condition most often associated with central nervous system disorders. At her age, it would likely be caused by a stroke or a brain tumor, and she wasn't showing any evidence of a stroke.

She removed her hand from her mouth, ignoring the smear of blood on her skin. "I'm childless myself," she told Toni. "I understand the pain you're feeling, and I wanted to help you feel better."

"That's not necessary," Toni said warily.

"Yes, you did nothing wrong." I hesitated, unsure of how to proceed without overstepping ethical boundaries. But if I was right and she had a brain tumor, she would need treatment immediately. "I noticed you have a slight eye tremor. It's probably nothing, but you should have it checked out."

Annabelle St. Crux's eyes jerked again, a lethal waltz played out in windows to her soul, and she suddenly stiffened. Her head bent back, the cords of her neck straining. Fine tremors ran though her like shimmers of oil on a hot skillet.

Fearing a seizure, I rushed around the counter, grabbed her, and eased her to the floor. I removed my jacket and placed it under her head. "Toni, we're going to need an ambulance."

Toni opened her purse. Annabelle's hand shot out and grabbed my wrist.

"No," she said, her voice little more than a papery whisper. "Please, no doctors."

"You don't understand," I said. "We need to get you to a hospital."

Annabelle's eyes rolled wildly. "I said no god-spilled doctors!"

"This is no time to—"

"*You horrid, cock-sucking bitch! We're not yours to do with—!*" Annabelle's eyes screwed shut. "You stop this right now."

"Oh, Jesus." I looked at Toni. "We need that ambulance."

Toni's hand dove into her purse. "I'm on it."

"*No...,*" Annabelle said. "Keep the...*run*...doctors away."

While Toni made the call, Annabelle's back arched obscenely, her modest chest rising up off the floor like a treat offered to a lover. Her lips peeled back and she made a gut-wrenching sound, somewhere between a frustrated wail and a terrified scream.

Toni kneeled next to me. "Ambulance is on its way."

"Help me turn her on her side," I said, and we maneuvered Annabelle around. "Did they say how long?"

"No more than a few minutes. Is she going to be okay?"

"I hope so."

Annabelle's chaotic mutterings continued. "*Water...stop...hate the water...shut up...afraid of it.*"

I felt my skin prickle in fear. "Stay away from her mouth."

Toni jerked her hands back. "Why?"

"Rabies. People with it hate water. If that's what she has, you don't want to be bitten."

Annabelle spewed more foul language, words worthy of a jaded longshoreman. She bucked hard, and I reluctantly had to grab her head to keep it from smacking on the floor.

"Oh my god," Toni said. "Rabies can do this?"

"I don't know, I think so. Where's the damn ambulance?"

Sirens sounded in the distance. They grew increasingly shrill, until they cut off in front of the store. The front door banged open.

I waved a hand above the counter. "Over here."

Two paramedics approached, followed by a policeman.

We made room for the paramedics. One held Annabelle, while the other shoved a stick wrapped with thick white tape in between her teeth.

"She was going on about hating water," I said. "She might have hydrophobia."

The policeman, a younger man with coal black hair, grabbed my elbow. "Come with me, please. I could use help. Ma'am, if you don't mind?" He beckoned for Toni to follow.

Outside, the officer opened the ambulance's bay doors. I helped him remove the gurney.

"Wait right here," he said, and returned to the store. Before long, the paramedics emerged with Annabelle St. Crux strapped securely to the gurney, still snarling and swearing.

Her wild eyes locked onto me. "Water is the beginning and the end," she yelled. "Remember that! *Remember it!*"

The paramedics loaded her into the ambulance and sped off, siren wailing.

The officer walked out of the store. He held out a shopping bag. "This yours?"

"Thank you," Toni said, accepting the bag. "Is she going to be okay?"

"Don't know," the officer said. "That'll be up to the doctors over at St. Mary's. I'm Kent, by the way. Kent Couttis."

"Brad Jordan. This is my wife, Toni."

Officer Couttis pulled out a notepad. "What happened in there?"

While Toni related our experience, I watched Officer Couttis scribble down her words. He couldn't have been more than twenty-five, with eyes the color of new steel and an open face that had not yet lost the softer edges of adolescence. He wore his uniform the way some boys wore their first suit to a formal school dance—stiff and uncomfortable, with his shirt sleeves a little too long and a neck hole that looked like an oversized pipe. He fidgeted a lot and sucked on his lower lip as he wrote.

Toni finished recounting the events of Annabelle St. Crux's seizure. Officer Couttis turned to me. "Can you add anything?"

"I think she might have rabies, or possibly a brain tumor." I described the nystagmus and her aversion of water. "You might want to radio ahead to the hospital."

Officer Couttis snapped his notebook closed. "You a doctor?"

"Ph.D., not MD. But I've had some training, and I interned in a hospital." I heard my own words and almost winced at how lame they sounded. "We were just trying to help."

"I'll let the hospital know of your concerns." He peered closely at me. "You sure you don't need an ambulance? You look like ten miles of badly laid asphalt."

I gestured to his notepad. "Do you need anything else from us? It's getting late, and we'd like to start for home."

"I've got your contact information. I'll let you know if I have more questions."

"Certainly." I slipped my hand into Toni's. "Feel free to call."

"Hold on a sec," said Officer Couttis. A blue SUV was racing our way, emergency lights flashing. It pulled to a stop next to us.

I recognized it as the one we had passed earlier, and out climbed the man I had seen readying himself for an afternoon of trout fishing. He had shed the waders and now wore a pair of faded jeans and hiking boots. Instead of a fishing pole, he sported a sidearm in a holster clipped to his belt.

"Whatcha got, Kent?" he asked.

"Ms. St. Crux had an episode of some kind." Officer Couttis gestured to Toni and me. "These folks called for an ambulance, and then stayed with her until it arrived."

"Episode?" the chief said, his white eyebrows climbing. "Like the kind I get?"

Kent Couttis shook his head. "Didn't sound like it."

"All right." The man turned and stuck out his hand. "Gordon Couttis. Chief of this little burg. Appreciate you helping our Annabelle."

"Couttis?" I said, exchanging handshakes and glancing at the officer, whose face had gone a deep shade of red.

"Kent's my boy," Chief Couttis said. "Fine young man. Me and the missus are proud of him."

"He handled himself well," I said. "I can see why you'd be proud."

"You folks here for the first time?" the chief asked.

Toni held up our bag of goodies. "We came to do a little shopping."

"We appreciate you sharing some of your hard-earned money with us. Every little bit helps."

"Dad?" Officer Couttis said, his voice barely above a whisper.

Gordon Couttis faced his son. The two shared the same steel eyes, though the chief's were more tarnished. "What?"

"Would you like to hear my report?"

"Are you gonna type it up?"

The younger Couttis nodded, and the elder Couttis gave his son a patient look. "Then I'll read it tomorrow, won't I?"

Kent Couttis's cheeks grew redder. He slipped the notebook into his pocket. "I'll go check on Ms. St. Crux. Maybe she's well enough to add to the report. Pleasure to meet you, Dr. Jordan. Mrs. Jordan."

Chief Couttis looked at me with surprise. "You a doctor?"

"Psychologist, but I know enough of the medical stuff to get in trouble."

"Me too," Chief Couttis said. "Been epileptic since I was a boy. You learn a lot when you're around the white coats all the time." He pointed to my face. "Someone did a number on your mug. Did it happen here?"

I touched my cheek. The skin felt warm from the bruising. "Traffic accident near Rock Mills. I'm lucky I walked away with only this."

Chief Couttis grimaced. "Hope they got the other fella. That is, if he lived."

"No dead bodies, Chief. We're all good."

"Do you mind if we go?" Toni asked the chief. "I'd like to get him home. He feels worse than he's letting on."

"Sorry, ma'am. I'm a bit of a talker." Chief Couttis looked me over a last time. "Ice those bruises, son. I hope you feel better."

"I'll call if I have any questions," the younger Couttis said. "Thanks again for staying with Ms. St. Crux."

"Please tell her we wish her well," Toni said. "She seems like a nice lady."

"Will do," he replied.

Toni led me away. She was right. The ibuprofen had worn off, and the pain had returned with a vengeance.

"Poor baby," she said, opening the car door for me. "You must be suffering."

I slid into the seat. Pain shot from my hip to my neck. "Try to avoid any railroad tracks."

While Toni climbed into the car, my eyes drifted to the *Star Fall Motel*, its sign now lit and flashing. The shooting stars looked like deadly asteroids hurtling toward the earth. God help the world should Bruce Willis die.

Toni pulled into the street. Chief Couttis and his son were standing in front of *Lost Desires*. I waved as we approached. Officer Couttis waved back. His father, however, leaned close to his son and said something. The younger Couttis, looking startled, pulled out his notepad and pen and started scribbling furiously.

He was staring at our car as he did.

* * *

We arrived at home well after the dinner hour. I put the Raggedy Ann doll on the table near the front door so I wouldn't forget to bring it to work. Next, I swallowed two more painkillers and drew a hot bath. Toni busied herself in the kitchen preparing a meal.

Lying in the tub, with the heat working its magic on my sore muscles, I thought about Annabelle St. Crux. The doctors would run a plethora of tests on her—CT scans, blood work, toxicity and drug screens, metabolic panels. They would check for swelling of the blood vessels in her retinas; a sure indication of a brain tumor. I didn't know a lot about rabies screenings, but I was sure the results would take at least a day to come back, likely longer than the doctors would want to wait. They'd start vaccinations against the disease immediately, without waiting for confirmation. I prayed she would be all right.

Closing my eyes, I sank into the tub until my chin touched the water. Warmth flowed into my limbs. My muscles loosened, the pain in my joints receded. I sighed heavily. I hated to see people suffer. Annabelle St. Crux, with whatever ailed her. Doug Belle, with his father forever gone and his mother seemingly incapable of coping with either her loss or her child's suffering. Frank and his financial straits. Kerry and her pregnancy. And Toni, my beautiful, wonderful, caring wife. Watching her suffer hurt the most. I hadn't made it any better by doubting her. I needed to let the past go.

The heat and the painkillers combined to make me drowsy, and my mind reluctantly wandered back to six years ago. The day Toni almost destroyed our marriage.

I was standing in the kitchen, slicing beef into thin strips to use for fajitas, when she said something I didn't quite understand.

"Say again." The chef's knife zipped back and forth across the meat. "I don't think I heard you right."

"An affair," she said. "I had an affair. With a man. Another teacher."

I stopped what I was doing. My wife, the woman I loved more than anyone, had had an *affair*? My mind suddenly ceased to function. I fumbled for something to say. What finally came out was pure stupidity.

"Oh, have I met him before?"

The blood drained from Toni's face. "That's it? That's your response?"

I set the knife down. It suddenly felt too comfortable in my hand. "Do I know him?"

"Yes," she whispered.

"His name?"

"Bryan Hinson."

"Hinson?" I flipped through my mental catalogue of her coworkers until I put a face to the name. "Short. Grayish hair. Teaches what, science?"

"Brad, please—"

"Is it him?"

"Do we have to—"

"Is it him?"

She looked away. It was all the answer I needed.

"Just perfect," I said, and went to the sink to wash my hands. The water was cold. I adjusted the tap until steam rose from the basin. I needed to feel something other than rage and hurt and terrible loss. My wife had had an affair. She had betrayed our vows. She had betrayed me.

"When did it start?" I asked, the skin on my hands turning pink under the hot water.

"It's hard to say." She turned so her back faced me. You didn't need a degree in psychology to understand what the gesture meant. "We've been talking for months. Mostly between classes, sometimes during lunch." She hesitated. "Occasionally over drinks after work."

I grabbed the soap and began vigorously scrubbing. "Go on. I know there has to be more. Did you sleep with him?"

Toni hesitated. "It seems so stupid now."

Her answer didn't surprise me. Fucking was at the heart of an affair. I swallowed back the words I wanted to spit at her, the rage I wanted to sling in her face, and focused on soaping up my hands. My skin had turned from pink to red.

"Look at what our lives had become," she said. "I'd leave for school before you were awake. You'd see patients late into the evening. Sometimes you didn't get home until after I was in bed. We barely saw each other. It wasn't what I thought our marriage would be like. I got...I guess I got lonely."

Pain, both physical and emotional, brought tears to my eyes. I let them fall into the sink. "So instead of telling me, you ran into someone else's arms. Perfect. I'm a therapist—I listen to problems for a living—yet you couldn't tell the person you claim to love that you were hurting."

"I wasn't sure how."

"You open your fucking mouth and tell me."

She was quiet for a moment. When she finally continued, her voice trembled. "The situation had changed. We were no longer students. We were working, money was tight. My job provided a steady income, but you needed time to build a clientele. I'm not making excuses either. I knew this would be the case going in. But I also saw the stress you were under. The last thing you needed was a whiny, complaining wife."

I remembered those days—scraping by to make mortgage payments, downscaling meals so we could pay this bill or that. To this day I refused to eat ramen.

"Then there was your dad," Toni said.

I stopped scrubbing my hands and frowned. "What's he got to do with this?"

"I knew how intensely he felt about his career. He valued success over everything, even your mother. If his intensity had rubbed off on you...." Her voice trailed off.

"You were worried about pushing me over the edge."

She turned to face me. "Yes."

Toni had met Doc Vader on many occasions. She had witnessed his rants about my mother's career choice, how his vilification of her had driven a wedge between him and his children, and how that wedge hadn't stopped his horrible behavior.

And I was his son: Luke to his Anakin. With genetics playing such a strong role in behavior, I understood her concern, not that it excused her behavior.

I turned off the water. Blisters had formed on the backs of my hands. "Why are you telling me this now?"

Toni bit her lip. "He's on his way over."

A small, previously-unknown part of me started to grin. "He's coming here?"

"I broke it off, told him we were through. He won't take no for an answer."

"Do you love him?"

"No, I don't. I don't think I ever did."

"Do you want a divorce?"

"No! Oh, god no! I'm so sorry this happened. I don't know what I was thinking."

I glanced at her wedding ring. "Is he married?"

"Not happily."

"So you two had more in common than just sex?"

She didn't answer.

"What do we do about your boyfriend?" I asked her. "He'll be here soon."

"He's not my boyfriend," she replied stiffly.

"Okay, your lover. Your paramour. Your fuck-buddy. Whatever you want to call him. What do we do about him?"

"I'll deal with him. I'm a big girl. I can clean up my own messes."

My eyes drifted to the knife. "I could deal with him."

"Oh, no. You stay here." She cupped my face in her hands. I resisted the urge to jerk away. "I know you're hurt. I wish to hell this had never happened, but it did. And it's over. I was terrified at the thought of losing you." Her lips brushed mine. "I love you. We'll work it out, same as we have any other time, I promise. Just give me a chance. Let me make it right."

A whirlwind of emotions blew madly through me, and for a moment I was overwhelmed by an urge to see my mother. I wanted to talk to her, to have her hold me, to run her fingers through my hair and tell me everything would be all right. But my mom had died months ago, her familiar comforts buried with her cancer-ridden body. My dad, distant as a far flung galaxy in the corner of the universe, saw nothing but himself and the torn rage he felt for a profession that had failed him. All I had left was Toni. She had hurt me, but through the pain, I also remembered how much I loved her. I began to cry.

"I don't know how I feel," I said, the words coming out in shuddering, wrenching sobs. "I don't know what to do."

"Then don't do anything." She pulled me into a gentle embrace. "Let me deal with this. We'll talk afterward."

I nodded into her shoulder.

The doorbell rang.

Toni pulled away. "I'll be right back. Please, stay in the kitchen."

I took her hands in mine and squeezed, firm enough she'd know I was hurting, but not hard enough to hurt her back. "We'll do this together. I won't pretend I'm not hurt or mad or jealous as hell, but you're my wife. You won't face this without me beside you. Maybe I should have been doing more of that from the beginning."

"I love you," she said. "I don't expect you to feel the same, but I hope one day to win your love back."

The doorbell rang again. I nodded toward the living room. "Shall we?"

I followed her through the living room to the front door. She took a deep, centering breath and opened it.

Bryan Hinson stood there, sweat beaded on his brow and dark blotches staining the armpits of his white button-down shirt. He was breathing heavily, his face flushed.

"About damn—!" He stopped when he saw me. "Oh, Brad. Sorry, I wasn't expecting you."

"I would imagine not," I said.

"Can I have a few minutes of Toni's time? We have a couple school issues to discuss."

"Say what you came to say," Toni told him. "I don't want to spend all afternoon standing on the porch."

That brought him up short. "Can't we, you know, go somewhere a little more private?"

I pointed behind me. "Would our bedroom do? I'm sure you'd feel more comfortable there. It's down the hall, last room on the left. I'll wait here. You may as well take advantage of all my amenities."

Hinson shot her a black look. "What's he talking about?"

"I told him," Toni said. "He knows everything. The lunches, the after school drinks, the sleeping together. Everything."

Bryan Hinson's eyes darted to me. He was probably gauging the likelihood of an ass-whooping. On a scale of one to ten, I put his chances at eight.

Then Hinson said, "She loves me, you know. She wants to be with me. Tell him, Toni."

His chances surged to thirteen.

"I won't," Toni said. "Because it's not true."

"Bullshit, you said it to me the other day."

"I never said I loved you," Toni told him. "Not once."

"Not once," I said, and slipped my arm around Toni's waist. I didn't feel like hugging her. I didn't feel like being in the same room with her. I also knew we'd never get past this unless we knocked Hinson back on his heels. "She told me, you know."

Toni stiffened, then tentatively slid her arm around me. She may not have known what to expect, but she knew enough to play along when she saw it.

"Oh, how cute," Hinson said. "You two, arm-in-arm, like nothing happened. Well, you can pretend all you want, but you can't erase the past." He turned to me. "You sure you want to stay with someone who cheated on you?"

I bristled. "You sure you want someone who cheats?"

"Leave him alone, Bryan," Toni said. "He's the one person who did nothing wrong."

Hinson smirked. "If he did nothing wrong, why'd you end up in my bed, with my cock buried deep inside you?"

The whoop-ass scale shot past twenty, and I bolted forward. My fist connected with Hinson's face, my knuckles exploding in pain, but I didn't care. I hit him again, this time in the gut. Hinson doubled over and started retching. Toni grabbed my arm and pleaded with me to stop. I shook her off. Pain and rage and betrayal and grief rose in me like a lava flow, consuming me, and I snatched a handful of Hinson's hair and pulled him up, my fist raised, ready to deliver another blow. Hinson looked at me, blood flowing from the corner of his mouth, his eyes wide, fearful. He raised his hands in a feeble effort to defend himself. It was such a pitiful gesture I paused, saw him for the coward he really was—the loser who used people as long as he got what he wanted. He reminded me of the kids I treated, poor, lost, mixed up children who were only now developing their moral compasses. Hinson was nothing more than an oversized kid; an emotional bully hiding in an adult's body. I wondered for a moment about his students and how he treated them. I would bring it up with Toni later, if we had a later.

I released Hinson. He quickly stumbled out of reach. "Go home," I said. "Apologize to your wife for being a scumbag. Beg for her forgiveness and pray she gives it to you. For her sake, I hope she doesn't. Oh, and one more thing—stay away from Toni. No contact, no emails, no texts, no friendly chats in the hallway at school. Nothing. I catch you sniffing around my wife again and there won't be enough of you left to bury in a shoe box."

Bryan Hinson tried to straighten, but my punch must've busted something inside him. Wincing, he wrapped his arm around his gut. "You fucked up, Jordan. Wait'll the cops get here. Let's see how well you defend her honor from jail."

I pulled out my cell and hit speed dial. "Hey, Frank," I said into the phone. "Got a guy here who wants to talk with you. Hold on." I held the phone out to Hinson, who eyed the device like it was a poisonous snake. "Who is it?" he asked.

"Frank Swinicki. Sargent, Rock Mills PD. His wife Kerry works with you too." I lifted the phone higher. "Go on, take it. Tell him you want to make a report. I'm sure he'll be happy to oblige."

Hinson hesitated, the scowl on his face deepening. He thought about it for a few seconds, then must have decided having a cop on speed dial might give me the advantage. "Come near me again and I will call the cops," he said, and limped into his car, a Corvette convertible. He had the top down. It looked like a chariot next to my Malibu.

Watching Hinson speed away, I thumbed the off button on the phone.

"Frank and Kerry are on a cruise with the kids," Toni said. "He isn't in cell range. Who did you call?"

I looked down at her. "Dell's Pizza."

"Good one." She grew somber. "I messed everything up. I can't believe I was this stupid."

With the crisis over, my hurt and anger returned. "You could have talked to me, let me know how you felt. It's not like I don't listen for a living."

She looked at her hands. They were knotted into fists. She forced herself to relax. "Do you think I could earn your forgiveness?"

"One day," I said, and stalked off.

It had taken a long time, but we did forgive one another.

I opened my eyes. The bathwater had grown cold, and my aches were returning. I got out, wrapped a towel around my waist, walked into the bedroom—

—and stopped, barely a step through the doorway.

The doll, Thumbkin, was propped on my side of the bed, facing me, as if waiting for me.

I walked over and picked it up. I could have sworn I'd left it on the table beside the front door. Yet here it was, at the other end of the house.

I turned the doll over in my hands. It didn't seem any different. Same cotton dress with white apron, same red yarn for hair, same cherub smile. Nothing seemed out of place.

Except for its eyes—those expressionless, black eyes.

They seemed to be staring at me.

I stared back. The doll's eyes were buttons. They had no pupils, no irises. There was no way you could perceive the doll as looking at you.

I couldn't shake the feeling it *was* staring at me, those lusterless eyes were taking in everything about me, every sensation, every memory, every love and every hate. The hairs on my neck rose. The sensation of being watched became so strong I turned, expecting to find Toni standing behind me, but I was alone.

Or was I?

I returned my gaze to the doll. I lifted it, brought its face so close to mine my breath blew its hair around in gentle wisps. I stared, and I waited.

I was about to give up, to chalk the whole mess up to post-accident jitters, when, for one brief, horrifying moment, its button eyes seemed to narrow, almost imperceptibly, and I sensed an intelligence behind them, a hateful, unfriendly intelligence.

Startled, I dropped the doll. It bounced off the bed and landed on the floor, face down. I backed away, images from a half dozen horror movies flashing in my mind—Chucky wielding a knife and cackling maniacally, the doll from *Poltergeist* dragging that poor kid kicking and screaming under his bed, Karen Black chased through her apartment by a vengeful voodoo doll sporting a mouthful of wickedly sharp teeth. Nightmare visions that had terrified me as a boy.

I stared at Thumbkin, waiting for her to move; to give me some indication she *could* move. When nothing happened, I shook my head. "Get a grip. It's a doll. That's all."

I heard footsteps coming up the hall. Toni stepped into the bedroom, a dishrag draped over her shoulder.

"Why are you standing there half-naked?" she said. "And who were you talking to?"

I pointed to Thumbkin. "Did you bring her in here?"

She picked up the doll and set her back on the bed. "She didn't get here on her own."

Relief swept through me. "Why'd you move her?"

Toni shrugged, her eyes lingering on Thumbkin. "I don't know. She seemed lonely sitting on that table. I thought she'd like some company before you cart her off to be mauled by your patients."

"Dolls don't have feelings."

"I know."

"There was no reason to move it."

"I know," she repeated. "I know, I know."

When she didn't say more, I touched her shoulder. "Toni, honey?"

She ignored my touch. Instead, she stared intently at Thumbkin, as if she were caught up in her thoughts.

"Hey," I said, gently shaking her. "Talk to me, babe."

She stood a little straighter. "Do you know what she wants?"

"Do I know what who wants?"

"The Green Queen." She passed a hand over her eyes. It was an odd gesture, one I didn't understand. "Do you know what she wants?"

"What Green Queen? Who are you talking about?"

"She wants something, you know. Something important. Do you know what it is?"

The voice was hers, but the cadence of her speech was off. It was like listening to two different people speaking at the same time, using the same vocal chords. The effect was unnerving.

"Brad?" she said, more insistently. "Do you know?"

I shook my head. "Why don't you tell me."

"She wants us. And with us, she wants the world." Toni peered at me, as if expecting an answer. When she didn't get one, the focus gradually returned to her gaze. A shudder ran through her. She looked around, as if disoriented, as if she had forgotten where she was. Her pale eyes found mine, and she gave me a smile. "Put some clothes on. I made chicken fettuccine. Let's eat before it gets cold." With a final, hesitant glance at the doll, she turned to leave.

"Honey?" I said, stopping her.

"Yes."

"Who's the Green Queen?"

"What are you talking about?"

"You mentioned someone named the Green Queen. You said she wanted the world. Who is she?"

"Green Queen?" she said with a laugh. "You sure you didn't hit your head yesterday?"

I watched her leave. My sense of unease had returned. I turned to the doll. She sat there, smiling at me.

Smirking at me.

Figure this one out, she seemed to be saying. *You try and figure this one out.*

The Green Queen; someone who wanted the world.

A Raggedy Ann doll, straight out of a child's cellar full of nightmares.

I shook off my unease. This was ridiculous, complete and utter nonsense. I'd let my nerves get to me. Grabbing my clothes, I told my self to stop being silly. There was nothing to figure out.

It was, after all, only a doll.

Chapter Six

After dinner, we retired to the living room. Toni took her spot on the sofa, wine glass in hand, the clear glass bell muddied by her fingerprints. I opted for the recliner, grabbed the remote, and clicked on the television. The same mindless drivel flashed by as I channel surfed. I settled on a documentary of the Beatles. On it, John danced with Yoko while George and Paul and Ringo sang about selfishness. I wondered if the irony of Lennon's behavior was lost on the others as they played. Did they understand the theater of life often displayed the parts of ourselves we held most secret? Probably not. That's why their music remained popular more than four decades later—it spoke to the same fears and insecurities and hopes we all faced, no matter the generation.

The documentary got me thinking, and not in a positive way.

"Honey," I said. "Can I ask you a question?"

"What's on your mind?"

"Bryon Hinson. Does he bother you anymore?"

She set the glass down. "Of course not. We settled that years ago. Why are you asking about him now?"

I hesitated. To confess that I had doubted her fidelity would hurt her deeply, but so would living with the lie buried deep inside me, festering, until I ended up dancing with my own Yoko.

"There've been no other incidents, with anyone else?"

"No! Jesus, Brad. Where's this coming from?"

"One more question—the Green Queen. Who is she?"

Her features darkened. "What queen? Why do you keep asking about a queen?"

I turned off the television. "You brought her up in the bedroom. You asked me if I knew a Green Queen. You told me she wanted the world. Don't you remember?"

"No, I don't. And what's this got to do with that douchebag Hinson?"

"They're not related."

"Then what's this all about?"

"The other day, when I couldn't get in touch with you after the accident." I hesitated, afraid for myself and for her. Neither of us would be the same after an insult like this; not for a while, at least. But there was no backing down now. "I thought...well, I thought maybe you were with someone."

Toni shot to her feet. "You still think that little of me?"

"I'm ashamed to say it, but at that moment, I guess I did."

"You *bastard*," she said, and stormed out of the room.

I hurried after her.

Before I could catch up to her, she slipped into the bathroom and locked the door.

I stood with my head pressed against it, the palms of my hands splayed flat against its painted surface. An inch of wood separated me from the woman I loved. It may as well have been a foot of steel.

"Honey?" I said, loud enough for her to hear. I waited, and when she gave no answer, I called out again. "Toni, honey? Talk to me."

"No," she said. "No, you don't get to do this on your turf. You don't get to play counselor, and I won't be your patient. This time, it's the other way around."

"What do you mean?"

"This time," she said, "you talk to me."

"All right."

"You'd better make it good."

Indeed, I'd better. "I suppose you want to know why I doubted you."

My question was met with silence, so I let out a sigh and plowed ahead.

"I love you. Let's start there. I love you, and I've always loved you." I pressed my palms more firmly against the door. "When you love someone, you lay bare everything you are, who you want to be, or who you hope to never become. Every defense is brought down. You're left naked, more than on the day you were born. The greatest rewards come with the greatest risks; you can't separate the two. With you I found my greatest reward, and in that, I took my greatest risk." I paused. "You still listening?"

"Go on," she said, the words muffled by the barrier between us.

"I'm not going to lie. What you did hurt. It hurt because you found comfort in another man's arms. It also hurt because I let your loneliness get that far; I couldn't or wouldn't see what was going on under my own roof. It hurt because I'd failed you, much more than you failed me."

I wrestled with the lions of silence for several moments before I heard her say, "You blame yourself?"

"To a large degree, yes."

"You never told me."

"Another error on my part."

"I don't understand. What's this got to do with Friday? Why did you think I was cheating?"

"Old insecurities never die," I said. "They only hibernate."

I heard a rustling noise, and when she spoke again, her voice sounded louder. She'd moved to stand next to the door. "Doc Vader," she said. "You're talking about your dad."

"I never did enough for him," I said. "None of us did, though I suppose Steve had the most success. His major was a hard science. Engineering may not be medicine, but at least you could produce concrete, verifiable results. When I chose psychology, Dad called 'bullshit' every chance he got. 'How do you know you healed anyone?' he'd say. And poor Penny—going into advertising was tantamount to selling out. Dad scoffed when she informed him of her major. 'You want to lie to people so you can steal their money?' I don't think they've had a decent conversation since."

I shrugged, even though Toni couldn't see the gesture. Maybe it was meant to comfort me. "Melissa and Christie got off easy. By the time they were ready to flee the nest, Mom was already sick, and I don't think the subject of their college careers was ever brought up. If Dad finds out Melissa dropped out to live with her boyfriend, the affront might be enough to pull him out of that hut in California."

"Go on," Toni said. "I'm listening."

I swallowed the lump in my throat. "Those kinds of messages get to you. They become so deeply ingrained in your psyche that they're part of your thinking. Every action, every decision, is run through the filter of 'have I done enough?' With Dad, I never did. His disapproval became a minefield he forced me to navigate. I would try, except every third step or so, I'd blow myself up. Eventually, as I grew older, I stopped trying. I accepted I would never be good enough to stand as his equal. What I didn't know until much later was I had quietly accepted the blame for my dad not liking me, or even loving me. I believed I had failed him."

"What about your mom? Estelle would've stepped in and told you guys how good you were."

"She did, as often as she could. But Dad had a powerful personality. Whenever you stood in his presence, he dominated you. Mom was simply too kind a person to overcome that kind of force. Don't forget, she had her own issues with him. Growing up in that house, every day was a tug of war, and more often than not, Dad won."

More sounds. I heard a click as Toni disengaged the lock, and the door swung open. She stood there, framed in light. I opened my arms and she stepped into them.

"I think I understand," she said, her face buried in my shoulder. "After I told you about the affair, you eventually blamed yourself for not having done enough, for driving me into the arms of another man."

I hugged her tighter. "Yes, I ended up wondering what I'd done wrong."

"That was years ago. Why bring it up now? Why think we had gone backwards so far?"

I kissed the tip of her nose. "It's an irrational belief. By definition, it doesn't make sense."

She squirmed out of my embrace. "I'm the one calling 'bullshit' this time. Don't treat me like a patient. Don't feed me vague, psychobabble answers. I want to know what was going through your head, what made you worry I was cheating."

Her eyes held a touch of defiance; not a lot, but enough. We had been through tough times together, and she deserved a complete and honest answer. The trouble was, I didn't have one.

"I don't know," I said. "Nothing you've done has hinted at a problem. You weren't on my mind while I was driving. I guess it was the accident. I could've died. You would've been left alone. Maybe it was enough to frighten me, and I overreacted. Like I said, I don't have a good answer." I smiled. "You did nothing wrong. I can't tell you how horrible I felt when I'd discovered what you'd been through."

Some of the fierceness left her expression. "I would never cheat again. You know that, don't you?"

"I know."

"I'd come to you first, tell you how I was feeling. I hope you'd do the same."

"I would."

"I feel bad too," she said, her words tentative. "You were hurt, and I wasn't there for you."

"We each carry our guilt. This will hopefully lessen it."

Toni grazed my bruised cheek with the backs of her knuckles. "When did you become such a philosopher?"

"After I read *The Fault in Our Stars*." I meant it as a joke, but she didn't take it that way, because she said, "I loved that book. It's tragic, how sadness can bring out the best in us."

"Not always," I said, thinking of my dad. "But in most cases, yes."

She slipped back into my embrace. "Do you miss your mom?"

"Every day."

"Do you think we'll have a child one day?"

"Absolutely."

"Do you think she's met him, our baby, up in Heaven? Do you think she's told our child about us?"

A vision filled my mind, one of my mother sitting in a field of bright blue flowers, the sun shining, with a child resting on her lap. Her arms were around him, holding him like she used to hold me, and they smiled as they watched butterflies dance around them. The pure joy on their faces warmed my heart.

"I hope so," I said. "I very much hope so."

"I love you."

"Love you, too." I kissed her forehead and stepped back. "It's getting late. What's say we call it a night?"

"Sounds good." She stepped into the bedroom. "No loving for you, though. I don't need you risking more injuries."

"Ooh, someone's full of herself tonight." I made a playful grab for her ass. The movement almost brought me to my knees. "Shit, you're right."

Toni folded down the bed sheet. "I always am. Besides, you had enough fun in the shower. That should hold you over for another day or so."

I slid into bed, and Toni slid in beside me.

"Good night, honey," she said with a kiss on my cheek.

"Good night." I closed my eyes and wondered what dreams, if any, may come.

* * *

An hour later I was still awake and trying to get comfortable enough to fall asleep, when my cell phone rang. It was my answering service.

"I'm sorry to bother you, Doctor, but I have a Desiree Belle on the phone. Says her son is a patient of yours."

My fatigued brain fumbled with the connections. Desiree Belle was Dee Dee Belle, mother of Doug Belle, my new patient from Friday. The one I was confident would never return after I offended his mother. I got out of bed and headed into the kitchen. "Sure, put her on."

After a short pause, I heard, "Mrs. Belle? I have Doctor Jordan on the line."

"Doctor Jordan, are you there? Oh, god." Dee Dee Belle sounded out of breath and on the verge of tears.

"I'm here, Mrs. Belle."

"Doctor Jordan, you have to help me. It's my son. I don't know what's wrong with him."

Again, a verbalized concern about helping her and not her son—the same issue I noted Friday. "Can you tell me what's going on?"

"It's Dougie. He's locked himself in the bathroom and won't come out. I've tried talking to him but he won't answer."

Young boys lock themselves in bathrooms for all sorts of reasons, some of which they may not want their mothers to know. "Is he upset about something?"

"Of course he's upset," she said, her voice climbing. "He's locked himself in the goddamn bathroom!"

"Mrs. Belle, I won't be able to help if you don't calm down. Please, take a moment and gather yourself."

I heard Dee Dee pull in a few hitching breathes. When she spoke, there was a slim measure of control in her voice. "We were reading a bedtime story. Dougie likes it when I read to him. We'd almost finished when he freaked out. He jumped out of bed, started screaming, threw the book across the room. Then he ran into the bathroom and locked the door before I could get there."

I couldn't help but notice the parallels between this and the situation earlier between Toni and me. Must be my night for bathroom drama.

"Do you know what upset him?"

"Everything was going fine. He just, I don't know, wigged out on me."

Doug had a history of impulsive outbursts, but they seemed to require trigger events—the death of his father, his strong sense of protection and solidarity with his friends. Reading in bed didn't fit into his pattern. I began to suspect his mother was hiding something.

"Could the story have set him off?"

"We've been reading the same story for weeks." She listed a young-adult adventure novel that was currently the hot item with kids, so I felt that part of the story was accurate. "He never had an issue with it before."

I ran my fingers through my hair. "Did anything unusual happen during the reading?"

"No, it was just reading."

"How upset is he? Do you think he'd try and hurt himself?"

"I—I don't think so. I mean, he's pulled at his hair, picked at his skin a little."

"Is there anything in the bathroom that he could use to hurt himself? Pills of any kind? Sharp implements?"

"No, nothing like that."

"Cleaning supplies?"

"Oh, shit." I heard her running, followed by her pounding on a door. "Dougie, are you okay? Answer me, Dougie!" Then, to me, "He's not answering!"

"Mrs. Belle, listen to me. You absolutely have to calm down. You're the parent, the one Doug looks to for structure and safety. By staying calm, you're showing him you *are* in control, and you'll be able to keep him safe. If you lose it, the situation will only get worse. Do you understand?"

Like a dog smacked down by its master, Dee Dee Belle responded with a tortured wail: "Why do you keep blaming me for things?"

"No one is blaming you," I said. "This is simply the job you took when you became a parent. You're the one in charge, and you're the one who has to stay in control, even when it feels like the world is falling apart." I took a moment to let my words sink in, and for her to gather herself. "I know it's been difficult since your husband passed, but that doesn't relieve you of your responsibilities as a parent. Doug needs you. You have to be there for him, to be the guiding force in his life. You can only do that if you stay calm."

Sniffles from the other end of the phone, and a few more ragged breathes. Finally, with remarkable serenity, she said, "You're right. I'm the only one Dougie has left, and I need to be there for him. I'm sorry for my behavior. I'll try to do better."

I paused, concerned about her mercurial emotions. Dee Dee Belle had gone from wildly upset to even-keeled in moments, which made me wonder about the possibility of bipolar disorder. If that was the case, her son could have inherited the trait. It would explain many of his symptoms.

"Mrs. Belle, would you please tell Doug I'm on the phone? I'd like to talk with him."

"Absolutely." Dee Dee said something to Doug. He responded. She came back on the line. "He'll talk to you."

"Excellent. You've done well," I said, hoping to reinforce her efforts at better parenting. "If Doug's willing to open the door, I'm willing to talk."

Dee Dee relayed the information. I heard the door creak open, the phone passed off, and the door immediately shut. A timid, terrified voice said, "Hello?"

"Hello, Doug."

"I didn't know my mom had your number."

"I have an after-hours service. She called them, and they called me."

"She shouldn't have bothered you. This is so stupid."

"Not at all. She did the right thing. Your safety comes first."

"What'd she think I was gonna do, kill myself?"

"Good question. Were you?"

"Fuck, no! I wouldn't do something like that."

"Let's keep the language clean." I wanted to see how he responded to boundaries. "No swearing this time."

I heard an irritated huff. "Sure, if you say so."

So, he wasn't angry in general or he would have responded with more resistance. That suggested the issue was likely between him and his mother. "Want to tell me what happened?"

"Not really," he said, his voice sullen.

"It might help."

"Doubt it."

"Don't forget, whatever you say is confidential. Strictly between you and me."

"Yeah, yeah, unless I'm really gonna off myself. I remember."

"Your mom doesn't have to know what we discussed."

"Like she's not listening at the door right now."

Sharp kid. "Yes, she probably is. Parents worry about their children."

"I guess."

"You don't believe that?"

"For some parents, sure. Not for everyone."

"I hear you," I said, letting him know he was not alone with his feelings. Isolation, and its ugly half-brother, hopelessness, were a child's worst enemies. Ask anyone who'd been bullied. "I've met my share of uncaring parents. Fortunately, they're few and far between."

"What's that mean?"

"I don't often run into them," I said. "Most parents I've worked with strike me as caring, even if they're unsure on how to show it."

Hesitation. "What do these kids do, the ones whose parents don't care?"

I took a steadying breath. This was the first significant question he'd asked me. "Most handle it well. They learn to tell their parents how they feel, what they're looking for from them. It's not an easy thing, either. It takes strength to be direct with your mom or dad. Especially if talking and sharing has never been encouraged."

"And the others, the ones who don't handle it well?"

"A lot of times the child will grow apart from his parents. He may head off to college, pick a school that's far away. He may come home to visit every once in a while. But eventually the need for contact fades, and he goes off and starts a life on his own, visiting Mom and Dad once a year or so."

Another hesitation. "Does it ever turn out worse? You know, like real bad?"

"You'll have to be more specific. 'Real bad' means different things to different people."

"You know, like run away or something?"

"Occasionally," I said slowly. "Those kids often end up in situations worse than they had at home. There are a lot of bad people in the world, child predators and such. Runaways tend to be their favorite victims."

"No way would I let a fucking pervert touch me!" Doug said, loud enough that I had to pull the phone from my ear. "No fucking way!"

I frowned into the phone. A strong reaction like that often meant something significant, and in this case, probably not something good. Putting the phone back to my ear, I heard pounding on the door, and Doug yelling at his mother to leave him alone. There was more pounding, and the sound of Doug's mother calling out to him. I couldn't hear the words, but they sounded concerned. I could see why. I'd be concerned too.

"You're paying this guy to help," Doug yelled. "So let him help."

His pleading seemed to work. The pounding ceased.

"Doug?" I said. "You still there."

"Yeah, I'm here." He sounded out of breath.

"Everything okay?"

"I dunno. Mom tried to come through the door, I think."

"I'm sure she's worried about you."

"Look, I better go. My mom's probably going nuts out there."

"A few more questions, if you don't mind."

"Nah, I think I'm done."

"All right. Two questions, quick and easy."

"Fine. Whatevs."

"One, do you have any plans to hurting yourself, or are you thinking about hurting yourself?"

"No," he said abruptly, like a twig snapping.

"Two, do you have any plans to hurt someone else, or are you thinking about hurting someone else?"

"No. Can I go now?"

I didn't want to stop the discussion. I'd hit on something, and I wanted to follow up on it, but I also didn't want to risk shutting him down. "One last question."

"What?"

"Can I call tomorrow and see how you're doing? No long talks, just to check in."

Another pause, the longest yet. "Yeah, sure."

"Thanks. Now, can I talk to your mom?"

He didn't bother to respond. I heard the bathroom door open, and Doug said, "He wants to talk to you."

"Doctor Jordan?" Dee Dee Belle said.

"I'm still here."

"Is Dougie gonna be okay? Did he say anything?"

"I don't think he's in danger of hurting himself or anyone else. Any more than that, I can't say."

"But I'm his mother."

"And I'm his therapist. Unless I think he's going to hurt himself or someone else, what he says stays between us." I had a hunch that Doug was listening. He'd likely put together his mother's words and figure out I was keeping true to the confidentiality agreement. "I do have one question for you."

"What?"

"Does anyone babysit Doug? A relative, or a neighbor? Someone in regular contact with him?"

When she spoke, her words were quiet, hard, and urgent. "Does this have anything to do with Dougie's outburst about perverts?"

"Mrs. Belle, please?"

"No, no one. I have a brother who comes by every couple months, but not regularly."

"No neighbors? None of your friends, male or female?"

"You think someone's been abusing him?" Her voice was filled with gall.

"I know no such thing. I'm simply gathering information."

"Sure, I have friends. None of them are left alone with him." She swore. "If someone's hurting him—"

"Let's not jump to conclusions. I'll know more after I've talked with Doug again." I opened the calendar app on my phone. "Can you bring him in sooner than Friday? Say, Monday afternoon at four? I'd rather not wait to see him."

"I don't think that's necessary." The woman couldn't have sounded more put out.

"His behavior could escalate if he doesn't deal with his feelings."

"Fine. I'll see what I can do."

"One more thing. I told Doug I'd call him tomorrow. I want to check on him. Is that all right with you?"

"Yes," she replied tersely. "Anything else, *Doctor*?"

"Keep an eye on him. Don't hesitate to call the service if you need me. If he gets really bad, call the police. Don't try to take him to an emergency room on your own." I never trusted parents to drive their children to ERs. There were too many opportunities for accidents or for kids to jump out of cars.

"I'll watch him."

"You can handle this," I said, doling out a slice of positive reinforcement.

"I don't have much choice," she said and hung up.

No, I thought as I wandered back into the bedroom. You don't.

"Everything okay," Toni murmured, still half asleep.

"Peachy." I settled back into bed, my abused muscles groaning in protest. "Just peachy."

Chapter Seven

It was the accident, all over again.

The massive long-hauler loomed in the rearview mirror, bearing down like a hell hound, headlights flaring, steam puffing madly from beneath its heavy cowling. Big. So *damn big*. It filled my eyes until I could see only the grill: metal teeth, menacing and vicious: chrome-plated death. Massive already, it grew in size until it blotted out the sun. I sat motionless, frozen but for the scream coming from my mouth.

Death had come for me. This monster was going to consume me whole. Into its steel gullet I would disappear, never to be seen again.

Oh, Toni! I'm so sorry!

Hands shaking like a man with a palsy, I fumbled for the seatbelt and hit the release and fell forward—and continued falling. I tumbled farther and farther, beyond the floor of the Malibu, beyond the tarmac, while above me, the long-hauler collided with my car in a cacophony of twisted metal, shattered glass, and exploding gasoline. The intense heat washed over my body like a sun's burning surf, searing fiber and follicle alike, until naked I fell through the limitless space now surrounding me, dark and cold and bespeckled with a host of stars.

I fell, timeless, until I saw a mass, orange with a churning skin of yellowish vapor. It spun in a lazy circle around an enormous red star.

A planet. It had to be a planet.

Toward that body I fell. I curled into a ball. I may not know much about physics, but I knew enough to understand friction. The atmosphere was dense; denser by orders of magnitude than the void through which I fell. I knew what would happen upon entry, when the heat found your bones and began to melt them.

With eyes clamped shut and knees tucked under my chin, I rolled and rolled until I felt the planet's gravity latch onto me. Nowhere abruptly became somewhere as I regained my sense of direction. My descent accelerated. Soon my body was buffeted by the hellish forces of the alien atmosphere.

The wind howled in my ears as I waited for the flame of entry to burn me to ash.

Except it didn't happen.

Instead, I felt an icy cold grip me, and I began to shiver. Icicles grew in my nostrils, along my grimacing lips. Frost knitted across my skin until it cracked and flaked away like so much snow, leaving behind a slick mass of raw muscle. Traitorous, my eyelids dissolved to dust and fled with their brethren.

I saw for the first time the planet's surface.

Mountains high and wide, deep valleys, treeless for as far as I could see. Long, curving coastlines of orange soil. There were no buildings, no roads—not a speck of intelligent design. No oceans or lakes or winding rivers or little streams. No water, or any other kind of liquid. Nothing.

This planet was dry: a desiccated husk.

And I was about to impact with it.

As the ground surged up toward me, my eyes caught a glimpse of something in the distance, near the peak of a tall mountain. A crackle of light, bright for a second, then gone, and then back, pulsing, over and over. I sensed immense power and wondered what it could be, but then had to let it go.

The planet occupied my present, and what would surely be my all-too-brief future.

Locked in an armor of ice I screamed.

And, as if in response, I heard my name called out.

"Brad!" someone shouted. "BRAD!"

I turned my head.

It was the Raggedy Ann doll—Thumbkin. It was falling with me, a scowl on its cloth face.

"Brad!" Its stitched mouth had pulled apart, leaving behind broken threads like diseased lips. "Look away, Brad! You weren't supposed to see this!"

"Wha—wha—wha—?" I grunted, my frozen lips and tongue rebelling, the words never fully forming.

The doll's face twisted in fury. "*LOOK AWAY!*"

Hurtling toward the ground, eyes locked on the doll and unable to move, I could only weep. The tears froze to my skinless face.

Perhaps sensing its failure, Thumbkin gave an enraged shriek. Her button eyes narrowed, the corners of her mouth bent into a sneer. "I should let you die!" she cried, and hurtled herself at me.

Her soft body, now hard as concrete, slammed into me as brutally as the long-hauler should have.

The impact pushed me and I tumbled away. The alien planet slowly retreated into the distance.

Sadness consumed me. I was going to sail through outer space forever. I would never see Toni again.

Then I hit—

* * *

—my head on something.

"Ow! Ow! Shit!"

I opened my eyes to darkness. Gone was the planet; gone, the swirling yellow atmosphere. I still felt, though, the bitter chill of outer space deep inside me.

I heard a click. Light flooded the room, causing me to blink.

I was in bed, with Toni next to me, staring at me.

"Brad, what's the matter?"

"Bad dream." I scrubbed my face with my hands. "A really nasty one."

She hugged me. We sat in silence. My heart gradually

downshifted to a more normal rate. The chills faded as the heat from Toni's body warmed me. I leaned back against the headboard. The pain I'd felt must have been my head knocking against it as I thrashed in my sleep.

"Want to talk about it?" Toni said, rubbing my shoulder.

"I was in space."

"Space?"

"Outer space." I related what I could remember of the dream. "The damn doll was there."

"You mean Thumbkin?"

I nodded. "She spoke to me."

"And?"

"She said I wasn't supposed to see something. The planet, I guess."

"You were going to hit the ground?"

"Just before I woke up."

She gave me a gentle shake. "Good thing we didn't test it, huh?"

"Test what?"

"Whether you die in life when you die in your sleep." She hugged me for a few seconds more. "What do you think it meant?"

"The dream? It didn't mean anything."

"You sound certain."

"It was vivid, and pretty terrifying, but it was only a dream. I wouldn't make more of it than that."

Her mouth twisted. "It sounded so strange."

"I've had stranger. Where is the doll, anyway?"

"On the table near the front door, where you left it."

I slid out of bed. "Be right back."

"Seriously, Brad. You're not—"

"I am," I said, and padded out of the room. It was almost midnight and the house was dark. I felt my way down the hallway until my fingers brushed against the light switch. I flipped it—for some reason, I half expected the lights not to work—and was relieved when the ceiling light came on. Squinting through the sudden illumination, I found Thumbkin where I'd left her—on the table with her back propped against the wall. Her cherub grin was intact; her smooth, serene face unaltered. There was no hint of the rage she had displayed in my dream. Then again, why would there be? I'd chided Toni for making a big deal of a simple dream, albeit a bad one, and here I was doing the same thing. I must be losing my mind.

Disgusted, I flipped off the light and fumbled my way back to the bedroom.

"Was it there?" Toni asked sleepily. She'd rolled onto her side, the covers brought snugly up around her shoulders.

"Yes," I said, and slipped between the sheets.

"Good."

"Night, honey."

"Night," she murmured.

I turned out the light but didn't fall asleep for some time.

When I did, I didn't dream.

Chapter Eight

The next morning, I was enjoying a cup of Seattle's Best and working at Sudoku puzzles when the phone rang. I glanced at the Caller ID and picked up.

"Kind of early for you, isn't it?"

"Get dressed," Frank said. "I'll be out front in ten."

"Something wrong?"

"I need a painting, and you're my canvas."

"What does that mean?"

"Just be ready." He hung up.

True to his word, Frank rolled up ten minutes later. I climbed inside.

"You look like shit," he said, pulling away from the curb. "Good."

"Gee, thanks. I love you too. Where are we going?"

"Culver," Frank said as we left the sedate streets of Rock Mills for the full-throated growl of freeway travel. He didn't use his flashers or his siren. Apparently, urgency wasn't a concern. "We're gonna exact a little revenge for the Malibu."

Culver was a small manufacturing town roughly thirty minutes north of Rock Mills. I'd been there on a few occasions, none of them memorable. "I don't get the connection."

"Remember the asshat who left the parts on the road?" Frank's lips peeled back into a predatory grin. "Well, I found him."

"What happened to not investigating?"

He pressed down on the accelerator. "Changed my mind. I drove to the Troop post yesterday. Figured they weren't doing jack shit about the accident, and I was right. Nothing going on, no plans to investigate. I finagled my way into the evidence room for a looky-look, found a piece of plastic molding with a serial number on it. Turns out it was from the bumper of a car. I tracked down the manufacturer, found out who sold it. Called *that* guy. He gave me the name of the guy who bought it. Then I called *him*. Guess what? His car's in for repairs. Had a fender-bender. I got the address of the repair shop from him. Hence, the road trip."

"You think it'll be open on a Sunday?"

Frank snorted, an ugly sound that would frighten a lesser man. "It better be. I called the fucktard myself and told him to be there."

"How long did this investigation take?"

"Dunno. Five hours, six maybe."

"Knowing you, it was more like eight, and now you're gone today. You squared this with Kerry?"

"She'll be okay."

"Which implies she isn't, at the moment, okay."

"I got a job to do, Paco."

"It didn't happen in Rock Mills."

He gripped the wheel like a man ready to do great bodily harm. "Don't you want to catch the guy who almost killed you?"

"And charge him with what? You can't even make an arrest. It's not your jurisdiction."

"I can't believe this. I'm trying to help and you're arguing with me."

"We agreed that finding who did this wouldn't change a thing."

"That doesn't turn a wrong into a right."

I waited a few seconds before saying, "What's this really about?"

Frank's jaw clenched, the muscles bunching like hammer blows, and for a moment I thought he would start shouting. Then the tension unwound from his shoulders, and he let out a thin stream of air from between his lips. "You always gotta do that, huh?"

"Friends don't let friends drive deranged. You're doing eighty in a fifty-five zone."

Frank glanced at the speedometer and swore. The car slowed.

Minutes later, we passed mile marker forty-two, infamous locally for the billboard advertising a local Christian college's slogan: GRADUATE WITH 'A's NOT AIDS. Culver was about fifteen minutes away, ten if Frank kept speeding.

"Trouble on the home front?" I said.

"Yep."

"The baby."

"Yep."

"Want to talk about it?"

"Nope."

"You just want to give a guy shit over something he doesn't know happened."

"Sounds about right."

"And that's going to make everything better?"

"Of course not, but it'll help keep me from throttling someone I love." He changed lanes to pass a slow-moving Prius with Indiana plates. "You gotta admit," he said. "What this guy did was pretty irresponsible. Sure, you didn't 'almost die,' but you damn well got your bell rung. What if it'd been a mom with a car full of kids, or an old couple on their way to their fiftieth anniversary party? You got lucky. Someone else might not have. This guy's gotta understand what he did was dangerous."

He had a good point. "You mentioned a painting?"

"A picture's worth a thousand words, right? Figured if this joker got a look at your mug, my message would have the proper emotional impact."

"What if he doesn't give a rip? What if he looks at me, laughs, and throws us out of his shop?"

"Then his day goes from shitty to fucked up real fast."

Frank took the exit for Culver and kept driving until he pulled into an aged parking lot with weeds growing from the cracked concrete. The building reminded me of a flea market hand-me-down: festooned with rust, flaking paint, and soaped-over windows. There were no other cars in the lot, and the flip sign on the door said CLOSED.

"Womblic's Auto Repairs?" I said skeptically.

Frank nodded. "Let's go introduce ourselves."

This part of town was eerily quiet, even for Sunday. The other businesses were closed. There was no traffic, no pedestrians.

Frank rapped loudly on the door, then tried the knob and discovered it was locked. "The son of a bitch better be here," he muttered, and resumed pounding. The wood rattled until, finally, the door opened.

The man was about my height and build, with wavy brown hair and a beard, both of which were shot through with streaks of gray. He glared at us with startled blue eyes. "What?"

Frank badged him. "You Richard Womblic?"

"Ricky," the man said, squinting at Frank. "No one calls me Richard. I hate it. Makes me feel like I'm back in kindergarten."

"Okay," Frank said. "Ricky. I'm Detective Swinicki."

"The badge gave you away." Womblic turned his attention to me. "And you are?"

"Brad Jordan."

Womblic's eyes lingered on my bruises. He opened the door wider. "Let's get this over with. I have work to do."

I followed Frank into the shop. Womblic led us through the lobby and into the garage, where two cars sat on hoists, their underbellies exposed. At the far end was a door, and beyond it, a surprisingly large workspace filled with radio equipment, a computer, a laser printer, and a large monitor. Photographs of various space-related objects hung on the walls. Most were prints of galaxies, a few looked like planets in our solar system, and one was of the Hubble Space Telescope. There were three more photos, each of Womblic with another person. In them he smiled broadly, an arm around the other person's shoulder and his hand shooting a peace sign. I pointed at one. "Is that Neil deGrasse Tyson?"

Womblic bobbed his head. "I went to the Hayden Planetarium two years ago. Got a chance to meet him. Nice guy. Taller in person than he looks on television." His eyes cut to Frank. "You like science—you know, space stuff?"

"What I would like," Frank said, "are answers to a few questions. I'm not here because I got nothing better to do."

"Yeah, yeah, I figured as much." Womblic dropped into a chair. There weren't any others, so Frank and I were forced to stand. "Can't imagine what this is about."

Frank took out a small notebook from his pocket, flipped it open, and made a show of searching through the pages. It was such a cliché move I almost laughed.

"Can you tell me where you were on Friday afternoon, between two and six?"

"Which Friday?"

Frank gave him an unfriendly stare. "This last one."

Womblic scratched at his beard. "Lemme think. I worked on an '84 Benz that needed new rotors. Then there was Mrs. Andrzejewski's Montana. It blew an overhead gasket. After that I ran some old car parts..." His voice trailed off. "Oh, wow. I think I know why you're here."

"I bet you do," Frank drawled.

"Look," Womblic said, his eyes owl-wide. "The trailer's tailgate is twitchy. I try to keep it secure, but sometimes it pops open. I swerved to avoid hitting a raccoon and some stuff fell out. It wasn't a lot. Not enough to cause a problem."

I lifted my shirt, exposing the ugly bruise on my chest. "Would you call this a problem?"

Womblic's owl-eyes widened. He leaned back in his chair. "Oh, man. I'm sorry, really. I didn't think there was that much on the road. What a screw-up. I guess you guys are here to arrest me." Womblic pulled a cell phone from his pocket. "Can I call my wife first? Let her know I won't be home for a while?"

Frank closed the notebook. "No need for that, Mr. Womblic. At least, not yet. But tell me, why didn't you stop and pick up the debris? It would have saved this guy"—he cocked a thumb at me—"his car and a lot of pain and suffering."

"Your car got totaled?" Womblic asked me.

I spread my hands. "There wasn't enough left to bury in a shoebox."

"You're okay, though?"

"Luckily. Had it been an older couple, or a kid who just got his license, things could've turned out badly."

That seemed to erode what little resolve Womblic had left. His shoulders slumped so much I thought they might break in the middle. "Guess you gotta take me in. Negligence, property damage, personal injury. Shit, Polly's gonna kill me. Can I get a copy of the police report? I've got liability insurance on the truck. I might be able to replace this guy's car." He slammed his fist on the desk so hard a stapler jumped. "Polly's gonna *kill* me!"

Ricky Womblic started crying.

I glanced over at Frank. He gave me a questioning look and I nodded. The guy obviously felt horrible about what had happened. It was time to end the charade.

Frank cleared his throat. "Look, Mr. Womblic, we—"

"Give me a minute," Womblic said. "I was going to take the family to the apple orchard later. Now I gotta tell them that I'm going to jail instead. What are my kids gonna think?"

"Mr. Womblic, please—"

Womblic bolted upright in his chair. His face went deathly pale. "Halloween's next week. I'm gonna miss my kids trick-or-treating!"

"Mr. Womblic," Frank said loudly. "Listen to me. I'm not going to arrest you. You are not going to jail. You're not going to miss anything."

Womblic paused, his chest heaving. He stared at us for a long moment, then his expression changed—disbelief replaced panic, which finally gave way to relief. He ran a shaky hand across his mouth. "I'm not going to jail?"

"No," Frank said. "Provided you file the insurance claim. The doc here needs his car replaced."

"Of course!" Womblic smiled. "Thank you. *Thank you.* I thought this was it. I was done, finished."

I pulled out a business card and handed it to Womblic. "You can reach me at this number."

"Sure, sure. Anything you say." He read the card. "You a shrink?"

"Psychologist."

Genuine concern, or maybe it was embarrassment, colored his cheeks. "I'm sorry, Doctor Jordan. Not cleaning up that mess was the dumbest thing I've ever done."

"Why didn't you?" Frank asked. "Clean it up, I mean."

This time Womblic's face flushed red. "I was in a hurry."

"In a hurry for what?" Frank asked.

"There was this, you know, show on cable. On one of the science channels." Looking down, Womblic shrugged. "I'd been waiting all week."

Frank's eyebrows rose. "You risked someone's life over a damn television show?"

I quieted Frank with a gesture. "What was the show about, Mr. Womblic?"

Clearly uncomfortable, he said, "Aliens."

"Aliens?" Frank said. "As in little green men?"

"They're gray," Womblic said. "Not green."

"I don't believe it," Frank said. "You're a fucking Roswell freak."

Womblic lifted his head. "Lecture me all you want about my mistake, but don't ridicule what I believe in."

"You saw the doc's face," Frank said. "How badly he's hurt. You're telling me it's because you had to see some bullshit program about E.T.?"

"There are over a hundred billion stars in our galaxy," Womblic said. "And over a hundred billion galaxies in the universe. That's over a hundred billion *billion* places where life could exist. It's not bullshit. It's fact. We are not alone." He turned his attention to me. "I'm not a Roswell freak. I don't think we're being visited by aliens. But something's happening out there, and there's a good chance we'll see it one day. Radio waves or some other kind of signal. We'll discover life on another planet. It'll be man's greatest achievement. I just hope it happens in my lifetime."

Frank grunted. "I bet you were pissed when they cancelled *The X-Files*."

I winced. Frank was a great guy, but sometimes he had the tact of a rhino.

"I'm a mechanic," Womblic said. "A grease-monkey with my head stuck in car engines all day. It doesn't mean I'm stupid, or I don't have passions. I don't know what your passions are, officer, but I would respect them. Too bad you can't do the same." He stood and pointed to the door. "I think we're done here."

Frank opened his mouth to say something. I cut him off. "Thank you for your time, Mr. Womblic. We'll get you a copy of the police report."

Womblic nodded coldly. "I'd appreciate it."

We left before Frank could do any more damage.

* * *

The rest of Sunday passed uneventfully. The next morning, I called my insurance agent, reported the Malibu's demise, and started the claims process. I also gave her the name and number of Ricky Womblic, so she could coordinate with his carrier.

My auto policy provided coverage for a rental car. Soon I was headed to the office in a newer model Impala. It wasn't the Malibu, but at least it was a Chevy.

I arrived at the office late. My eleven o'clock scowled but didn't hesitate when I motioned for him to join me. He was here to work on his frustration tolerance. Waiting was good practice.

During lunch I checked my schedule and remembered Doug Belle was coming in at four. He'd had the outburst Saturday night and needed to be seen. When I'd called yesterday to check on him, he'd seemed in better spirits.

I looked over at my chest of toys. Thumbkin stared back at me.

Despite my misgivings, I'd brought the doll. The dream had rattled me, but it had been just that: a dream. To let an irrational fear take over made little sense. Best to confront it head on.

I breezed through the next three appointments. Four o'clock rolled around. I checked the lobby.

No Doug.

I returned to my office and dictated session notes. Ten minutes later, I checked the lobby again.

Doug Belle was a no show. Not a complete surprise. I'd had doubts about ever seeing him again.

I'd almost reached my office when I heard my name called.

Dee Dee Belle hurried down the hallway with Doug skulking behind her.

"I'm sorry, Doctor Jordan." Reaching back, she grabbed her son by the arm and hauled him forward. "I hope we're not too late. Dougie didn't want to come." She stared at my face. "What happened to you?"

"Minor traffic accident," I said. "Don't worry about being late. Mondays are slow, and you're my last appointment. We'll get our time in."

"Great," Doug muttered and stomped into my room.

"How's he been?" I asked when Doug was out of earshot.

"Sunday was fine. We didn't read. Today he was at school. I didn't get a call from them, so that's good."

"Did he mention what upset him the other night?"

"He wouldn't talk to me. I tried, but he shut me out. I even tried ice cream." She began picking at her coat. "I don't understand. I love him so much. I want to help him feel better, and he won't let me."

"Everyone grieves at a different pace. Don't push. He'll come to you when he's ready. Until then, there's not much you can do except be his mother. Let him know you're there, and you'll keep him safe." I gestured to the lobby. "I'll bring Doug out when we're done."

Dee Dee Belle shot me a wounded look. "I don't like being kept in the dark. Can't I sit in?"

"It's too soon," I said. "Doug and I need to build a better rapport before I invite someone else in."

"I'm not 'someone else.' I'm his mother."

"It wouldn't be in his best interest."

She glared at me, then grinned awkwardly, as if she'd been caught doing something improper. Except, I caught a hint of something in her look. Was it desperation? Vulnerability?

No—it was fear.

Dee Dee Belle was afraid.

"Is there something I should know?" I asked.

Dee Dee hesitated. "I love my son, Doctor Jordan. He's gone through so much this year. We both have. When Tink deployed, I knew there'd be risks."

"Tink?"

"My husband. His name was Bill, but in the Marines, everyone gets a nickname. With the last name of Belle—"

"'Tink' is short for Tinker."

She nodded. "They tell you about the dangers, the risks of having a Marine for a spouse. You never think it'll happen to you."

"Losing him must have been devastating."

"I can't get my husband back," she said, squaring her shoulders. "Is it too much to ask for my son?"

"Let me work on it." I steered her toward the lobby. "I'll do my best, I promise."

As she walked away, Dee Dee Belle had the wooden gait of a person close to collapsing from the burdens of a difficult life. Maybe I would bring up the therapist idea again. She could use someone in her corner.

In my office, I found Doug cross-legged on the floor, his head bent in concentration. He had set up a battalion of G.I. Joe figurines. One side contained several fallen warriors, while the other mounted an attack. He held one figure tightly in his fist and issued commands in the low, gravelly tone kids sometimes used to sound like adults.

"Hold your ground, men. The enemy can't win if we stand together." His hand swept out and knocked over more green plastic soldiers. "That's it, kill the bastards!"

I watched from the doorway as he engaged in a mock battle, the hero figurine in his hand issuing orders and generally obliterating the enemy. He eventually looked up and saw me. Embarrassed, he scooped up the G.I. Joes and dumped them into the plastic box with the rest of the toys.

"Sorry," he said. "Didn't mean to touch them without permission."

I eased into my chair. "You didn't have to stop."

"I was killing time while you talked to my mom."

"There are a lot of toys in the box. Interesting you chose the G.I. Joes."

"Right," he said. "You think it has something do to with my dad."

"People gravitate to the familiar. Your dad was a Marine." My tone softened. "The figure in your hand, the one in command. Was he supposed to be your dad?"

Doug shifted uncomfortably. "I guess so."

"He must've been a brave man."

"Bravest I ever knew."

"Kind of like you."

Doug raised his head. "What do you mean?"

"Your friend, the one with the harelip."

"Johnny Richardson?"

"If I remember right, you stuck up for him. 'Got his back,' I think was how you put it."

"That's nothing."

"I doubt Johnny feels the same. I bet he'd say you were the bravest kid in school."

Doug looked away. "Like I said, it's nothing."

"I also think your dad would be proud of you, standing up to bullies."

"If you say so." Doug's gaze wandered to the toy chest. He picked up Thumbkin. "Was this here last time?"

"I bought her over the weekend. It's her first day here."

His mouth twisted. "Her?"

"She's a Raggedy Ann doll. Her name is Thumbkin."

"Stupid name." He turned the doll over in his hands. "What's it supposed to do?"

"Anything you want."

"Not big on directions, huh?"

"I like to keep things open-ended."

Doug stared at Thumbkin. No, that wasn't quite right. He seemed to be staring into her, into her button eyes, his concentration so intense his face seemed to lose some of its focus. It was as if he had left this room behind and gone elsewhere.

I called his name. When he didn't answer, I touched his

shoulder. "Hey."

Doug's head whipped up, his eyes wide. For a moment, I saw the same fear in him that I'd seen in his mother. Then it was gone. "What?"

"You okay?"

"Yeah, sure. I'm fine." He frowned. "Why?"

"You kind of zoned out."

"I did?"

"Looked that way," I said. "Do you remember what you were thinking?"

"No," he said. "I don't."

I thought for a moment. "You up for something?"

He eyed me suspiciously. "What?"

"Saturday night. You were in bed. Your mom was reading and you got upset."

"Yeah."

"Pretend the doll is your mom. Tell her what upset you. Say to the doll what you would like to say to her."

"That's dumb."

"Any more than playing with green plastic men?" He scowled, and I raised my hand. "Think about it. Is talking to a doll any different than pretending a G.I. Joe is your dad?"

Doug seemed to consider this. He sat on the ground, fingers working at the doll, thumbs pressing into its soft body. The minutes passed. His hands clenched into fists. Thumbkin crumpled in his grip.

"Why'd you do it?" he whispered.

I wasn't sure if he was talking to me or the doll.

"Every time," he said. "Every *damn* time!"

The doll, then. And by default, his mother.

"Do what?" I asked.

"I wanted to hear a story. That's all. And you had to ruin it."

"You're doing fine, Doug. It's just talk. Nobody gets hurt. Nobody knows what you said."

Doug's fingers dug into Thumbkin. "Kids need protecting. Ain't that right, Doctor Brad?"

"Yes, they do."

"Like Johnny. He needs protecting, so I protect him. That's how it should be, right?"

"In a perfect world. Sometimes, the world isn't perfect."

Doug lifted one shoulder. "I guess not."

He grew quiet. Silence was a powerful therapeutic tool. People tended to remember the last words spoken before a prolonged silence. I wanted Doug to remember his reply.

After enough time had passed, I said, "Other than your friend, do you know anyone else who needs protecting?"

Doug's fingers continued to work over the doll. They pressed and plied. The course fabric of her skin warped. Her smiling face twisted into an ugly sneer. The boy was struggling with something.

"Doug?"

"No," he said, a bit too sharply. "Nobody."

Fair enough. He wasn't ready. "What else would you say to your mom?"

Another long pause. "I'm sorry."

"For what?"

"For not being the person she wants me to be. For not being *him*."

"Your dad?"

"She misses him a lot." He looked at me. "You know she keeps his dress uniform on his side of their bed? She stuffed it with newspapers, like it was some kinda creepy mannequin. She even pinned his medals to the shirt. She's got his gloves and hat and shoes and everything. It's like he's there but he isn't."

"Do you think she talks to him the same way you're talking to the doll?"

"I heard her late at night, whispering in her room. It's sad."

"It is."

We spent the next few minutes talking about anything but his father or mother. After running out of reasons to avoid the obvious, Doug said, "I hate him. I've never said this before, but I hate him. I hate him so much."

"You're angry he left."

"Why'd he have to go? He coulda been a cop or a taxi driver

or anything else, but no, he had to serve God and country, and now he's dead. Why'd he have to die?"

"I don't have a good answer. All I can tell you is the pain lessens with time."

"How much?" Doug said, snot running down his nose. He lifted Thumbkin and twisted her violently in his hands. "How much time will it take—?"

The office lights flared bright, too bright. I squeezed my eyes shut. I heard a sizzle and a pop, like a transformer blowing. The air filled with the sharp stench of ozone.

I opened my eyes. Doug lay on his back, his eyes staring blankly at the ceiling. Blood trickled from one nostril. Thumbkin, her dress scorched, had fallen from his hands and lay crumpled next to him.

"Doug!" I grabbed a wad of tissues and held them to his bloody nose. "Doug, are you okay?"

He didn't respond. I checked for a pulse and found one, and he was breathing. I shook him. "Doug? Come on, buddy. Say something."

I was getting ready to call for help when Doug groaned. He coughed weakly. His eyes found mine.

"Doctor Brad?"

"Here." I offered him my hand and helped him to his feet, then handed him a tissue. He pressed it to his bloody nose.

"Do you feel dizzy, nauseous?" I said.

"No, just tingly, like I got an electric shock or something." He prodded the doll with his shoe. "What did that thing do to me?"

It was a good question.

If only I had an answer.

* * *

Doug recovered quickly.

He didn't want me to tell his mother about the incident—he thought she would overreact—but this wasn't something I could keep from her. Turns out he was right, not that it made my day any easier.

"Oh my god, Dougie!" she cried when she saw the crimson smear across his upper lip and down the side of his face. "What happened?"

"He's all right," I assured her as she hugged her son. "At least, he seems fine."

Doug squirmed in her embrace. "Mom, please. Doctor Brad's right. I'm good."

She released him. Her face was pale. She turned to me. "What did you do to him?"

"There was some kind of power surge," I said. "The lights, I don't know, they flared somehow. We heard an electrical discharge. Doug ended up on the floor with a bloody nose."

"Doctor Brad couldn't have done anything to stop it," Doug said. "Anyway, you know I'm tough. A little zap ain't gonna hurt me."

He gave her a disarming smile. Dee Dee Belle didn't return it.

"I tell you I want my son to feel better, and you try to electrocute him. What were you doing, playing with electrical cords?"

"Mrs. Belle—"

She pointed her finger at me. ""Don't say a word—not another word. And count yourself lucky if I don't sue your ass." She grabbed Doug by the arm and hauled him away. "Come on. You're getting checked out by a doctor. A *real* doctor."

I stepped forward. "Mrs. Belle."

She kept walking.

"Mrs. Belle, please."

This time she stopped, her face still warped with outrage. "What?"

"Doug's appointment Friday. I'd like him to keep it." I glanced at Doug. "Before whatever happened, we'd made progress. I'd like to continue."

"You almost kill him, and now you want me to bring him back? You're the one who needs a shrink."

She turned to go, but Doug stopped her, his face strangely calm as he slipped from her grasp.

"The doc's an okay guy. I wanna come back. Can we keep the

appointment?"

Dee Dee Belle glared at her son. He calmly returned her look.

Mother and son, engaged in a battle of wills.

"Please?" Doug said. "I think it's helping. You know, the talking."

I refrained from commenting. She was angry—definitely at me, perhaps at herself—and I didn't want to provoke a reaction by trying to sway her decision.

Dee Dee Belle's glare gradually softened. She again took on the slump-shouldered look of a woman who had wanted so much from life and had achieved almost none of it.

"Let's have you checked out first, then we'll see about Friday."

Doug floated a ghost of a smile. "Thanks, Mom."

"I'll call you about Friday," she told me.

"Absolutely. Please let me know if the doctors find anything."

"You'd better hope they don't," she said, and left with her son in tow.

* * *

Having finished my appointments, I grabbed Thumbkin and headed home. I wanted a closer look at the doll.

I picked up dinner on the way. Chinese—noodles for Toni, rice for me. She liked hers spiced hot enough to hurt.

When I walked into the house, Toni's school bag was on the kitchen counter and her laptop on the table. Papers were spread in front of the computer, with the school's grading program open.

I checked the clock. Just past six.

"Honey?"

"In the bedroom."

"Be right there." I placed the food and the doll next to her work bag and grabbed a couple beers from the fridge.

I found Toni tucked into bed, her hair damp from a bath, a smile on her face. I popped the tops on the beers, sat on the edge of the bed, and handed her one.

"Thanks," she said. "You're the best."

"Rough day?"

"When isn't it?"

"Which one this time?"

"Trinity."

"Ah, yes. The entitled child. What now?"

"A teacher saw her bite another student. We confronted her and she denied it. We told her we had a witness. She said the teacher was mistaken, she would never bite anyone. Kids these days must think we're stupid."

"Did Morgan suspend her?" Morgan Day was the school principal. A decent guy, if a little soft on discipline.

She made a rude noise. "He tried, but when we called Trinity's mother to tell her about the incident, she demanded a meeting after school. Trinity lied, over and over, and her mother believed her. She refused to listen to the teacher who saw the incident, refused to believe her precious little angel would ever do something so horrible. She refused to accept the suspension. She even hinted we were targeting Trinity because of her color."

The race card, played more often than a one-eyed Jack in a euchre game. "What'd Morgan end up doing?"

"What he always does—he backed down. At least he warned them that another incident would be taken seriously, up to and including expulsion. Trinity's mom smiled and said we'd better do a better job watching the other students."

"It's women like her that keep me in business."

Toni grimaced. "I don't know what's up with kids today. They have this outrageous sense of entitlement. What'll happen when they become adults? The real world will mow them down until there's nothing left but bloody stumps for ankles."

"I've got a clue for you—they're going to *be* the real world. That's the scariest part." I nuzzled her cheek. "Mmm, you smell good."

She caressed my face. "It's the soap I bought in Emersville."

"You liked it?"

"A lot. Loved the bath. Best I've had in a while."

I took in her aroma. "Did you ever place the scent?"

"Some sort of floral, but at the same time not." She gave me a sexy grin. "It made me feel tingly."

I paused, thinking of Doug and how he had felt *tingly* after his incident with Thumbkin. The coincidence unnerved me, and my stomach did an unpleasant little flip into by bowels.

I took a steadying breath. Stupid coincidence: that's what it was. I pushed the memory aside and took Toni's hand. "I brought dinner. Let's eat while it's still hot."

"I'm not hungry. At least, not for food." She turned back the covers. She wore one of my t-shirts and nothing else. "Plenty of room in here, mister."

"You hate cold Chinese."

"Not as much as I'd love some hot Brad." She slipped out of her shirt. I was more of a leg man, but the sight of her full breasts with their hard, pink nipples sent a shiver through me. I cupped her face in my hands and stared into her eyes. They were beautiful. Soulful and eternal. I loved them. I loved her.

We kissed. There was no tentativeness, no hesitancy, just urgency and passion.

Her fingers worked at the buttons of my shirt, the buckle of my belt. Soon I was naked and in bed. Her hands stayed busy. They pinched my nipples, slid down my stomach, found my excitement. My hardness. She gently stroked me, moaning into my mouth, her tongue exploring.

My skin tingled where she touched me. It added a sense of intoxication to my excitement, and I felt myself grow harder. Harder than I've ever been. Hard enough to explode.

"Jesus, Brad. I need you inside me."

I rolled on top of her, my lips traveling to the curve of her neck. I kissed her again and again as I entered her. She rocked her hips. I responded by thrusting, driving into her, back and forth, back and forth. I felt her clamp down on me. The tingling sensation swelled, driving me on.

"Whatever you're doing," I said. "Keep doing it."

"Oh, baby. You feel so good."

I pounded harder. Toni, normally a passive partner, responded by bucking against me, riding my length. We kept going, meeting thrust for thrust, until she shuddered in one of the most intense orgasms I'd seen her have.

Her skin glowing, she grinned at me. "Okay, lover. Your turn."

Gripping my shoulders, she rolled me over in one smooth motion. I stayed buried in her the whole time.

It was so fucking hot.

She sat up. Her hair was mussed, her skin damp with excitement, her eyes shining with passion. In the glow of the hallway light, she looked like a goddess.

She began to grind her hips. As she rode me, her hands caressed her breasts, her fingers tweaked her already taut nipples.

"You like this?" She gripped my cock with the walls of her vagina.

I grunted. It was all I could manage. Words would not have done the experience justice.

"How about this?" Grinning impishly, she reached back and gently massaged by testicles. "You like this too?"

That did it. I felt a tightness in my groin, a churning that signaled my impending eruption. I swelled to the point where it was almost painful.

"Oh, baby." Toni clamped down again. Her skillful fingers urged me on. "Oh, baby. Give it to me."

My hands shot to her hips, holding her down as I reached my climax and shot ribbon after ribbon of white into her. The spasms continued until I thought I would pass out. The musky-sweet scent of our love filled the room.

I pulled Toni into a hug. With her knees bent, the embrace felt a little awkward, but I wanted to experience the warmth of her skin on mine, her breath on my cheek. She buried her face into my neck.

"I love you," I whispered.

"Love you right back," she said. "That was amazing. I don't think I've experienced anything like it before."

"You were amazing. The things you did to me."

"We were both amazing." She giggled. "My god, you've never felt that big before. I thought you were going to split me in two."

"I almost passed out at the end."

"My stud." Toni swiveled her hips. "Oh, wow. Look at you, lover boy. Still hard as a rock."

She was right. My excitement hadn't subsided. I remained buried inside her.

She twitched her muscles and I groaned. We hadn't had a back-to-backer in years.

"Let's see how far we can take this," Toni said, and began working her magic on me.

Needless to say, I was enthralled.

* * *

After a third round of lovemaking, Toni curled into a ball and fell asleep.

Stunned at what had transpired, I couldn't sleep. What I needed was a cigarette. Since I didn't smoke, I settled for a beer.

I retreated to the kitchen, wearing the t-shirt Toni had borrowed and my boxers, and ate reheated Chinese with chopsticks.

I loved my wife, but we had been married more than ten years. Time and familiarity had blunted our passions. Twofers were a thing of the past, and I'd never gotten it up three times in rapid succession, even as a youth.

As wonderful as we had felt, as amazing as our lovemaking had been, it had felt unnatural, almost forced. Or maybe *induced* would be a better word.

The thought made me pause. Certain drugs effected sexuality. Little blue pills for erectile dysfunction, the over-the-counter infomercial crap bought by gullible men who wanted to become love stallions—they might work on the mechanics of sex, but they did nothing for passion. Older compounds like cabergoline and bromocriptine could induce a sense of eroticism, and they were reputed to cause multiple orgasms in men and women, but they were difficult to acquire, let alone find a way for us to ingest them.

Then there was the tingling sensation. It had followed Toni's touches; where her body came into contact with mine, my skin almost burned with excitement. Maybe she passed something on to me, inadvertently drugging us both into an act of unrestrained love.

I thought back to what Toni had done during her day: school, meeting, bath.

Soap.

My pulse quickened. It had to be the soap. Annabelle St. Crux had given it to Toni during our visit to Emersville, saying she wanted to help us.

Could the soap contain a chemical, one passed on by touch, one that could enhance our arousal? A kind of transdermal roofie?

And soap wasn't the only thing we'd procured in Emersville.

My eyes cut to the counter.

Thumbkin, with her big black-button eyes fixed on me.

Thumbkin, with her scorched dress, as if she had withstood a massive electrical charge, one that had stunned me and rendered Doug Belle incapacitated.

I grabbed the doll and laid her on the table. A ceiling light shone from above, illuminating the surface. I felt like a doctor about to perform surgery in an operating theater; or worse, a medical examiner about to conduct an autopsy on a murdered child. I took a pull from my beer and wiped my mouth with my hand.

Three long scorch marks marred Thumbkin's apron. A jagged burn like a scar skittered along her moon face, beneath her left eye and across the tip of her triangular nose. It gave the doll a menacing look, as if she had emerged from a barroom brawl, bruised and battered and looking to kick more ass.

I lifted the apron. The blue cotton dress beneath had burned through in spots, the charred holes looking like blisters in an ocean. Hints of smoke scratched at my sinuses, drawing tears from my eyes. The acridity seemed too intense, given the amount of time that had passed; I shouldn't have been able to smell anything.

I flipped the doll over. More holes. I stuck my finger into one. The stuffing felt soft, puffy. Everything you would expect. I pushed my finger in further and found more batting. Certainly nothing that would cause a spontaneous combustion. It seemed, in all respects, a stuffed doll.

Then I felt a sharp, slicing sensation and jerked my finger out.

Blood covered the tip. I wiped it away with a napkin. There was a small incision across the pad of my index finger.

Something inside the doll had cut me.

I grabbed a pair of scissors and carefully cut away part of the dress, exposing wads of gray cotton shot through with blue and red threads, parts of which were burned away. I gently pulled the batting apart.

That's when I found it, buried in the center of the doll's chest like a heart: a metal lattice-work construct, about an inch long and shaped like an egg, with holes like honeycombs cut into the surface and a small, jagged hole near the middle.

I pushed it around with a chopstick. Whatever it was, it looked delicate. At first I thought it might have been constructed of wire filaments, the metal was so thin. On closer examination, I discovered there were no windings at the intersections, and the metal was flat instead of rounded. Not wire, then: the egg had been fashioned from a single piece of metal.

I picked it up. It hardly weighed anything. The surface was shiny, like silver or aluminum. Where the lattice had broken, the metal ends stuck up, needle-like. I must have cut my finger on one of those edges.

Holding it between my fingers, I squeezed. Not hard, but enough to test its strength.

The egg held its shape.

I squeezed harder. The egg didn't warp or bend or twist. Given the metal's slenderness, I should have been able to flatten it.

Setting it on the table, I hammered at it with the blunt end of a chopstick.

Nothing.

We owned a steel meat tenderizer. I got it out and hammered at the egg a couple times.

It didn't even scratch the metal.

A worm of fear, cold and wet, slithered up my spine.

I was going to need help on this one.

Chapter Nine

"What do you think it is?" Frank said, holding the tiny lattice-work egg up to his eye.

It was the next day. After rescheduling my morning appointments, I called Frank asking for help. We met in his office at the police station. Manila file folders covered his desk. Despite the transition to computers, Frank couldn't break with tradition. Each of his cases had to be printed out: reports from officers or the M.E., evidence chains, photos of the crime scene, transcripts from interrogations. He then assembled everything related to the case and stuffed into a folder. Talk about old school.

"Not sure," I said. "I found it inside a doll I bought. A patient was playing with her when she short-circuited. Knocked the poor kid out cold."

Frank glanced at me. "Her?"

"I meant the doll, Thumbkin."

"You gave it a name?"

"It's a matter of convenience."

"It's fucking weird." He returned his attention to the egg. "Metal looks thin. You said you tried hammering it?"

"Couldn't raise a scratch."

Frank set the egg on his desk. "What was the kid doing when it happened?"

"He was angry. His dad died recently. He was twisting the

doll as he talked about it."

"Hard enough to break this thing?"

"You mean, harder than hammering it with a meat tenderizer?"

The lines on his forehead deepened. "Yet it broke while surrounded by soft cotton."

"If it made sense, I wouldn't be here."

The sounds of a busy police station filtered through the closed door. Footsteps, terse conversations, the muted squawk of a police band radio. Frank's office held the dry paper scent you would more commonly associate with in a library.

"What about having the metal analyzed?" he asked.

"I suppose Steve could find someone to do it." Steve was my brother, the engineering professor over at Ann Arbor. He probably knew people who tested metals. "Except I'm not sure I want him involved."

"You two have a falling out?"

"No, nothing like that."

Frank waited. I was holding back, and he knew it.

I shifted uncomfortably. "You have coffee in this place?"

"You're stalling."

"A cup of coffee. Please?"

Grunting, Frank left the office. He returned with two Styrofoam cups and set one in front of me.

"Okay, Paco, you got your fix. Now fess up. Why don't you want your genius brother involved?"

"Two reasons. First, whoever did the testing would have to use University equipment, which means requisitioning time. I'm not sure he could swing it for work outside of his research."

"Why don't you let him worry about that?"

"Sure. He says no, it's no. But I know him. He'd insist on helping. He'd get the tests run."

"Which leads to your second concern."

"I'm guessing the tests would require some use of energy."

Frank sat up straighter. "That worries you?"

"A little," I said, and sipped my coffee.

When I didn't continue, Frank threw me a look that would

have broken the resolve of a far stronger man. "Don't jerk me around, Paco. I deserve better than that from you."

He was right. I should be more up front with him, but we were wandering into dangerous territory filled with unknown threats. He had a wife and family, with a baby on the way. I owed my caution to them as much as to him.

Without him, though, I wouldn't get far in solving the puzzle of the egg.

Like it or not, he was the detective in this duo.

I pointed to the egg. "Do you see a battery in that thing?"

"No, I don't."

"Yet it released an electrical charge strong enough to blow a hole in it. How much energy would it take, given I couldn't scratch it with a tenderizer?"

I could almost hear the wheels turning in Frank's head. "You're worried a test might cause another discharge."

"Wouldn't you be? It doesn't have a battery, yet it held a powerful charge. What if it's still holding a charge, and we add energy to it? Who knows what damage it could do."

Frank picked up the egg. "It doesn't look like much, does it?"

"That bothers me too."

"A delicate latticework object made of metal so thin it's like parchment. It has nothing inside, yet it produced an electrical charge strong enough to knock a kid out."

"That pretty much sums it up."

"The analysis—you're worried the results might be unusual?"

"The thought crossed my mind."

The phone on his desk rang. Frank let it go to voicemail.

"You bought the doll in Emersville?" he said.

"Yes."

"Kerry bought one there."

"I know."

"The store had a lot of tourist crap mixed in with a few solid works and a variety of toys."

"*Lost Desires.*"

"That's the place." Frank drummed his fingers on the desk. "You know what we need to do."

"Oh, yeah."

He shoved the egg in his pocket. "You with me?"

I downed the rest of my coffee and tossed the cup in the trash. "Where else would I be?"

* * *

Tuesday morning. Everyone in Frank's family had left for school: the kids for class; Kerry for work. We had the house to ourselves.

I'd been here almost weekly for years. I knew it as well as I knew my own home, and it had always felt welcoming. Today, I sensed an unease—a displeasure—as we walked through the front door. I stopped, my skin puckering into gooseflesh.

"You feel that?" I asked Frank.

He turned to stare at me. "Feel what?"

"I don't know. A sense. An impression, like someone isn't happy we're here."

"Don't start losing it, Paco."

I put my hand on his shoulder. "I'm not kidding."

Frank stared at me for a moment, then reached into the folds of his jacket and withdrew his sidearm. The sight of him holding a gun in his own house unnerved me further.

"Stay here." He left to check the house. It didn't take long. When he returned, he had holstered his weapon. "Nothing."

"It's probably nerves." I felt foolish, like a kid entering a haunted house attraction on a dare and immediately bolting for the exit. "Don't mind me."

"Tell me if it gets worse." He headed down the hallway. I followed.

The living room looked much the same as it did on Friday night, with empty snack bowls and water glasses on the floor. There was only one difference.

"Where's the doll?" I said.

"It was there when I left this morning." Frank gestured to the painted wooden chair in the corner. "Same as any other day."

"Maybe Kerry moved it?"

"I don't see why she'd —"

A loud crash came from the kitchen, followed by a clattering like an avalanche of metal.

We ran into the kitchen. The cupboard doors were open, their contents thrown onto the floor. Stock pots, sauté pans, a pressure cooker. Even the silverware had been tossed out. A solitary spoon rocked back and forth.

Frank's gun was back in his hand.

"Police!" he said. "Step out where I can see you! Keep your hands up!"

I felt a prickling at the back of my neck — an impression, like someone was watching me — and turned. I caught a flash of movement, low to the ground, a flutter of cloth heading down the hallway.

"There," I said, and pointed.

We charged out of the kitchen. The hallway led to the bedrooms and a bathroom. The doors were open. We couldn't tell where the intruder had gone.

"What'd you see?" Frank asked. He'd stopped before he reached the first door.

I looked nervously at him. "I think it was the doll."

"This isn't the time for games."

"You're holding a gun. I couldn't be more serious."

Frank hesitated. "How can a doll move?"

"Find it, and maybe you'll find your answer."

A sense of foreboding settled over the house like a wet wool blanket, suffocating us, weighing us down. Frank's grip on the gun tightened.

"This is stupid," he said. "I refuse to believe a doll can move. It has to be something else. Some*one* else." He advanced on the first door. "Shout if you see anything."

He stepped into Nathan's bedroom. I heard him shuffle around, open what must have been a closet door. He emerged moments later and shook his head. I started to tell him a doll that size could hide anywhere, but he held a finger to his lips.

I nodded my understanding.

Frank checked the twins' room and the bathroom. Both were

empty.

That left his and Kerry's bedroom.

Gun gripped in both hands, he stepped inside.

The hostility I'd sensed earlier exploded. It grew quickly, spilling into the hallway. The animosity was so powerful, so terrible, it soured my stomach.

Frank shouted—no, he *screamed*. A terrified scream. A sound I'd never heard him utter in all our years together.

The gun went off with an ear-shattering crack.

Out of Frank's bedroom ran the doll. It loped toward me on all fours, its tiny face twisted in rage. Bits of yarn protruded like broken teeth from a mouth that was no more than a slit in the fabric of its face. It saw me and snarled.

Stunned at the sight of a doll moving, I froze. It almost cost me my life.

The doll leapt with surprising strength, launching itself at my face, its tiny mouth open. Although it was made of soft cotton, I sensed it could do real, serious harm. I sensed it could kill me.

Frank barreled out of his bedroom, gun pointed at the ceiling. His face was pale, almost pasty.

"Brad!" he shouted. "Get down!"

His voice brought me out of my shock. I dropped, rolling when I hit the carpet.

The doll sailed over me. Frank leveled his weapon and fired. A second concussion of sound punched at my ears.

The doll disintegrated in an explosion of sparks and smoke.

Ozone stung my eyes. An electric charge passed over the surface of my skin, making my nerves twitch. Bits of charred cloth fell to the ground like volcanic ash. A button landed on my cheek. I swatted it away.

Frank approached. He was talking, but his voice sounded fuzzy, like it was coming from the far end of a long, long tunnel.

I pointed to my ears. "Can't hear you."

"Are you all right?" he shouted.

"My ears hurt."

"The gunshots." Frank went to holster his firearm. His hand shook so much it took him three tries.

I picked up a scrap of cloth. It felt impossibly light. "You shot it."

"I know."

"You shot it, and it blew up."

He helped me to my feet. "What'd you want me to do, let it get you?"

"It exploded," I said in wonder. "The damn thing *exploded*."

"Must've hit the power cell. It caused an electrical discharge similar to the one in your office."

"A power cell? That's what you think the egg-thing is?"

"Has to be. What else could make the little fucker move?"

"You know there's more to it than that."

Frank grimaced. "I know. Like, how did its arms and legs move? What caused those weird facial expressions? Most importantly, who was controlling it?"

I puzzled over his words. "You think it was radio controlled, like a toy race car?"

"Nothing else fits."

"The range on those things isn't far."

"Whoever did this heard the shots. He's long gone by now."

The doll had loped on all fours, and had reacted when it saw me.

"Frank?"

"Yeah?"

"Do we have technology that sophisticated?"

* * *

The doll's remains were spread out on Frank's dining room table like a museum exhibit. We found scraps of burned cloth and cotton. We also found two pieces of parchment-thin, metal latticework.

What had us stumped were several filaments so thin they resembled the threads of a spider's web. Frank took one in his hand. He could bend it, twist it, or tie it in a knot. What he couldn't do was break it. It seemed perfectly elastic, and perfectly indestructible.

"Any idea what it's made of?" he said, holding one up.

"Doesn't look metallic. Some kind of fiber optic cable?"

"Possibly. You find anything like this in your doll?"

"No, but I wasn't looking."

We checked the rest of the evidence (for want of a better word) and found nothing else we would call unusual. Frank made two piles, one for the explicable, one for the inexplicable. He went into the kitchen and returned with two quart-sized plastic storage bags. He dumped the cotton and cloth into one, the metal and filaments into another, and sealed both.

"We're not scientists," he said. "We won't get anywhere trying to puzzle through the physical evidence. I do want to examine your doll, see if it has any of these filaments running through it. After that, we may have to call on your brother."

"Fair enough."

Frank caressed the cigarette pack in his shirt pocket. "Why make the damn thing move? Before that happened, we had no reason to believe it was more than a simple doll."

"The house was supposed to be empty. Maybe we caught the guy off guard."

"Doing what, running around looking in my underwear drawers? Technology like this has to cost major bucks. Why not use it in the boardrooms at Apple or Google, or the halls of Congress, or the White House? Places with valuable information." Frank grumbled deep in his throat. "We don't have state secrets. We're not worth spying on."

"Which means spying wasn't the objective. It had to be something else."

"Motive usually boils down to power, money, or sex. Information is power, and it looks like we've ruled that out. I'm not missing anything valuable. Are you?"

"We barely have two quarters to rub together."

"The expression is 'two nickels.'"

"Inflation," I said. "Seriously, Toni has some jewelry, and I have a pocket watch my grandfather gave me. They might be worth something, a few thousand dollars to the right people. That's it."

"Not nearly enough to cover the cost of losing a valuable piece of technology. The return has to outweigh the risk. The money aspect doesn't play right to me."

"That would leave sex."

"They aren't blow-up dolls, Paco."

"No, but you're expecting another baby. I assume the process involved sex at some point."

Frank gave me a frosty look. "I'm not into threesomes with a doll, either."

"That's not what I meant." I gave him the PG-13 version of last night's sex marathon. "Did anything like that happen to you and Kerry?"

To his credit, Frank didn't blush—he didn't even bat an eye—but when he spoke, anger choked his voice. "I didn't know what was happening. Kerry had taken a bath to relax. I found her in bed. The kids were out of the house. We hadn't had alone time in ages, so I slipped into bed. Before I knew it, we were going at it like teenagers. I'll spare you the rest of the details, but our baby came out of that love-fest."

"Did you feel anything, any sensations you'd call unusual?"

"We keep coming back to that word, unusual." Frank scratched at his cheek. "I do remember a tingling sensation across my skin. It seemed to, I don't know, excite me. Sound familiar?"

"Very familiar."

"You said Toni had a bath before your romp?"

"She did."

"We have a connection." Frank glanced at his watch. "I gotta go. I've got a meeting at one with the district attorney. We'll have to pick this up later."

My first patient wasn't until two. That gave me enough time for lunch and to make a few phone calls. I wanted to check in with Dee Dee Belle and ask about Doug. "Meet at my place around eight? We can check out Thumbkin."

Frank lifted his bulk from the chair. "You might want to reach out to Steve. See what it would take to get these analyzed." He picked up the bag containing the metal fragments and the filaments and handed them to me. The other one he left on the table. "Something freaky's going on, Paco. Watch yourself. And don't let your guard down."

"You, too." I looked at the remains of the doll which had impossibly tried to attack me.

For the first time in my life, I wished I owned a gun.

Chapter Ten

I arrived at my office and started making calls. I left Dee Dee Belle for last. She answered on the third ring.

"What can I do for you, Doctor Jordan?" she said, her tone unfriendly.

"How's Doug? Did he get a green light from the doctors?"

"He's fine, no thanks to you."

I took the jab, and prepared for more. Her son had been hurt while in my care. I would expect no less. "There were no lasting effects?"

"He had some numbness in his fingertips, but that's gone."

"Nothing else? No episodes of dizziness or disorientation? No fugue states—"

"What?"

"Walking and talking but not being aware of it, like he's sleepwalking."

"No, nothing like that."

"Is there a family history of epilepsy?" I recalled yesterday, where Doug zoned on me. "Any neurological disorders at all?"

"What's with all the questions?"

I told her about the episode, and my concerns for Doug. "Some forms of epilepsy can result in explosive or unusual behavior. I want to make sure we're considering all the options, Mrs. Belle."

She paused. "Can't brain tumors do the same thing?" Her voice grew fearful. "Do you think that's what he has?"

"Has he complained of blurred or double vision, uncontrolled vomiting, or smelling burned rubber all the time?"

"No. At least, not to me."

"Then a tumor's unlikely," I said. "An old doctor friend of mine once said, when you hear hoof beats, think horses instead of zebras. Let's focus on the horses before we look for the zebras. Now, is there any family history of epilepsy?"

"Not that I know of."

"Have you noticed anything else, anything that stands out after yesterday's session?"

"He had trouble sleeping last night, but that's been going on for weeks. Dougie can have such terrible nightmares."

"About what?"

"I dunno, stuff."

"Anything specific?"

"No," she said stiffly.

I jotted a note reminding me to ask Doug about his nightmares. Maybe they would help bring to light whatever was bothering him.

Also, I didn't trust Dee Dee Belle to tell the truth.

"Is there anything else?"

"Have you decided whether you'll bring him Friday?"

"Not yet," she said, and hung up.

* * *

I had four appointments, which meant I didn't finish until after six. I called Toni, asked about dinner plans, and mentioned Frank's visit later in the evening.

"Why don't I make soup and a salad?" she said. "Keep it simple."

"Sounds good. I'll see you soon. Love you."

In the parking lot, I headed for the rental. Darkness had spread over the sky like an ink stain, blotting out the warm glow of the setting sun. Mindful of Frank's warning, I kept my eyes open, reached my car without incident, got in, and fired up the engine.

Half an hour later, I pulled into my driveway. Toni had dinner waiting. I opened the beers. We clinked bottles.

"What kind of trouble are you into now?" she asked as we sat at the table.

"Trouble?"

"Frank's coming over on a weeknight, at eight o'clock. It has to be trouble."

"We want to check on something." I finished the soup and switched to the salad. "How was work?"

"It was fine. What are you checking on?"

"Nothing, really."

"Then quit being defensive and tell me."

"I'm not being—"

"Frank's coming over and you won't tell me why. I ask you and you avoid the question. I confront you and you play dumb. Cut the crap. We treat each other better than this."

I set down my fork. What was I supposed to tell her? We bought a doll that almost electrocuted a patient? Our best friends owned a similar doll that could run and sneer and leap and Frank blew it away in a blaze of fireworks? Someone might be spying on us with strange technologies? Frank thought we might be in danger?

Dinner conversation, Rod Serling-style.

She was also right. We should treat each other with more respect, but at the expense of worrying her, or worse, frightening her?

Like most quandaries, the answer could be found somewhere in the middle.

I filled her in on the dolls, leaving out the parts about them moving (or, in Thumbkin's case, possibly moving) or the potential surveillance. I opted for Frank's explanation for the lattice-work eggs.

"There were batteries inside the dolls?"

"We think they're batteries," I said. "It's the only explanation that makes sense."

"Batteries to do what?"

"That's why Frank's coming over. We need some good, old-fashioned detective work."

My cell started ringing. It was my answering service.

"Doctor Jordan?" The woman sounded slightly irritated. "I have someone asking for you. He won't tell me his name, but he sounds young. Says it's an emergency."

I told her to put him through. "This is Doctor Jordan."

I waited for a reply. When none was forthcoming, I said a little louder, "Hello, this is Doctor Jordan. Who is this?"

More silence. I was about to hang up when I heard a sniffle, soft but full of sorrow.

"Hello?" I said, more urgently. "I can hear you. You sound upset. Please, can you tell me who you are?"

More sniffles, definitely male sounding. I ran though my patient list. One name rose to the surface.

"Doug?"

The line went dead.

Swearing, I found Dee Dee Belle's number and punched it in. She answered immediately.

"Another call?" she said. "What is it this time?"

I explained the call to my service. "I think it was Doug. Is he home?"

"Where else would he be?"

"Is he with you right now?"

"No, he's in his room, drawing I think."

"Could you please check on him?"

"I assure you, he's fine."

"Please, I want to make sure."

"Whatever." I heard footsteps. A door opened. "Dougie, it's your doctor. He wants to know if you're okay." A murmured reply. "You're not upset or anything?" Another string of clipped murmurs, like lemmings falling off the edge of a distant cliff. "All right, honey. Go back to your drawing. I'll come by later and we can have story time."

To me, she said, "I told you he was fine."

"Better to be safe," I said. "The alternative is often bad. Does

Doug have a cell phone?"

"No." Dee Dee put as much irritation into one syllable as was humanly possible.

"Is there a house phone nearby, one he could use without you noticing?"

"Doctor Jordan, we've determined Doug is fine. I think we're finished here."

"Wait, before you hang up. You said Doug was working on a drawing. Do you remember what it was?"

"Oh Christ, I don't know. Kid stuff. Who actually looks at that crap?"

Parents who care, I thought. Parents who want to know what their children are up to. Not, apparently, in Dee Dee Belle's world.

"Thank you for checking on him," I said. "One last thing. Could you do me a favor?"

"You're unbelievable."

"Could you bring some of his drawings on Friday? Sometimes they're helpful in determining what's going on inside a person's head."

"Fine. If we come on Friday, I'll bring them."

The line went dead for the second time tonight.

"Is everything okay?" Toni asked. She worried about my patients almost as much as I did.

"I hope so." I glanced at my watch. "Frank should be here soon. Let's clean up these dishes and—"

All the lights went out at the same time, plunging the house into darkness.

Chapter Eleven

"What the hell," I said, rising so fast I knocked my chair over.

"Brad," Toni said fearfully.

A hissing noise, like something burning, came from the direction of the front door. Light as bright as a welder's torch blazed, followed by the sound of metal thudding onto the floor.

It had to be the door's locking mechanism.

"Call the police," I told Toni, and bolted for the door. "Then run."

"Brad, no. It's too dangerous."

"Do it." Concern for my wife outstripped any other thought; if I could keep the intruder at bay long enough, she might escape unharmed. "Go."

I reached the foyer as the front door banged open.

A figure entered, cloaked in shadow and menace. It looked like a man. A *big* man. He filled the doorway. Others huddled behind him. I couldn't tell how many, but there were a lot.

"Get out," I yelled. This went against everything I'd learned from Frank about safety—don't confront, don't attack, let the thieves take what they want—but I was furious. How dare they invade my home! Rational behavior flew out the window. "The police are on their way."

The big man advanced. The others flooded in around him. Bathed in shadow, flowing as they seemed to be, it was like being attacked by a horde of Azkaban's Dementors.

I searched for something I could use to defend myself but couldn't see well enough.

The big man loomed in front me.

Out of options, I took a swing at him. The impact felt like hitting a slab of marble.

The big man lifted me by my shirt and slammed me into the wall. My head knocked painfully against the sheet rock.

Two of the Dementors glided down the hallway toward the bedrooms. The others seemed to float behind the big man. None were as large as the fellow who had me by the shirt.

I struggled against his grip. He was stronger, and my efforts only seemed to infuriate him. He slammed me against the wall again. My teeth clicked together. Blood flooded into my mouth.

Desperate, I kicked but only managed a glancing blow, hardly enough to stop him. The man lifted a beefy arm, his fist hanging in the air like the blackest, bleakest comet, ready to crater my face.

I prepared for the worst.

A figure flew out of the dining room. I recognized Toni's enraged scream as she swung something at my captor. I heard a satisfying *thunk*. The big man grunted, released me, but didn't fall. Whatever she had hit him with, it hadn't been enough to incapacitate him.

The other Dementors flowed left and right, intending to either cut off our escape or surround us and attack.

We'll see about that, I thought grimly, and bull-rushed the big man—the one I assumed was the leader. I rammed my shoulder into what I'd hoped was his chin. He gave an angry hiss.

In full "mama bear" mode, Toni struck again. There was a meaty *thwock*, like a cantaloupe breaking open, and a Dementor collapsed. She kept swinging. The invaders fell back.

Heart galloping, I snapped my foot up, hoping to connect with the leader's crotch. Faster than I thought possible, he snatched my foot and lifted. Off balance, I couldn't protect myself. The big man must have known this. With punishing brutality, he drove a foot into my chest. I went down in a heap.

"*BRAD!*" Toni yelled as Dementors surrounded her. She tried keeping them at bay with her weapon, but their superior numbers outmatched her elemental ferocity. Someone hit her. Another grabbed her arm, preventing her from swinging. A third came up from behind and wound an arm around her throat. She gave a gurgled cry and stopped struggling.

I couldn't get up. I tried, but I couldn't. With air wheezing from between my lips, I hugged my arms to my chest and hoped to avoid further injury.

The big man loomed over me. From my vantage point, he looked ten feet tall and scary as hell.

"You got it?" he called out.

The Dementors who had glided down the hallway reemerged. One held up Thumbkin.

"It's missing the proximity lock."

I could feel the big man's eyes on me. I knew he was close to losing control. Fury oozed from him like scalded oil.

This is it, I thought. We're going to die.

"Where is it?" the big man asked, his voice a surprising tenor as supple as Roy Orbison's.

"Don't know what you're talking about? Where's what?"

"The proximity lock. Where is it?"

"What the fuck's a 'proximity lock'?"

A new sound intruded on the scene.

Sirens.

The big man gestured. Several invaders glided out the door. Two carried their downed comrade. The one holding Toni clubbed her to the floor and followed his brethren.

I was left alone with the big guy.

He took a step toward me. The toe of his boot rested against my chin.

"Dig any deeper," he said, "and we'll kill you and your cop friend."

The big man kicked me hard in the ribs and left.

Whimpering in pain, I curled into a ball and waited for the cops to arrive.

* * *

For the second time in a week, a paramedic was examining me. He held a stethoscope to my back.

"Breath sounds are pretty good bilaterally," the paramedic said. His name was Ray Kingston. His daughter was in Toni's third hour. "No sign of a pneumothorax. Still, you might have cracked a rib. Want a ride to the ER? It's on the city's dime."

I shook my head. I had other things to worry about than pain.

Toni sat across from me on the sofa, an icepack on the back of her neck. At her feet lay the frying pan she had used to bludgeon the attackers. She'd been medically cleared.

Outside, red and blue lights blazed with unsettling urgency. Officers were posted inside the house and out. CSU techies gathered evidence, took pictures, and dusted everything for fingerprints. A clear plastic bag contained the door's lock with about an inch of wood still attached, the edges charred by whatever had burned through it.

"Gas chromatograph might pick something up," a techie had said. "A trace of some chemical. We'll have to wait and see."

A detective strode through the door, a man named Dillon who I'd met through Frank. We shared a rather low opinion of him.

"Any word on the Swinicki's?" Toni asked him.

"Just got off the phone with Kerry." A thirty-year veteran, Detective Dave Dillon had the tired look of someone who could smell retirement lurking around the corner and couldn't wait to turn in his shield. "She and the kids are fine. We have a patrol car sitting out front. They should be safe."

I lifted myself out of the chair. The pain made me grimace. "What about Frank?"

"We're still looking for him."

"You don't know where he is?"

"We're searching right now," Dillon said. "Frank's one of us. We won't stop until we find him."

"Did he make his meeting with the D.A.? What time did he leave? Surely you know—"

Detective Dillon's expression hardened. "This is a police

matter. I'm not obligated to share information with you."

"Cut me some slack, Dave. He's my friend."

"You want information, file a FOIA request, same as everyone else."

"Freedom of Information Act? That's your answer?"

"The best one you're getting."

I snorted in disgust. "You know something. You're a real asshole."

"Tell me," Detective Dillon said, his cheeks reddening. "Are you privileged in some way? Does knowing Frank make you a *de facto* cop? Wait, do you have one of these?" He flipped open a leather wallet and held it to my face. "Do you have a badge? Do you? No? I thought not." He held the badge up long enough to make sure I didn't miss the message and put it away. "I'm the detective, you're the civilian. Authority flows from me to you, not the other way around. Get used to it."

Toni came to stand next to me. "Brad's right. You are an asshole."

Dave Dillon smiled sweetly. He had the upper hand and knew it.

"This is getting us nowhere," I said, barely keeping my tone civil. "How about we focus on finding Frank instead? What can we do to help?"

"Let's go over your story, while it's still fresh in your mind."

We suffered through his interrogation. I'd not shown such restraint in years.

"Any idea why they took the doll?" Detective Dillon asked. "Why not something valuable, like a television or a DVD player?"

"You're the detective," I said. "Responsibility for the investigation flows from me to you, not the other way around. Figure it out for yourself."

Dillon's eyes narrowed to hard, angry points. "If you know anything relevant to the investigation, you need to tell me. Is there something special about the doll, something that would prompt a reaction this extreme?" He gestured to the broken door. "Withholding information will only slow the investigation."

The words leapt to my lips: *Okay, if the doll is anything like*

Frank's, it moves around as if it's possessed. And the damn thing's evil. Think that'll help narrow down your lists of suspects?

I didn't say it, of course. He wouldn't have believed me. Instead, I said, "No idea. It's just a cheap doll."

Dillon held my gaze. I could tell he didn't believe me. Even Toni looked at me askance. I didn't care. Something dangerous was unfolding. Our home had been invaded, our persons assaulted, our property stolen. Frank was missing. My patient had been shocked by a metal egg with no visible power source. I was having strange dreams about outer space, dead planets, and falling stars.

No, no way was I going to share anything with Dillon the Dickhead. Let him go pound sand with a conventional investigation.

I stared silently back at him, my face expressionless.

Dillon shook his head and sighed. "Play it that way if you want, but if I find you're withholding evidence, you'll be looking at jail time. And if Frank's dead, I'll nail you as an accessory after the fact."

Heat rose to my face. "Frank's not dead," I said, my voice loud enough to carry throughout the room.

Movement around us ground to a halt. The patrolmen, the shift sergeant, the CSU techies, even the paramedics were watching the confrontation. I stood ready to refute any challenge to Frank being alive.

Dillon's eyes cut to the men standing nearby, and his jaw clenched. He knew he'd made a mistake. He spoke of the death of a fellow officer before it had been proved. Cops were a superstitious bunch, and that kind of talk could put you on the outs with them, sometimes for the rest of your career.

Frank would still be alive if Dillon hadn't opened his fuckin' yap!

Life as a cop, even in a backwater burg like Rock Mills, exposed you to dangerous situations. Being on the outs with the people protecting your back didn't help your life expectancy.

I now had the upper hand. Dillon knew it, which posed its own dangers. I'd seen men lose their shit over lesser provocations.

The seconds stretched until I thought time would break.

Someone coughed—one of the officers outside, I think—which was enough to break the silence that had fallen over the house.

Dillon made a show of examining his notepad. "Any idea what a 'proximity lock' is?"

"Not a clue," I said, genuinely puzzled. "Proximity makes me think of nearness, something close by."

Toni nodded. "Lock could mean to secure, or fasten."

"Fixing something in place," Dillon said. "Locking it down. Keeping it nearby." He walked, clicking his pen, seemingly lost in thought. His path led him down the hallway. Toni and I followed. "Is the proximity lock the doll itself, or something inside it?"

The metal latticework egg—*it* had to be the mysterious proximity lock.

Whoever had come for the doll was expecting to find the egg.

When did I last see it? Sometime today, I was sure, but where? I wanted to smack myself in the head.

Then I had it: Frank's office. I'd brought it to show him, and he'd slipped it into his pocket when we left.

Frank had the egg.

I stopped walking.

Frank had the egg!

Toni touched my shoulder. "What's wrong?"

My thoughts raced. The invaders had come looking for the egg. They knew about Frank's involvement. Knowing I didn't have it, they would go looking for him.

Would they kill him to obtain it?

I broke out in a cold sweat. I needed to find Frank, and I had a good idea where to start.

"Brad," Toni said. "Talk to me."

My head snapped up.

"We need to leave," I told her. "Right now."

Chapter Twelve

I drove slowly through Emersville.

Coming here had been a brash idea. Frank would have called it lunacy and berated me on the dangers of following such a crazy hunch. But Frank was missing, and this town was the only lead I had.

Toni sat next to me, gazing out at a street mostly devoid of cars. On the way over, I explained how Doug Belle had been shocked by Thumbkin. I related my encounter with Frank's doll, and how it had tried to attack me. I didn't leave out a single detail. If she wanted to ride shotgun, she needed to understand the dangers.

She had balked at my words, questioning my assumptions, countering my arguments. Finally, she accepted what I'd told her. There were no more doubts, no more hesitations.

That was Toni: once you convinced her, she backed you fully.

I parked in front of *Lost Desires*. A sign had been tacked to the door.

CLOSED UNTIL FURTHER NOTICE

"You think she died?" Toni said. I assumed she was referring to the owner, Annabelle St. Crux.

"Either that, or she's very ill." I wasn't sure which was better. Like funeral clothes kept in a box on the top shelf of a closet, a dignified death often wore better than an undignified life.

Toni popped open the car door. I joined her on the sidewalk.

"*Lost Desires* is the distribution point," I said. "The place where the planning ends and the mischief begins. If we could get our hands on another doll. Wait here while I check something."

I made sure nobody was within eyeshot, then jogged up the steps and tested the door.

Locked, not that I expected different.

There were four panes of glass set into the upper half of the door. It wouldn't take much to break one, unlock the door, and slip inside.

Unless the store had a security system, in which case we'd find ourselves in a jail cell, and the search for Frank would end.

The thought of cops triggered something in my brain. I stepped back from the store. "Maybe we should go to the police. We were beaten, our property stolen. A man is missing. Crimes were committed, possibly by people living in Emersville. Chief Couttis might be able to help. He's here to serve and protect. Besides, we could use an ally."

Toni bit her lower lip. "I don't think the cops are a good idea."

"Why not?"

"Either they know about what's happening, or they don't. If they know, talking to them will only tip off the people we're looking for. They'll know we're interested in Frank and the dolls. If they don't, how are you going to keep them from locking you up in a hospital room with padded walls?"

I took a moment to digest what she had said and could see she was right. No cops. At least, not yet.

"We'll go it alone for now," I said. "But if we find any sign of Frank, or evidence that people here are responsible for his disappearance, we call the police. I don't care if they're Rock Mills PD or Emersville. Going in half-assed and undergunned will only get us killed."

"Agreed."

"Where do we start?"

Toni smiled. "Buy you a cup of coffee, sailor?"

* * *

Black and Brewed did a brisk business, even after the rest of Emersville had rolled up the sidewalks for the night.

The interior was decorated in cold chrome and glass and plain, white paint. No posters on the walls. No long counters where patrons could plug in their laptops and Facebook with the world. No sugar-coated pop music dripping from speakers in the ceiling. Nothing like the half a zillion Starbucks across the nation. In fact, it resembled more an ice cream parlor than a coffee shop.

Toni and I stepped up to the counter, where a jittery young man wearing a Maroon 5 shirt asked us what we would like.

I peered at the menu tacked to the wall behind him. Nothing fancy. Just coffees, teas, a handful of espressos, a few lattes, and one or two children's drinks.

"Small black coffee?" I said. "Toni?"

"The same, please."

The kid drew off two cups. We sat at a table near the back. Conversations flowed around us like a babbling stream. I checked my watch.

"Almost eight-thirty. I'm surprised the place is this full."

Toni looked around and shrugged. "Hipsters have invaded the 'burbs. We should all be afraid."

"None of the faces look familiar."

"Why should they? We've only met three people. Annabelle St. Crux, the police chief, and his son."

I thought of Dementors gliding through my house. It had been too dark to see their faces, though two would show signs of injury: the big guy I hit and the one Toni took down with the frying pan. The latter likely needed hospital care. The leader, on the other hand—I hoped to catch him here.

"What now?" Toni asked. "We can't pull up Frank's picture on your cell and ask if they've seen him."

"I don't know. I've never done this before."

"We need a place to start. That's all. A place to start." Toni's grimaced. "I only wish I knew where."

I pulled out my phone and checked for messages. "No word from anyone on Frank."

"Send him a text. See if he answers."

I did. He didn't.

"Let's think for a minute," said Toni, coffee mug in her hands. "If Frank's here, in Emersville, where would he be? Where could you safely hide a cop?"

I considered her question. "Someplace secret, like a basement or warehouse. It'd have to be secure, where no one could wander in and find him."

"Jail cell?"

"Doubtful. Cops record the activity in them. Helps protect against claims of abuse or neglect. I'm sure the surveillance is time-stamped, too, making a cover up more complicated. Whoever did this will want to keep it simple."

"Okay, no place with a camera, which rules out most stores." Toni pointed above the service counter to the dark glass-domed security camera affixed to the ceiling. "They've gone up everywhere."

I stared at the camera. "Maybe we're looking for a house rather than a—"

Four people entered the coffee shop. Two men and two women. Three of them were unremarkable.

The fourth was big. Really big, with a skull-shaped earring in his left lobe and the left side of his face scraped raw.

I shot to my feet.

Like a herd of water buffalo scenting a lion, they stopped as one. The big guy's face twisted in recognition or revulsion. He turned and shoved the others out the door.

"Come on." I grabbed Toni's arm and pulled her up. "It's him."

Toni hadn't seen our attacker—her back had been to the door—but she didn't argue. Running after me, she said, "Who are you talking about?"

I didn't answer. My focus remained locked on the guy with the earring. I didn't want to lose him.

We were half way to the door when an elderly couple rose, the man lifting a coat so his wife could slip her arms into it. Both looked terribly frail and moved as slow as an old silent movie played at half speed.

Worst of all, they blocked the quickest route from the shop.

Cursing, I stutter-stepped left, hoping to circle around them, but another table of patrons stood. Young hipsters (one wore a black knit cap filled to capacity with his crinkly hair), they made a show of leaving a tip and gathering their possessions.

"Dammit, get out of the way!"

The hipster in the cap looked calmly at me. "Chill, man. There's no fire here."

I skidded to a stop. Toni halted next to me.

Every customer in *Black and Brewed* stood and moved to block the exit. They stared at us, their pale faces expressionless.

A chill crept up my spine. I had seen a movie years ago called *Village of the Damned*. All those kids, cute as could be, had stared at George Sanders with the same dead-eyed, vacant expressions we were getting.

"Get out of the way," Toni said, unintimidated. She'd had years of experience with unruly classrooms and knew the exact tone to take.

A few of the younger patrons, those who had been out of school for perhaps a year or two, shuffled uncomfortably. The rest stood rock still, their faces inscrutable.

"I told you, man," said the hipster, a smirk on his face. "Chill."

"Why are you doing this?" I said. "Why are you protecting him?"

The hipster moved to stand in front of me. "Who?"

"The guy who just ran out of here. Big as a pickup. Scrapes on his face."

"Nobody ran out of here." He turned to face the crowd. "Anybody see a guy run out of here?" When no one replied, he turned back to me. "See, man. You're mistaken. No one was here." His smirk faded. "Sit down. Finish your coffee. We pride ourselves on our brew."

Toni stiffened beside me. She wasn't used to this kind of treatment from someone more than fifteen years her junior.

Several of the patrons noticed her reaction and turned to face her. Their expressions didn't change, yet I could sense the threat, even if I couldn't see it.

These people were capable of violence.

"We're leaving," I told the hipster. "I suggest you get out of the way."

"And if I don't?"

"Then we'll let Gordon Couttis handle it."

The hipster's eyebrows climbed his forehead. "You know the chief?"

"Met him last week. Nice guy. I'm sure he'd love to hear that a group of his law-abiding citizens assaulted two tourists in his town." On an impulse, I pulled out my cell. "Shall we call him?"

He glanced at my phone. Sweat had broken out along his upper lip, and his eyes held less certainty. "You're bluffing. You don't have his number."

"It's 9-1-1, you moron." I lifted my shirt, exposing my new wounds. "The guy you let get away may have done this, and if he did, I'll push for an obstruction charge against you. Think about it. Jail time, a court trial. How much money would it take to defend yourself? Lots, I'm guessing." I lowered my shirt. "You sure you want to push it?"

The room was completely still, completely quiet.

We looked like a tableau of a riot moments before the fighting broke out.

The hipster motioned for the others to sit.

"Go," he said. "Leave. No one here will stop you." His smirk returned. "No one here would've."

Bullshit, I thought as I grabbed Toni and led her out of the shop. They might have stopped short of killing us, but they would definitely have stopped us.

Which led to another thought.

How many people in Emersville were involved in this mystery?

* * *

There was no sign of the big guy with the scratched up face.

"Did you see what he was driving?" I asked Toni.

She shook her head. "You can't see the parking lot from inside the shop."

I shook with rage. The crisis had passed and emotions rolled over me like a battering ram. Why were they protecting this guy? Was the whole goddamn town involved?

"Look." Toni pointed at the long window that fronted *Black and Brewed*.

Faces filled the glass. Every person inside the shop was staring at us.

A sea of expressionless, doll-like faces.

I don't know which was more terrifying, those blank stares, or the fact they all stood, motionless and unblinking.

Both, I decided. Both frightened me.

"Come on," I said. "We'd better leave."

"I think you're right," Toni replied, and we crossed the street.

I'd unlocked the 4Runner when I heard the sound of a car

approaching. The noise was distant, low and throaty, but quickly turned into an angry growl. Headlights appeared, two glowing eyes in the darkness. The car raced down the street, the engine shedding decibels as the driver accelerated. It shot past us, pulling enough air in its wake to ruffle our clothes.

A car racing through Emersville was an odd sight this late in the evening, when most of the town had called it quits for the night.

The more amazing sight was the driver.

"Brad," Toni said, her voice holding as much amazement as I felt. "What's she doing here?"

I hadn't been seeing things. Kerry Swinicki, wife of the man who currently held the top spot in my own personal Amber Alert system, had just sped past us like Jeff Gordon high on crystal meth.

"What's she doing here?" Toni repeated.

I climbed into the car and cranked the ignition. "Let's find out."

* * *

Kerry had a good mile lead on us, and she was already driving the Explorer's pistons as hard as they could go. Luckily, the road was a straight, inky line, and we had no trouble seeing her progress.

The older 4Runner, however, struggled to keep up, let alone gain on her.

"Do you think she left the kids alone?" Toni said worriedly. "Do you really think she could?"

I checked the mirrors, half expecting blue-and-red lights to appear in the distance. When none did, I nudged the speedometer past eighty. Ahead, Kerry's brake lights flashed, and her car sped around a corner and out of sight.

"Dammit." I stomped on the accelerator. "Dammit, dammit, dammit."

We raced down the road. The hum of the tires grew to a strained whine. Street lights flickered past us. I gripped the steering wheel so tightly my hands ached.

"I don't understand any of this," Toni said. "Why isn't she home, waiting for news of Frank?"

"Maybe she heard something," I said, slowing the car so it didn't spin out on the curve.

"Okay, then where are the police?"

I'd slowed, but not enough. The 4Runner skidded sideways. The steering wheel slipped in my sweaty grip. Toni let out a shriek and grabbed the handle bolted to the ceiling.

I eased up fully on the accelerator and let the car have its lead. It soon regained its traction. We were back hurtling down the road.

Toni let go of the handle. Her hands trembled as she smoothed back her hair. She looked like she'd aged a year in two minutes. "Where did she go? Do you see her car?"

"Nothing. I don't see a damn thing." Scaling back the speed, I looked out the window. Trees formed a dark, impenetrable wall along my side of the road. "Keep your eyes open," I said, pointing out her window. "Let me know if you see anything."

We had traveled almost five miles when Toni smacked the dash with the palm of her hand. "We lost her."

I was about to suggest we turn around and search from the other direction when I saw a flash of red. It came from the woods, not too far ahead of us. I grabbed Toni's arm. "Did you see that?"

"What?"

"A brake light, I think, in the woods. There has to be a road or a path nearby." I slowed the car, my eyes straining to see through the darkness. Then I spotted it: a narrow dirt path winding its way from the road. "Look there, off to the left, between those pines."

"I see it. Where do you think it leads?"

"Only one way to find out." I slowed the car to a crawl and snaked it between the trees. Branches scraped the sides of the 4Runner and crunched under its tires. The uneven ground jostled us as we slipped into the woods. I turned off the headlights, plunging us into darkness.

"What are you doing?" Toni whispered.

"I don't want to tip her off that we're here."

We waited five minutes for our eyes to adjust. The wink of moon helped.

"Can you see?" I asked Toni.

"Barely." She gestured out the windshield. "Looks like it curves left up there."

The 4Runner edged along the path. Twice I had to stop abruptly before we hit a tree, but after another ten minutes of creeping forward, we came to a clearing and I parked the car.

A lake spread out before us. The moon's reflection floated like a white scar on its smooth surface.

Parked off to one side, tires almost touching the water, was Kerry's Explorer.

Toni opened her door. "Do you think she's in there?"

"Nowhere else to go." I climbed out of the 4Runner. Crickets chirped, frogs croaked. The night air carried the scent of dead leaves and algae and...something else. Something sour and unpleasant. "What's that smell?"

"Farts," Toni said. "It smells like cow farts. When I was a kid, I used to ride horses. Each weekend, Mom took me to a stable outside Kalamazoo. They had cattle and pigs as well as horses. The place stunk to high heaven." She looked at me. "It smells just like cow farts."

I almost laughed, except it wasn't funny. Cow farts contain methane, and methane was flammable. "Where do you think it's coming from?"

"My guess is swamp gas. Stagnant water mixes with decaying organic matter and releases methane. There's probably a cutaway or a bog somewhere along the shoreline where the water accumulates."

"Methane's flammable, right?" I asked, just to make sure.

"I wouldn't recommend lighting a match."

Great. "Let's check on Kerry."

We found the Explorer empty and the doors locked, with Kerry's cell phone and purse on the driver's seat. Her jacket lay draped over the front seat.

"Are the keys in the ignition?" I asked.

"No," Toni said. "Wherever she went, she took them with her."

"Good. She plans on coming back."

Toni looked at me curiously, then her eyes widened and her mouth dropped open. "No, not Kerry. She wouldn't do that to her family."

I stuffed my hands in my pockets to warm them. "Think about it. The isolation, where no one would find her right away. Her personal possessions left behind. The trauma of Frank missing, especially if she learned something terrible had happened. It could have overwhelmed her." I paused. "But I don't think that's the case here. She took her car keys. She intends to come back."

Toni remained worried. I couldn't blame her. There was no good reason for a person to come here at this time of night, yet Kerry had come, in a rush, and leaving behind important, possibly life-saving items like her jacket and cell phone.

"Where do you think she went?" Toni said. "There's nothing out here. No people, no other cars."

"I don't think a little light would hurt." Pulling out my cell, I tapped an icon and the tiny bulb in the back lit up. I held the phone low to the ground. "Let's see where she went."

The light revealed damp earth with irregular patches of grass, a few twigs, a scattering of rotting leaves, and footprints. They led away from the car and toward the lake. We followed them until they stopped at the edge of the water.

Stopped—or went in.

I lifted my phone. The light wasn't powerful enough to see more than a foot or two in front of us.

"Wait here." I hurried back to the car, cranked the ignition, and flipped on the headlights. The powerful beams shot out across the water.

I rejoined Toni. "See any sign of her?"

She shook her head. "She did it, didn't she? She walked out into the water." Her voice cracked. "She killed herself."

I put my arm around her and held her tightly. I didn't say anything. Sometimes silence says it all.

Her shoulders shook as she began to cry. "How could she? How could she do that to the kids? To us?" Her knees buckled, and I had to catch her to keep her from falling into the water. "Oh god! Her baby!"

I held my wife. I had to bite my lip to keep from crying.

Only one thing could have pushed Kerry to something this drastic.

Frank Swinicki was dead.

Chapter Thirteen

We reported the emergency, after which we called the Swinicki's. Nathan, the oldest, answered. He sounded frantic, wondering why their mom had run off, and where their dad was. I calmed him down the best I could and asked if a neighbor could come watch them. He said he would call Mrs. Collins next door. She'd covered in emergencies before. He sounded near tears when he hung up.

Twenty minutes later, the cavalry arrived. A police cruiser, an ambulance, and a florescent yellow rescue vehicle wound their way toward us. Once they cleared the woods, an officer popped out of the cruiser and hustled over to us. The ambulance parked off to one side. Two men jumped out of the rescue vehicle and quickly unpacked wet suits, scuba tanks, masks, and powerful underwater spotlights.

The officer introduced himself as Ted Sytniak. His gaze drifted to the lake. "It's been what, almost an hour since she went in?"

"You think they can find her?" I pointed to the men donning the wet suits. "It's almost pitch black, and the water's likely to be murky."

"They know what they're doing," Sytniak said. He was tall, stocky, with hair so pale it was almost invisible. "How'd you folks find your way out here?"

"My best friend," Toni said, wiping her eyes. She had been almost inconsolable while I phoned the police. Only a tremendous effort and an iron will had allowed her to keep it together. "We saw her racing through town and followed her."

"Your friend would be"—he checked his notes—"Kerry

Swinicki?"

"Yes," I told him. "Her husband's a detective with Rock Mills PD."

"Why isn't he here?"

I related the disappearance of Frank and my suspicion about Kerry learning of her husband's death. "It would explain why she did what she did."

"Have you checked to see if there's news?" Sytniak said.

Checked? Christ on a cross, I could be stupid. "I didn't."

"Let me see what I can find out." Sytniak lifted a phone to his ear and began talking.

While the officer made his call, Toni and I watched the divers wade into the lake, their black wet suits barely visible in the darkness. They disappeared under the water, their lights glowing algae green as they searched for Kerry's body.

Annabelle St. Crux's words suddenly came back to me.

Water is the beginning and the end! Remember that! Remember it!

I stared out over the lake. It didn't seem possible, but had the old woman been trying to warn us—had she pulled information from the future and related it to us in the present?

It didn't make sense. Then again, neither did the existence of dolls that tried to kill you.

"I still can't believe this," Toni said. "How could she do that to an unborn child?"

"Friday night's card game," I said, deciding to keep with the mundane and explicable. "She'd been behaving oddly. The inappropriate joke, the emotional outburst. Maybe something was wrong back then." Gestational depression wasn't uncommon, though Kerry hadn't shown signs of it with her other pregnancies. "Maybe this wasn't as sudden as we think."

Officer Sytniak approached. "I talked with a Detective Dillon. There haven't been any developments in the Swinicki case. To the best of his knowledge, no one told Mrs. Swinicki her husband was dead." Sytniak frowned. "You sure it was your friend you saw?"

"Run the plate," I said, gesturing to the Explorer.

"I did," he said. "It's hers."

"Then what's the problem?"

"It's strange," Sytniak said. "Three Rock Mills residents come together at the shore of a little-known lake miles from their homes.

One is missing, having apparently killed herself by drowning, while the other two stand by and watch. If you ask me, something doesn't add up. Especially given the fact there was no news on her husband."

There was a hardness in his voice I didn't like. "We didn't watch her drown."

"Yes," Toni said. "She was already in the lake when we arrived."

Officer Sytniak turned to her. "How do I know that?"

"Because we told you," Toni said.

"Do you have anyone to corroborate your story? Any other witnesses?"

"Out here?" she said, her exasperation building.

"Exactly. All we have to go on is your word. It may not be enough." Sytniak paused. "We may have to dig deeper, find out exactly how you ended up here."

Toni rocked back on her heels. "I can't believe this. My best friend is dead, and you're questioning us?"

The situation was quickly spiraling out of control. I made a calming gesture with my hands. "We're on the same side here. We can do better if we cooperate."

Toni and the police officer glared at one another. Several seconds passed. Surprisingly, the officer caved first.

"You're right," he said with a sigh. "I have two points I'd like to make." He had reeled in his attitude. He now sounded more deliberate than suspicious. "First, until we find a body, we can't be sure she's dead. Second, it's my job to ask questions. It's what I do. It doesn't mean you're sitting at the top of the suspect list, provided we do find a body, but you were here when she went into the water, or soon afterward. You're an eye-witness of sorts. You're going to be questioned about your presence, and should the evidence point that way, your involvement." His voice softened. "Sorry if I was abrupt. We haven't had a death like this since I started the job. There have been hunting accidents, floaters who turn up after ice fishing ends, but nothing suspicious." He looked back toward the trail. "I called the chief. He should be here soon."

"Then what?" I asked.

"A lot will depend on whether we recover a body."

"She was pregnant," Toni said. "Six weeks."

The three of us were quiet for a moment. Whether it was respect for a dead child or remorse for a mother pushed beyond her limits didn't matter. Grief was a shared penance: like food set out at a wake, you sampled it because your soul craved comfort, not simply because you were hungry.

Officer Sytniak interrupted the silence. "Do you mind if I ask some questions?"

Toni nodded glumly, and I said, "Sure."

We described the events that occurred in Emersville, including the bizarre encounter at *Black and Brewed*, and how we followed Kerry's mad dash to the lakeside. Toni turned away when I got to the part about following Kerry's footprints to the water's edge.

"That's when we called you," I said. "For the record, if we were involved, the police would've been the last people we called. No one knew we were here. No one saw us drive into the woods. We could have slipped away unnoticed, with no one the wiser. The fact we called should speak to our innocence."

We heard an engine. Headlights knifed through the trees. Before long the SUV we'd seen on our earlier visit rumbled out of the woods and parked next to the police cruiser.

"Chief's here," Officer Sytniak said. "He'll want to talk to you both. And yes, I'd already thought about the call. But people do strange things to try and hide their guilt. Besides, we don't work off of assumptions. We work off of evidence. It's not a matter of being insulting, or not believing your story. It's a matter of being thorough. You don't want us doing a half-assed job, and we don't either. Nor would this poor lady's husband, should he turn up. He's on the Job. He'd want us to stop at nothing to find out what happened. I hope you understand."

"Thank you," I told the officer. "We appreciate your help."

Toni, less charitable than I, simply nodded in agreement. Still pissed, her arms were wrapped tightly around her body. I knew from experience that it would take her a while to calm down.

"If you'll excuse me." Sytniak walked toward Chief Couttis, and the two began talking in whispers.

I hugged Toni. "You okay?"

"No." She rested her head on my chest. "If she didn't receive news about Frank, why would she do something like this? Why would she leave behind her children, or murder her own baby? Her kids were her life. None of this makes sense. We're missing something. I can feel it." She shivered. "Until we see her body, I'm not giving up on her."

"I wouldn't expect less. The same goes for Frank. We owe it to them, and to the boys. We won't quit until we have proof they're gone."

There was a splashing out on the lake. We turned, but could see nothing.

"It's so dark out there," Toni said.

"The lake's big. She could be anywhere in there. The odds of them running across her are pretty small."

"I know."

Chief Couttis approached. He wore a black nylon jacket with Emersville PD on the chest. His expression was grim, his gray hair tousled, as if he had been in bed and the call had robbed him of a night filled with pleasant dreams.

"I'm surprised to see you two again. This is what, twice in a week?"

Toni stepped up to meet him. "How's Annabelle? We saw the sign on her store. Closed indefinitely."

"Not well, I'm afraid. The doctors at St. Mary's transferred her to the hospital in Grand Rapids for specialized care. Brain tumor. Neuroblastic something-or-other."

My ears perked up. "Neuroblastoma multiform?"

"Yes, that was the name." Chief Couttis's eyes narrowed. "Is it serious?"

"Not a very high survival rate, I'm afraid. I wish it had been something different."

"Annabelle used to babysit my boy, back when he was in grade school. You remember Kent? Responded to your emergency call?"

We told him we did.

"He and Annabelle got along great. She used to make these pinwheel cookies for him. Had raspberry jam in the center. Me and the missus used to hide them, so Kent didn't polish them off in one sitting. Christ, that kid was a handful." His voice grew gravelly, as if a pebble of grief had lodged in his throat. "He's going to be heartbroken if she dies."

Toni said, "We'll send prayers her way."

"Thank you, ma'am. I'm sure she'd appreciate it. But she's not the reason you're here. Can you tell me what happened?"

We recounted for the second time the events of the evening.

When we got to the incident at the *Black and Brewed*, he stopped us.

"Who was the kid? Can you describe him?"

"About twenty, twenty-two," I said. "Thin build. Long hair stuffed into a knit cap."

"Shit-eating grin?"

"You know him?"

Chief Couttis nodded. "Cyrus Kline. Dropped out of college when the classes got hard. Now he drives a Hi-Lo for *Grant Textiles* outside of town. Likes to stand up to anyone he sees as an authority figure." His tone hardened. "Kid needs his clock cleaned. I wear the badge, which means it can't be me. Hell, with my luck, somebody'd record me tap-dancing on the little shit's head and *bam*, suddenly I'm a YouTube star. Cameras in my face, lawyers up my ass. Not the way I want to sail off into a happy retirement."

I sympathized with the man. I'd witnessed the shift from respecting the police to reviling them. "What about the rest? They stood there, like they wanted to keep us from leaving."

"Might be coincidence, Doctor Jordan. No reason they'd all interfere."

"They did interfere," Toni said. "They blocked our way. And they stood at the window and watched us leave." She gave a little shudder. "It was creepy."

"I'll look into it for you," he said. "Doesn't sound like any laws were broken, but I don't like anyone bullying out-of-towners. Emersville survives on their greenbacks. We get us a bad rep, suddenly the cash flow dries up and this place ends up a dust bowl. Not gonna let it happen, not on my watch." He paused. "Tell me, how is it you two are back in the center of another crisis, given you are, in fact, tourists?"

More splashing came from the direction of the lake, but I didn't let it distract me. The sudden shift in the chief's questioning was meant to catch us off guard. I was sure of it. I had been expecting it. Hang out with cops long enough and you learn a trick or two about police work.

"It's like we said," I explained. "We were in town. We saw our friend's—"

Couttis held up a hand. "That's the part I don't get. You told Ted you were assaulted earlier. Someone broke into your home, knocked you around some, and stole your stuff. Yet here you are, far from

Rock Mills and looking like you had a run-in with a hay combine. Damn strange if you ask me. I guess that's my question: why come here after something like that?"

Chief Couttis's question did put me on the defensive. This part of our story was hard to explain without giving away what we knew. If the police were in on the conspiracy, outright telling the chief could land us in a jail cell or worse, but I couldn't see any way out. I had been asked a direct question, and the chief expected a direct answer. I would have to tell the truth, but not necessarily the whole truth.

"The doll," I said. "It was the only thing stolen."

"What doll? What are you talking about?"

"I bought it at *Lost Desires*. Someone broke into our house and all he took was the damn doll, the one I bought here, in your town. We came to see if we could find out who did it. And we think we found him."

"Found him? Where?"

"*Black and Brewed*. We were trying to catch him when the place went all *Twilight Zone* on us."

"Describe him," Couttis said.

"Tall, brown hair cut close to his scalp, big as a hay combine."

"That could be any number of people. Any distinguishing features? Scars? Tattoos?"

"He was wearing an earring. A steel skull. 'Bout the size of your thumb."

Couttis suddenly looked wary. "You sure about that skull earring?"

I nodded. "Hard to miss, and not something I'd make up."

"I suppose not." The chief started rubbing his hand up and down on his pant leg, as if he were wiping a stain from his palm. "I can't believe it. What the hell was he thinking?"

"Who?" Toni said. "What was who thinking?"

"His name is Conrad Hunter," Couttis said. "Goes by Connie. Lives up on Longmeadow, next to the library. Drives an F150. Big blue mother with knobby wheels and a muffler that rumbles like an earthquake."

"I remember him," I said. "He drove past *Lost Desires* while we were talking to your son. Mirrored sunglasses hiding half his face. Expression about as friendly as a wood splitter."

"That's him."

"How do you know him?"

Chief Couttis turned to face me. Every pore on his weathered face was visible in the moonlight.

"He's our mayor, Doctor Jordan. Connie Hunter is our goddamn mayor."

* * *

An hour later and the divers were still searching for Kerry's body.

The night had turned cold. Frost covered the car windows like white mold. Even the frogs and crickets had packed it in for the night. The only sound was the occasional splash coming from the lake.

Toni and I paced the shoreline in an effort to keep warm. Officer Sytniak approached us. He had donned a heavier coat. "You should go home. There's nothing you can do here."

"Any word from Chief Couttis?" Toni's voice shook from the cold.

"No, ma'am. Not sure we'll hear from him again tonight."

After learning that the man who beat me might have been Emersville's mayor, Chief Couttis had become all business.

"I need to talk to Connie," he had said. "See if he has an alibi for today."

I agreed. "If he doesn't?"

"I'll have to turn him over to Rock Mills for questioning." His face twisted into a grimace. "Implicating a mayor, especially a popular one like Conrad Hunter, doesn't come without risks. I'll have to be careful. Connie might look like a brute, but he's sharp as hell. He won't balk at giving me trouble, putting up roadblocks. He might even consider dismissing me for harassment. I don't think he'd do it—there's not many people in this town qualified to run a police department—but like I said earlier, I'm facing retirement in a few years, and I don't want to go out on a sour note." He walked to his car. "It won't stop me from doing my job, though. I'm a professional, same as him."

"What does he do?" I called out.

"What else?" the chief had said. "He's a lawyer."

Officer Sytniak snapped on his flashlight, bringing me back to the present. He cast the beam out over the lake. Mist rose from the surface and drifted in lazy, hypnotic swirls. As I stared, my eyelids began to droop, and I had to shake myself to keep from dozing off.

"Seriously, folks," Sytniak said, bringing the Maglite around until it illuminated our faces. "There's no need for you to stay. If we find anything, we'll call."

"I'd like to stay," Toni said, blowing into her hands, "but I'm not sure if I can last much longer. I feel like I could collapse at any moment."

Looking at her, I noticed how pale she had become. Her cheeks were bone-white except for the dark smudges under her eyes, and there was a trace of blue around her lips.

"Honey," I said, alarmed by her appearance. "Are you all right?"

She nodded weakly. "Just tired. Too much going on, not enough rest. I'll be fine by tomorrow."

"There's the *Star Fall Motel*," said Sytniak. "It's back in town. You could stay there. If something turns up, you'd be nearby."

My skin crawled at the mention of the motel. My nightmare from the other night returned—me falling through space, a dead planet spinning below me, and Thumbkin, sailing alongside me, scolding me. *You weren't supposed to see this!*

"Maybe you could sit in the car with the heater on," I told Toni. "Bailing now feels like giving up on Kerry. I don't want to do that. Not to her, and not to Frank."

"The motel is a few miles away," Officer Sytniak said. "You could be back in a heartbeat if we needed you. And truthfully, I'd prefer you go. Until we know otherwise, this is a crime scene, and since you were the last to see Mrs. Swinicki alive, you're a party to the investigation."

I opened my mouth to protest. Sytniak help up a hand. "It would be in your best interest to leave. A prosecutor could start wondering why you stayed behind, and you don't want that kind of attention. Please, go take care of your wife. Get some rest. I've got both your cell numbers. If there are any developments, I'll call."

"If you find her out there"—Toni pointed to the lake—"will you let us see her before you take her away?"

"I doubt it. For the same reasons you shouldn't stay, you also shouldn't see her. You don't want first-hand knowledge of the evidence. It's to protect you as well as the integrity of the investigation." Officer Sytniak considered. "With her husband missing, we will need someone to positively identify the body after the M.E. is finished. You might be asked to drive over to St. Mary's. Would you be up to it?"

"Absolutely," Toni said.

"If you need us, we'll be available," I assured the officer. "I hope it won't come to that."

Sytniak's eyes met mine. "She's been gone a long time. Her car is here. So is her purse and her phone. If she's not in the water, then where is she?"

His tone was calm but also certain, and I understood what he was telling me.

She's given herself to the lake, and the lake has accepted her gift. She won't return to this world in the same condition she left.

I needed to brace myself for the unpleasantness ahead. Standing here cold and shivering wouldn't help.

"Come on," I said. "Let's go warm up."

"You'll call?" Toni asked Sytniak. "When you find her, you'll call us?"

"Yes, ma'am," Office Sytniak said. "You have my word."

With the 4Runner's heater blowing full blast, we drove away. Neither one of us spoke.

I pulled into the *Star Fall Motel*. We rented a room, staggered inside, and crawled into bed. Toni fell asleep almost immediately. I lay awake, my mind mulling over the day's events. I've always had trouble turning off my brain.

Half an hour later, my phone rang. I answered without looking at the screen, assuming it was Officer Sytniak calling to inform us they'd found Kerry's body.

"Hello?"

"Paco?" Frank's voice sounded too loud over the phone's tiny speaker. "Where the hell is everyone?"

* * *

Frank arrived at the *Star Fall Motel* in record time.

I opened the door for him. He charged into the room, disheveled, his face looking more hound-dogged. I caught a whiff of fast food grease on his clothes as he brushed past me.

"Take me to the lake," he said. "Take me now."

I followed him. "Frank—"

"No," he said. He was breathing heavily, almost panting, and had the "close-to-the-edge" look of someone who was about to blow. "Take me to my wife."

"Frank, listen to me." I kept my voice level, my tone reassuring. He didn't need anything adding to his distress. "We'll fill you in on everything, but it'll take time. Sit down. Catch your breath." I paused, then added quietly, "I don't think we have to hurry."

He stared at me with red-rimmed eyes. "She's my wife. I need to be there."

"I know. First, though, you need to calm down. Let us tell you what we know. You can tell us where you've been. Then we'll take you to the lake. Agreed?"

"I am calm," he said through clenched teeth.

"You need to trust me. A level head works best. It's the only way we'll figure out what happened, and what to do next."

"Goddammit, Paco! Don't feed me this shit! I want—"

Toni stepped up to Frank. Her face was still pale, she still looked haggard, but she managed a smile. Reaching up, she grabbed his blocky, Polish head, brought it to hers, and lightly kissed the tears on his cheeks.

"We all loved her," she said. "We love you, too. Never forget that, Frank. Never. Now sit down. The lake will come soon enough." Without a protest from Frank, she led him to a chair and sat him down. "Take a moment to grieve. You owe yourself that much."

There was a box of tissues on the stand next to the chair. Frank grabbed two fistfuls and pressed them to his face. We watched as he started rocking in the chair. He didn't make a sound as he cried.

Toni rested a hand on his shoulder. "Don't hold back. Let it go. Let her know how much you'll miss her." She bit her lip to hold back her own tears. "Let her know how much you loved her."

It was too much for Frank. He hunched over, his face buried in his hands, his broad shoulders heaving, and screamed. He screamed his wife's name. He screamed his kids' names. He screamed for the unborn child he would never know. He screamed with the naked, tormented grief people never know how to put into words. He screamed until his voice grew hoarse. When his screams turned to sobs, Toni knelt beside him and held him. He turned and buried his face into her shoulder. Gently stroking his hair, she consoled him.

"It'll be okay. Just let it out. We understand."

The immediacy of his grief finally ran its course. Frank sat up and wiped his eyes with the tissues. It didn't do much good. They were soaked with his tears.

Toni snatched a few more from the box and handed them to him. "You did well. We're proud of you."

Frank wiped his face dry and blew his nose.

"We're here for you," I said. "Anytime, anyplace. For any reason."

"I know."

"Better?"

"A little. Tell me what happened."

Toni and I related the events of the night. The tale didn't take long.

"The police are searching for her," I said. "The lake's big and deep. It could be days before they find her."

"Just the same," Frank said. "I'd like to be there. I'm having a hard time believing this happened. It's so unreal. Until I see something, until I see her..." Frank slumped back in the chair, his bulk making the legs creak. "She was alone when she died. She shouldn't be alone when she's found. I can do that much for her."

"We'll head out in a few minutes." I asked Toni to run to the motel's vending machine and grab some sodas, preferably with caffeine. After she'd left, I turned my attention to Frank. "Have you talked to the boys?"

"Earlier," he said. The hard-nosed cop had fled, leaving behind a vulnerable father of three newly-motherless children. "They're all freaked out. Particularly Nate. He sees himself as grown up, but he's a kid. It'll change tomorrow. Death has a harsh way of shoving us into adulthood, whether we like it or not."

"Did he say why she left?"

"Only that she was talking on her phone when she abruptly hung up, threw her jacket on over her pajamas, and ran out of the house."

"Without saying a word?"

"She just stormed out."

"Whoever was on the other end of the call might know why she left, or why she did what she did." My eyes met his. "Her cell phone's in the car."

Toni returned with the sodas. Frank, impatient to get going, drank his down in three large gulps. Toni sat on the edge of the bed. The color hadn't returned to her cheeks, and when she drank her soda, her hand trembled. "I'm going to sit here for a minute. I don't feel so hot."

"It's been a long night," I told Frank. "Everyone's exhausted."

"I hear you." His scowl softened. "I appreciate what you've done. Thank you."

I informed Toni about Kerry's phone conversation, the one she'd had before she rushed out of the house. "We need to look at her phone and find out who she talked to."

Toni set her soda on the nightstand. "Do you mind if I stay here?" She looked at Frank. "It's not that I don't care. It's that I'm so damn tired. Maybe I'm coming down with something."

"Sure," Frank said, and I added, "You'll be all right by yourself?"

"An hour or two of sleep will do me good." She kissed me on the cheek and whispered, "Promise you'll call if you learn anything."

I returned her kiss. "Get some rest. We won't be long."

As we climbed into Frank's Charger, I saw the lights go out in the motel room.

"She okay?" Frank asked as he pulled out of the parking lot and sped toward the lake.

"I hope so." The interior of the Charger was warm from Frank's mad dash to Emersville. I remembered how cold it was at the lake and cranked the blower. "Where were you? We called your cell over and over and got worried when you didn't answer. It's not like you to go off the grid."

Frank looked sheepish. "Damn phone died again."

"For fuck's sake, Frank."

"I know, I know. I'll get a new one as soon as I can."

I brushed aside my frustration. "We'll deal with that later. For now, tell me where you were."

"After leaving the DA's office, I grabbed lunch and went over my notes. The case is a murder charge involving an ice chipper and a bottle of drain cleaner that goes to trial in two weeks. Jakobson, the D.A., wants me up on the facts."

"And it took all night?"

He gave me an unfriendly stare. "I was about to head home when I overheard a call on the police band. Kid missing from his home, mom in a panic, thinks he's been kidnapped. I decided to help." He shook his head. "We came, we searched, we found no evidence of foul play. Likely the kid ran away. I would too, if I had her as a mother. What a loon. Anyway, we put out an Amber Alert. Last I heard, the kid was still missing."

"You're not worried?"

"Kids run away all the time. He's probably at a friend's house, hiding in the basement. Figures if he gives his mom a fright, she'll buy him a video game or some such shit. I see it all the time." Frank sailed around the curve in the road and approached the lake's access road. He slowed when I pointed it out and nosed the car into the gap between the trees. "The kid's mom gave me a bad vibe. Wouldn't budge from the kidnapping angle, even after I explained how most missing kids are runaways."

"Did you call the FBI?"

"Not enough evidence to suggest a kidnapping. I'm telling you, the kid ran away."

"What about the dad?"

"Dead."

"Recently?"

"A few months ago. Died overseas. Active military. Poor bastard was blown up by one of those IEDs. Iraq, I think."

Father died overseas. Mother a little off. Boy willing to run to get away from her.

Ding ding ding.

"This kid who ran away, is his name Doug Belle?"

Frank's eyes widened. "Jesus, Paco. He's one of yours?"

There was no sense in denying it. "When did his mom report him missing?"

"Around eight. They'd finished dinner and the kid went to do some homework. When she checked on him, he was gone."

"No note? Nothing to suggest he wasn't coming back?"

"Clothes were still there. So were a few of his dad's medals, which he keeps in his room. Can't see him leaving without those."

We approached the beach. Frank hit the Charger's flashers, letting the cops know he was one of theirs.

"He called me this evening," I told Frank as he parked next to an Emersville PD cruiser. "At least, I think it was him."

"When was this?"

"Around six."

"Did he say why he called?"

"That's the strange part. He didn't say a word. I'm sure it was him, though."

Frank hesitated. "What can you tell me about him?"

"Sorry, you know the rules."

Frank killed the engine and pocketed the keys. "He's missing, Paco. Any information you can provide might help us find him."

I thought about Johnny Richardson, Doug's friend with the harelip. "There's not enough reason to break confidentiality. If the situation changes, I'll see what I can do."

"Fair enough, I guess." Frank climbed out of the car. "Who'd you say was in charge here?"

"The guy standing by the shore. Name's Sytniak. See what you can find out. I'll stay here and keep warm."

While Frank went to converse with the officer, I checked my phone for calls from my service. Finding none, I tapped in the Belle's home number. While I couldn't reveal anything to Frank, there was nothing in the rules about intervening myself.

Dee Dee answered on the first ring and practically shouted into the phone.

"Dougie? Is that you? Where have you been?"

"It's Doctor Jordan, Mrs. Belle."

A surprised pause. "What do you want?"

"I saw the Amber Alert." No sense getting into the details of my association with the police. "You haven't heard from Doug?"

"No, and he's been gone for hours. I don't know what to do. I want my little man back."

"Do you know why he'd run away, why he'd suddenly leave like this?"

Another pause, longer this time. "He was mad," she finally said, not mentioning the kidnapping story. "He gets so mad sometimes. I don't understand why. I mean, I know he's upset about Tink, but why take it out on me? It's not like it was my fault."

The sudden shift from concern for her son to concern for herself wasn't surprising, but it was depressing. The narcissistic elements of her personality would hinder her forming a lasting bond with her son. Neediness would overshadow her love for him, and he would suffer for it.

"Have you tried calling Johnny Richardson's house? Doug spoke pretty highly of him. Maybe he went there for a while."

"Who?"

"Johnny Richardson? Boy in his class? They hang around together?"

"Oh, him."

"You know who I'm talking about?"

"Yes," she said coldly. "Dougie wouldn't go there. I don't like him hanging around with that boy."

"I don't understand. It sounded like they got along well enough."

"That boy is trouble."

"In what way?"

"He's, you know, *deformed*." She whispered the word, as if speaking it were an offense to God, and she didn't want Him to hear.

My heart sank. "You mean his harelip?"

"What else do you think I mean?" Dee Dee Belle's voice coiled with anger. "He's got a future, my Dougie does. He's going to be a football star. He needs to make friends with kids his own caliber. Hanging around with some kid who could be in a 'fix my face' charity commercial is disgusting. It'll scare away people, important people, like scouts and agents." She gave an irritated huff. "Dougie needs to stay here with me. I can protect him. I can make sure he becomes the man he's supposed to be, one Tink would be proud of. No, my son is not with that...that *retard*."

Listening to Dee Dee Belle spout her prejudices made my want to vomit. The woman was vile. She couldn't even stomach using Johnny Richardson's name.

"You should try Johnny's house," I said, setting aside my personal feelings for the woman. "Doug might be there. You could bring him home. Everything else can be dealt with later."

"I told you, my son—"

"Is missing," I said, cutting her off. "The police are looking for him. If a simple phone call can end this, you need to do it." I took a steadying breath. "If you don't call them, I will. The police can check the Richardson house for Doug. I'm sure they'll also want to know why you didn't mention his friend."

"You'll be breaking confidentiality," Dee Dee Belle said. "Do it and I'll sue you!"

"Doug has an Amber Alert out. I have to assume he's in danger.

Any assistance I provide would be protected by law." Apparently finished with Officer Sytniak, Frank approached the car. I held up a finger and pointed to the phone. He nodded and moved away. Returning my attention to Mrs. Belle, I added, "Doug's safety comes first. I'm sure you understand."

"All right, I'll call" she said, her tone caustic. "But know this— you're fired. I'll find another therapist to help my son. Someone who's more professional."

She hung up before I could respond. Not that I minded. Sometimes I had a hard time holding my tongue.

I met Frank by the shore. He was looking at the water.

"Who were you talking to?" he asked, his breath misting in the cold air.

"Wrong number."

He turned to look at me. "You called the mom, didn't you?"

"Don't know what you're talking about."

An evil grin spread across his face. "Get anywhere with the bitch?"

"You should be getting a call soon." The moon was setting across the lake. Waves caused ripples of argent to slither across the surface. "What did the officer say?"

"Nothing good," Frank said, and lost his smile. "They haven't found her. The divers are getting cold. I think they're going to call it and try again in the morning." He swallowed hard. "Maybe she'll, you know, surface by then."

By *surface*, I think he meant *float to the surface*. "What about the car? Did you get her cell?"

"They won't let me." He kicked at the sand with the toe of his shoe. "Claim it's part of the evidence."

"Is it?"

"Yes, it's part of the fucking evidence."

We stood for a while, watching the water.

"I can't imagine how you're feeling," I said, breaking the silence.

"How do I tell the kids?" Frank said. "How do I keep Nate from blaming himself for not stopping her? How do I keep him from developing...what do you call it?"

"Survivor guilt."

"Yeah, survivor guilt."

"They'll need to talk to someone. I'll get you a name."

"Maybe I'll need one too."

"Two names. It's not a good idea for you to see the same therapist they do."

"If you think it's best." He drew in a breath and let it seep out from between his lips. "How did I fuck the puppy on this one, Paco?"

"What do you mean?" I said.

"How did I miss the signs? How did I not see it coming? Where was my head, if I couldn't see how depressed she'd become?" He stuffed his hands into his jacket. "How did I fuck the puppy?"

"Maybe Nate's not the only one prone to survivor guilt."

He lifted one shoulder in a half-hearted shrug. "I guess we're all in the same boat. Kerry kills herself, and the people who love her are left to pick up the pieces. It's not fair."

The significance of his words was not lost on me. "You said it out loud. You admitted her death is real. That's how the healing begins."

"How long will it take?" he said. "How long before I start to feel normal again?"

I left his question unanswered because there was no answer. Everyone was different, and healed at different rates.

"We'll worry about this later, after—"

Frank's cell chirped, followed immediately by mine. I didn't know who was calling him, but Toni's name came up on my screen.

Frowning at one another, we answered our respective phones.

"Hey, honey," I said.

"Brad," Toni said breathlessly. "Get back here, right now."

"What's wrong?"

"It's Kerry." Toni let out a squeal of laughter. "She's here."

"What?"

"She's wet and she's cold but she's here and *she's alive.*"

My head spun. "We'll be right there."

I hung up and turned to Frank. He was finishing up his conversation.

"I'm leaving," he told me. "And you're coming with."

"Frank, wait."

He didn't seem to hear me. "Your patient, Doug Belle. We found him."

"There's something I need to tell you."

"He's in a marsh, about a mile from his home." He started for his car. "We need to get there pronto."

I hurried to catch up. "Why? What's going on?"

"He's armed with two knives and a gun, says he's going to kill himself, says he won't talk to anyone but you." He opened the car door. "Get in, Paco. You're on the clock."

"Frank, hold on." I reached in and took the keys from his hand. "Listen to me."

"What the—? Have you lost your mind? The kid needs you."

I lifted my phone. "The call was about Kerry."

His face paled. "What about her?"

"It was Toni. Kerry's with her."

"Say again?"

I smiled. "Your wife is alive."

Chapter Fourteen

Frank notified the rescue crew that his wife had apparently turned up alive. They called off the search, and Officer Sytniak informed Frank he needed to speak with Kerry. Frank told him he would arrange a meeting, but not until tomorrow. When Sytniak balked, Frank explained how a crime had not been committed, and Sytniak could not force an interview. Tomorrow would have to suffice. The officer didn't look happy, but he agreed. "Tomorrow it is."

We climbed into the Charger and left, stopping at the motel long enough to confirm Kerry Swinicki was there, and she was alive. We told our wives about my patient and the danger he faced.

"Go help the poor kid," Toni told me. "He needs you."

"We'll talk when you get back," Kerry said. Her face was pale, her pajamas soaked. Her eyes looked haunted, like she had traveled a great distance and didn't like what she had seen. "I'll explain everything."

"Damn right you will," Frank said with a touch of anger. "You scared the hell out of everyone."

Kerry winced but didn't apologize.

"I'll put her in a hot shower," Toni said, and started herding Kerry toward the bathroom. "Warm her up. See what I can do about drying her clothes. The motel's vending machine has candy bars. I'll get her a few. She needs to eat."

She shut the door on us—and a potential argument.

Frank and I climbed back into the Charger. Rock Mills was thirty minutes away. With his flashers going, we could make it in under twenty. Frank called the officer in charge and told him we were on our way.

"Where do you think she's been all night?" Frank asked tightly.

"She's alive and that's what matters. Do you still have the metal egg, the one from the doll?"

Frank blew through a red light, not that there was much traffic at this hour. "Sure. Why?"

I filled him in on the details of the break-in, how the burglars were looking for something called a proximity lock. "They took Thumbkin, but it was missing the egg. I think the egg is the lock. It's what they came for." Frank ran another red light. He may have been concentrating on the road, but I knew he was also listening. "I thought they'd found you, maybe killed you to get it. The guy who beat me up said he would take it that far. It's why Toni and I were in Emersville. The dolls came from there, so we thought we might find you there."

"Went Delta Team on me, huh? Search and rescue operation?" He removed the egg from his pocket, the metal glinting red in the Charger's dash lights, and dropped it into my hand. "Here you go."

That it weighed almost nothing still surprised me. It contained no gears, held no power source, yet something had punched a hole in it with a force stronger than anything we could replicate. What function it performed, what job it was intended to do, was a dark mystery.

"A lock fastens something in place," I said. "Or secures a door, so no one can open it."

"It also stops a mechanism from engaging," Frank said. "Think the lock on a gun. It keeps the weapon from firing."

"It could also mean homing in on a location, like locking onto a target."

Frank gripped the wheel tighter. "I don't like the sound of that one."

Neither did I. "What does proximity have to do with a lock? By definition, something locked would have to be nearby. Again, unless it is some kind of homing device." I pocketed the egg. "We need to find the person who assaulted me. He'll have the answers."

"One crisis at a time," Frank said, taking the exit for Rock Mills. "The marsh is a few blocks from the kid's house. We'll be there soon."

He glanced at me. "Time to open up. What's the kid's issue? Why's he threatening to off himself?"

"Doug's basically a good kid who lost his father and has been acting out his anger and depression over the loss. Fighting, letting his grades fall. The kind of externalizations you'd expect from someone his age. But threatening to kill himself would be a radical departure from his previous symptoms."

"He never talked about suicide?"

"Not with me, and his mother never reported it."

Frank grunted. "What's your take on her?"

"Lots of narcissistic traits. Self-absorbed, emotionally immature, explosive if confronted. Likes to call Doug the man of the house now that her husband is dead. She doesn't want the responsibility of adulthood, so she forces it on him." We were coming up on the marsh. I unbuckled my seat belt. "Did she give you much trouble?"

Frank turned a corner. Several police cruisers crowded the end of the street. He parked behind one. "Other than the kidnapping fantasy? Yeah, she didn't want us looking in his bedroom. Had to threaten her with child protective services before she'd move away from the door."

"What'd you find?"

"That's the kicker—we didn't find anything unusual. Posters on the walls, some video games. School books. And bottles of lotion. I think your patient has a serious skin problem."

Frank's badge got us past the security perimeter, and we quickly found the officer in charge. Lieutenant Ricky Weston stood near the front of the line of cars. Dee Dee Belle lingered beside him, wearing a bulky coat over her silk pajamas. She'd combed her hair and had taken time to apply makeup. As she talked to Lieutenant Weston, she lightly touched his arm and smiled.

My stomach turned.

Dee Dee Belle was flirting.

"Lieutenant Weston!" Frank shouted, having seen the same display and undoubtedly reached the same conclusion.

With a look of relief, Ricky Weston stepped away from Dee Dee. Her eyes trailed hungrily after him. When they fell on me, though, her teeth clenched, and her face turned red. She was not happy to see me.

"Where's the kid?" Frank said when the Lieutenant was close

enough.

"About twenty yards into the marsh," Weston said. "He's got the gun in one hand and a knife in the other. He has the second knife stuffed into the waistband of his pants. We've been trying to talk to him, get him to drop the weapons. He's not having any of it." He turned his attention to me. "Says he'll to talk to you and no one else."

"Any idea why?" I asked him.

Weston shook his head. "Won't tell us."

"Did his mother talked to him?"

"Once, when she got here. The kid started screaming, telling her to go away. He wanted nothing to do with her. She gave up, a little too easily if you ask me." Weston snorted. "Since then, she's been too busy looking for a boyfriend to worry about her kid. The lady's a piece of work."

If Dee Dee Belle had designs on Ricky Weston, they had just crumbled to dust. She wouldn't be finding a relationship with him.

"Has he said anything?" I asked.

"Oh, he's talking, but not to us." Lieutenant Weston suddenly looked uncomfortable. "It's like he's having a conversation. He turns his head when he talks, like someone's standing next to him. He talks, and then waits, and talks again. It's the creepiest thing, Doc."

A breeze kicked up, carrying Doug's voice from the marsh. His talk was gibberish, his words a mishmash of subjects, a combination of exclamations and pleadings that made little sense. I thought back to the boy I'd met less than two weeks ago; the boy who could kick ass in Connect Four and chew bubble gum like a pro wrestler. Doug Belle was more tormented than I thought.

"I need to talk to him," I said.

"First thing's first." Frank motioned to another cop, who brought over a Kevlar vest. Frank handed it to me. "Put this on."

"He's not going to shoot me."

"The kid's got a gun, Paco. No jackie, no talkie. Them's the rules."

I reluctantly slipped on the bulky vest. I expected it to be heavy, like carrying sacks of sand, but it weighed no more than a winter jacket. "Satisfied?"

Frank looked at Weston. "Take us to the kid."

We headed toward the marsh. Dee Dee Belle, who had been glaring from her position several yards away, saw us move and stormed over. She'd covered about half the distance when she lost a slipper, almost fell, and had to wave her arms to retain her balance. In the process, her robe slipped off her shoulders and the hem fell into the mud. She jerked it up. The embarrassing display didn't improve her mood as she stopped in front of us.

"What's he doing here?" No one had to ask who she meant.

"Your son asked for him," Frank said. "Doctor Jordan agreed to come. He wants to help."

"He's not Dougie's therapist anymore."

"He's also here at my request."

"I don't want him near my son."

"Stand aside, Mrs. Belle," Frank said.

Dee Dee Belle didn't budge. "He's already done enough damage. Get him out of my sight."

An anguished howl came from the marsh, followed by a series of high-pitched yips like coyote calls.

"Frank," I said in warning.

"I hear you." Frank pulled himself up to his full height. "Lieutenant Weston?"

"Sir."

"Remove Mrs. Belle. If she resists, put her in cuffs. If she fights you, lock her in a car. Under no circumstances is she to go near the marsh. Got it?"

"Yes, sir." Ricky Weston took Dee Dee Belle by the arm. "Ma'am, if you'll please come with me."

Dee Dee Belle stiffened. "Take your goddamn hand off me!"

Ricky Weston began dragging her away. When she tried kicking him, he pulled the cuffs from his belt and snapped one open. It made a sound like knuckles cracking.

The dramatic gesture got Dee Dee's attention. She stopped struggling. With a glance back at me, she said, "This is your fault. I'll make sure you lose your license over it."

Apparently finished with her threats, she allowed herself to be led away. The woman was probably already plotting how to get Lieutenant Weston into her bed.

Good luck with that.

Frank and I proceeded to the marsh. He stopped about twenty feet from the edge.

"Here you go. Do that voodoo you do best." He put a hand on my shoulder. It felt like a final, "gee shucks" gesture from the warden before he sent you to ride the lightning. "Help the kid, but don't risk your life. Keep a safe distance. If it looks like he's gonna start spreading lead, this session ends and we try something else."

"What does that mean?" I said, stepping forward. "Something else?"

"We take him down. There are two sharp shooters trained on him."

I froze. "He's a kid."

"He's a kid with a big ass gun, and it's my job to make sure he doesn't hurt anyone." He hesitated. "I know this sounds cruel, but a suicide's safety comes last. Doesn't matter if he's a kid, if he looks like he's going to shoot, we stop him." His voice softened. "I hope you understand."

"I understand," I said. "I just don't like it."

With the protective weight of the vest bolstering my courage, I went to talk to my patient. Ex-patient, actually.

The marsh was part of a vast wetland stretching from Portage Lake along the Clancy River to Lake Michigan. A popular spot with hunters, the marsh was also dangerous. Poisonous snakes swam in the murky waters. Bears hunted along its shores. Wander in too far, step in the wrong spot, and you sunk up to your knees in soft, mucky earth. More than a handful of inexperienced hikers had been found dead because they couldn't get free and had suddenly found themselves at the bottom of the food chain.

Tonight the waters were calm with patches of ice floating on the surface. Twenty paces out, illuminated by the police lights trained on his thin body, Doug Belle stood waist-deep in the water. Like a waif in a Dickens story, he wore a grimy shirt of alternating blue and red stripes. Mud speckled the skin on his arms and spread like leprosy across his face. His right hand held the gun, a nickel-plated semiautomatic with half the barrel submerged in the water. Clutched in his left fist was a Bowie knife almost as long as his forearm. The hilt of a smaller knife stuck out from the waistband of his pajamas.

Head tilted back, eyes closed, he swayed back and forth, like he was listening to a symphony only he could hear.

I called out, "Doug? It's me. It's Doctor Brad."

He stopped swaying. His cracked lips peeled back until all of his teeth showed. "The distance was too great. Some things cannot be changed, no matter how smart you are."

He sounded exhausted, and I wondered when he had last slept.

"Doug, open your eyes. Look at me."

"In the end, it was easier to go through than across." He chuckled, a horrid, gurgling sound. "Did I say easy? Moving worlds would have been easier, yet I succeeded. I found the way." His face twisted in revulsion. "And how does she reward me for my work? She sends me here. Here!"

"Do what, Doug? What did you do?"

"I saved them," he said. "Only later did I realize I'd saved the wrong ones."

"The wrong ones?"

"Her people. That bitch, I should have killed her."

My heart sank. Doug was in worse shape than I'd thought. His speech was filled with confabulations, a mixture of fact and fantasy some psychotics used to build structure around their delusions, and it signaled a deeply disturbed person. How had he deteriorated so much in such a brief amount of time?

Doug suddenly lifted the gun. It looked like a cannon in his slender hand. He pointed it at the sky and shouted, "I deserved better from her!"

Alarmed, I stepped forward. Marsh water sloshed over my shoes, soaking my feet. "Doug, put the gun down. I can't help you if you don't put the gun down."

A loon sounded in the distance. Doug tilted his head. "It was our greatest accomplishment. Some said it cemented our genius. Ask the Stranded, though, and I bet you'd hear a different story. I doubt they'd be so charitable."

The stranded? It sounded like a proper name, and psychotics rarely had the wherewithal to create specifics like names. Their delusions rambled too much.

"Doug, put down the gun and we can talk. I want to hear more about this success."

He chuckled again and finally opened his eyes, now deep-set and bruised. He wiped at the snot running down his nose. "She'll come for you. Like an unstoppable force, she will come and she will gather you together like the cattle you are and she will destroy any who don't fit her purpose. What she'll leave behind will be unrecognizable, a distorted shadow of who you were and the world you knew. In the end, your lives will be forfeit. If you had souls, I would pray for them."

I tried to parcel out truth from delusion. "Who will come?" Certainly it couldn't be his mother.

A tremor like a seizure shot through his body. He shook his head violently, like he was denying a truth. This went on for several more seconds, and when he looked back at me, his anguished expression had been replaced with one of stark terror. "Doctor Brad, I can't take it. I can't listen to the voice anymore. It tells me things. Bad things. It tells me about her." He raised the knife to his tear-streaked face. "I don't want to hear any more."

"Doug." I took another step into the water. "Listen to me. I can help you, but you need to let me try. Together we might be able to stop the voice, but we can't until you drop the weapons."

His hand trembled as he said, "It's too late. She's here, and no one can stop her."

"Are you talking about your mom?" Given the woman's relentless narcissism, my next question should have been asked much earlier. "Did she hurt you?"

Doug made a whining sound, like a wounded puppy. "Don't make me tell you. Please, don't."

"I won't make you do anything." I kept my voice calm despite the alarm coursing through me. Doug's distress was escalating. I didn't want him to lose it completely.

Doug's hand wavered. I thought for a moment he might drop the knife. Then his grip tightened, and he pressed the blade against his cheek.

"I'm a kid, right? A kid. School taught me about stranger danger, but what if the danger lives under the same roof with you? What're you supposed to do then?"

"The lotion bottles in your room," I said, a horrible suspicion coming to mind. "More than one boy would need. What did she do with them? Did it have something to do with story time? Is that why you would get so upset."

I heard a scuffle behind me, and Dee Dee Belle shouted, "You shut up about that, Dougie! That's Mommy time, and these filthy people have no business knowing about Mommy time!"

Frank barked an order. More shouting, this time from Lieutenant Weston. He was ordering Doug's mother to get into a patrol car.

"You're my good boy!" she yelled. "I love you more than

anything! You keep quiet! You—"

A car door slammed, cutting her off.

Doug let out a broken sob. "I told her to stop, but she wouldn't. She kept going and going." He drew the knife down his cheek, drawing a line of blood. It dripped onto his shirt and into the water. "She'll never stop."

I charged into the water. Doug leveled the gun at me. "Don't make me kill you."

"Don't shoot!" I called out, more to the police than to Doug, and stopped. "Don't shoot," I repeated, more softly. "We can talk from here, Doug. Just put down the gun. I don't want anyone getting hurt."

"She wanted me to be him," Doug said, tears mixing with the blood. He moved the knife to the other side of his face. "She wanted me to be my father. She said she missed him so much, but at least she had me."

The blade skittered along his cheek, slicing open his skin. Blood flowed.

"She'd touch me while we read, told me it was good for us to be in love. When she finished the story, she would smile and put me in her mouth. Told me it was a reward for being good. I cried and told her to stop. She said I needed to behave—to be her good boy—or she would tell my friends what we did. Then she told me we should, you know, do it. That it would prove our love."

He paused. "The lotion was for me, because we couldn't d-d-do it like real adults. She said it would be a sin. We could only do it from behind, *in* her behind. The lotion helped me fit." He brought the blade to his throat. "I threw up the first time, right onto her back. She made me keep going. She turned me into something dirty, and I hate her for it. But more than my mom, I hate the other one. I hate her for what she's doing, and for what she's planning."

I risked another step toward him. If I could get close enough...

"Doug, please, you don't have to do this. Anything can be fixed if we work together."

Doug's hand tightened on the hilt. "You know who I mean, don't you?"

Another step. "Put the knife down."

"It's her, Doctor Brad," he said, his voice barely above a whisper. "It's the Green Queen."

I froze. How could he know about the Green Queen?

"Don't let her get you!" Doug cried, and jerked the blade across his throat.

I charged forward, threw my arms out to stop him, but I was too far away. The blade bit into his skin, peeling it back like lips to reveal pale cartilage and muscle. Blood fell in a red sheet down the front of his shirt. His other hand clenched involuntarily and the gun fired. The round flew harmlessly into the night. Then his legs folded, and he sank into the march.

By the time I reached him, blood had stained the water crimson. The paramedics arrived. They tried to save him, worked on him there in the water, but it was no use.

Doug ended up on a gurney in the back of the ambulance, a sheet pulled over his pale face.

From the back of the patrol car, Dee Dee Belle screamed and pounded on the glass. No one paid her any attention. For a narcissist, it was the worst punishment imaginable.

Frank came up and draped a blanket over my shoulders. I nodded my gratitude, and he walked away without saying a word.

* * *

Frank had an hour or two of unpleasant paperwork staring him in the face. He attacked it with the appetite of a man rich in anger. A child had died on his watch. Suicide or not, he would blame himself. I had no doubt he would experience nightmares about this night for years.

Sitting in Frank's Charger, I found my own demons scratching at the door with long, bloody nails.

For a therapist, work long enough in the field and you eventually had to deal with a suicide. Someone who placed his care in your hands, who trusted you to make his pain go away, found himself ultimately with nowhere to go, overwhelmed by despair on a scale no human should have to suffer, but some did. Despite your best efforts, your patient's depression worsened. The vegetative symptoms, the ones you could see like sleeplessness and poor appetite and withdrawing from others, became a standard of living— a prison cell more formidable than any created with concrete and steel—and along with it, a crushing sense of hopelessness, a bleak view of the future where there was no out, no chance for improvement, no reason to continue living.

In my years of practice, Doug Belle was the third patient to end his own life.

He was also the youngest.

Turning my back on the circus of rescue workers, police, and now the news media, I turned the car's heater on full, and cried for the young boy for whom I had grown so fond.

* * *

With my eyes now dry, I opened up the recording app on my smartphone and dictated what had happened. Whether or not Dee Dee Belle followed through on her threat to sue me—unlikely, given what her son had publicly proclaimed—I wanted a record of the events leading up to Doug's suicide.

Resting my head in my hand, I recalled as accurately as possible the gibberish Doug had spoken, his rambling statements about success and punishment and going *through* rather than *across* something. Perhaps I could make sense of them later, once I had examined them in light of his mother's sexual abuse.

I hesitated at his mention of a Green Queen, debated leaving it out, but ultimately decided to keep it.

But more than my mom, I hate the other one. I hate her for what she's doing, and for what she's planning.

Don't let her get you.

Toni had also mentioned a Green Queen. It had happened last Saturday, after I'd noticed Thumbkin had been moved and asked her about it. Her expression had grown strangely distant as she gazed at the doll. When she spoke, I hadn't recognized the voice as completely her own.

"The Green Queen...she wants something, you know, something important...she wants us, and with us, she wants the world."

The car grew cold despite the heater. How could my patient and my wife, two people who to the best of my knowledge had never met, share the same delusion?

Perhaps it wasn't a delusion. Perhaps they had, in fact, known one another. He was a student, and she a teacher.

I pulled up Toni's number on my phone. It didn't take long for her to answer.

"Honey, do you know a student named Doug Belle? Eighth grader? He's new to the district."

She hesitated. "Where are you?"

"Rock Mills, remember? My patient?"

"Who's with you?" She sounded cautious, almost afraid.

"No one," I said. "I'm sitting by myself in Frank's car."

"The chief's not there?"

"Barry Trumble?" I said, referring to Rock Mills's head lawman. "He's probably somewhere nearby, but I don't see—"

"No," she replied. "Not Barry. I'm talking about Chief Couttis. Is he there?"

I frowned. "Why would Gordon Couttis be here?"

"Look around, will you? Do you see him?"

"Wait. Why am I looking for Couttis?"

"Just do it!"

Maybe it was her tone, or maybe I'd had enough drama for one night, but whatever the reason, her words grated on me. "No, I won't. Not until you tell me why you think Emersville's chief of police would be here, forty miles from his town, at a crime scene unrelated to his duties, in the middle of the damn night. Better yet, why are you worried he'd be here?"

I listened to dead air for too long before she said, "Oh god, your patient. He died, didn't he?"

"Yes." I leaned forward until my head rested on the steering wheel. "Killed himself, not ten feet in front of me. Cut his own throat."

"I'm sorry, Brad. I know you did your best."

"His name was Doug Belle. Did you know him?"

"I don't think so. Maybe he went to Strohm, or one of the charter schools?"

The hard plastic steering wheel was digging into my forehead. I sat up and rubbed at the sore spot. "Toni?"

"I'm here."

"Who's the Green Queen?"

"Didn't you ask me this the other day?"

"Any idea who she is?"

"I don't get it. What's a Green Queen?"

"Doug mentioned her before he killed himself. That's why I asked if he was in your class. You sure you've never heard of her?

She's not a character in a book?"

"None that I've heard of."

"And your concern about Couttis?"

"Kerry's been talking. Something bizarre is going on in Emersville, and I think Gordon Couttis may be involved. Also the mayor, Conrad Hunter. And Annabel St. Crux. Hell, I think just about everyone here is involved."

"Involved in what?"

"Not on the phone. When you and Frank get back. You should hear it from Kerry. I'm bound to miss something. And...and I'm having trouble believing it myself. The things she claims are going on in this town, what the people are planning, what they're doing."

"You make it sound like a conspiracy."

"It is. On a scale you can't imagine."

The ambulance pulled away, its lights flashing but no siren wailing. Doug Belle's dead body lay in the back. Soon he will be put in the ground, his frail body encased in wood and darkness and lost hopes. The thought sickened me, and I turned away from the sight.

"You're scaring me, honey."

"I know," she said. "Get here when you can."

"As soon as Frank's done."

"And Brad?"

"Yes."

"Bring a pregnancy test."

* * *

Frank stopped at an all-night drug store so I could buy a pee stick.

"Let me guess," he said, pulling onto the highway. "Your period is late."

"Something like that," I said, and filled him in on the conversation with Toni.

"A town-wide conspiracy?"

"It would seem so."

"Kerry knows about it?"

"Ditto."

"Did Toni say what kind of conspiracy?"

"She wouldn't talk about it on the phone. She sounded

frightened."

"Bullshit. Your wife could stare down a pit bull."

"I used to think so."

"And that?" He pointed to the E.P.T. kit cradled in my lap.

"Your guess is as good as mine."

"Real helpful, Paco. Real helpful."

We rode the rest of the way in silence. When we hit Emersville's borders, Frank popped the flashers and blew through every stop sign and red light until we arrived at the *Star Fall Motel*. He pulled in next to Toni's 4Runner.

"Let's find out what this is about," he said, and tried the door to room 12.

Locked.

"Hey!" he called out. "Open the door."

No one came. He tried again with the same result.

Frank drew his gun and pounded on the door with it. The noise was louder, harsher. "Kerry, it's me!"

"I'll get a key." I ran for the manager's office, only to find that door also locked. The lights were on, and I could see the lobby and front desk through the thick glass door, but it appeared deserted.

"Hello!" I shouted. "Hey, anybody?"

After about a minute of yelling, I gave up and returned to Frank. "The office is locked and looks deserted."

Frank squinted at the door. "I'm probably gonna regret this." He brought his foot up and kicked the door. The impact was powerful, but not enough to open it. He kicked again. This time the aging wood shattered near the lock with a crack loud enough to make me wince. The door swung open. Darkness filled the room. Frank flipped on a light.

The place was a mess. Bed tossed, sheets strewn on the floor, the lone lamp broken and resting against the wall, its shade torn. Only a small table and chair remained upright.

"Stay here," Frank said. Holding the gun barrel up, he stepped into the room. "Police! Anyone here?"

It took him less than twenty seconds to secure the room.

"No sign of the girls," Frank said. "Try Toni's phone. Kerry's is still in her car."

I punched in my wife's number. It went right to voicemail. "Hey, call me as soon as you get this." My heart sank as I looked at the mess. "They're gone. Taken, by the looks of it."

"Tell me something I don't already know." Frank holstered his gun. "Toni's car is still here, which means they were driven off in someone else's vehicle, and without a night manager, I doubt we'll have a witness who can identify the car." He glanced through the open doorway. "The parking lot is blacktop. No chance of tire tracks showing at least a direction they were taken." He considered. "We need more information, and I think I know a way to get it."

Frank stepped over to the nightstand and picked up the phone.

He punched in three numbers.

* * *

The officer who responded to the call wasn't Sytniak, but a matronly woman named Jacaruso. Her dark, Mediterranean eyes narrowed when Frank badged her.

"There's been an abduction," he said, and gave her a judiciously-edited version of what happened. "I want to talk to Chief Couttis. Seems he can't control what's going on in his town."

Frank in full-bore imitation mode was a formidable sight. Officer Jacaruso, however, stood her ground. "Did you do that?" she asked, pointing to the broken door.

Frank visibly restrained himself from shouting. "I had reason to believe a crime was being committed."

"And getting a key from the manager would've taken too much time?"

I stepped forward. "We tried. The office is closed."

"The lights are on," she countered.

"The door's locked," I said. "I didn't see a night manager."

Jacaruso gestured to the bed, the lamp. "Did you do this, too?"

"No," Frank said though clenched teeth. "It's part of a crime scene."

"At this point," Jacaruso said coolly, "I'm assuming everything here is part of a crime scene, including the door." She nosed around the room, examining the broken lamp and glancing in the bathroom. "You already admitted to breaking and entering. How do I know you didn't toss the place?"

"Toss it and then call it in," Frank said. "Did they weed out the smart ones for this job?"

Jacaruso stiffened. "You know how the law really works, Detective—everyone is guilty until proven innocent. Prove your innocence and I'll move on to other lines of investigation. Fight me on this and I'll crawl so far up your ass I'll find last night's dinner. Are we clear on this?"

"My wife is missing," he said. "A second woman is also missing. Given the state of this room, I believe they were taken against their will. That is the fucking 'line of investigation' you will follow. The longer it takes for you to mark your goddamn territory, the greater the chances I will never see my wife again. If it comes to that, I'll have your badge. I fought a State senator, Officer Jacaruso. You don't intimidate me." He took a moment to compose himself. "Call your chief. Wake his ass up if you have to. I want him here pronto. His town is falling apart, and I'm here to help him pick up the pieces."

Police officers have a code, a certain politeness they follow when interacting with one another. Some, like Frank, comply if it suits their purpose, or they stomp it to dust if it doesn't. Others, mostly those new to the force, tend to follow, even if it means relinquishing authority. To her credit, Officer Jacaruso fell into the former.

"Nice try, Detective," she said, though the words came with a slight smile. "Give me your word you didn't toss the room, that you're here to find your wife, and, I'm assuming, his wife." She nodded to me. "Then we can move on."

Frank eyed the woman. "How many years pushing a car, Jacaruso?"

"Eighteen, next February."

"Never bucked for a command position?"

She shook her head. "Passed on every offer. Can't stand sitting behind a desk. Plus, you know how hard it is to carry wearing a pants suit? I refuse to keep a gun in my purse."

Frank chuckled. "I hear you. Yes, you have my word. Neither I nor Doctor Jordan contributed to the crime scene. I take ownership of the door and nothing else."

"Have you touched anything, moved anything?"

"No, ma'am. The scene is intact. You will, though, find our fingerprints. Brad and I stopped here earlier to check on our wives. We probably touched something the CSU boys'll examine."

"Good," Jacaruso said, and pressed a button on the mic attached to her shirt. "Base 2, this is 41. Come in."

"41, this is Base 2."

"Jerry, call the chief. Tell him we have an incident at the *Star Fall*. There's a Rock Mills DT here. He wants to talk to Couttis pronto."

"You sure, Val? It's almost three bells."

"Do it, Jerry."

"Aye aye, ma'am."

"Jerry's former Navy. Good man, but still hasn't lost the sea talk." As she scanned the room, I noticed the lines at the corners her eyes, the slight pouches under her jawline. Office Jacaruso was older than I had initially thought. "When was the last time you spoke to your wife?" she asked Frank.

"About three hours ago, here in this room. Brad talked to his about an hour ago."

She turned to me. "What was the conversation like?"

Toni's phone call, her concern that Chief Couttis might show up at a crime scene forty miles away, still bothered me. Also, she'd mentioned a conspiracy involving most of the city.

Could Jacaruso be part of it?

I decided to try something. Reaching into my pocket, I found the metal egg and casually removed it.

"One of my patients was in crisis," I said, bouncing the egg in my hand as if it were some kind of good luck token. "The police asked for my help. Toni called to see—"

I dropped the egg.

Officer Jacaruso watched it bounce on the threadbare carpet. It rolled momentarily, wobbling, and came to rest between her feet.

Her face tightened. Her eyes darted to me, to Frank, back to me. Then her lips peeled back into an angry snarl and she went for her gun.

Frank struck first. He snatched her hand and twisted. Jacaruso kicked. I had to jump back to avoid one in the nuts. Frank clamped his other hand on the back of Jacaruso's head and twisted his fingers into her bun. He wrenched the officer up until her back arched.

"Grab her gun," he said.

I reached out, but Jacaruso twisted and thrashed, making it impossible to get near her.

Frank yanked her head around. "Hold still!"

Jacaruso complied, sort of. She spat at me when I took her gun.

"What should I do with it?" I asked, wiping the wetness from my face.

"Pop the clip and take it," he said. "Leave the rest."

Shrieking, Jacaruso brought her hand up. Frank darted his head back, narrowly avoiding a fist full of knuckles. Jacaruso squirmed and clawed and kicked like a wild woman. Frank struggled to hold her.

I stepped in front of Jacaruso and lifted her service revolver until the barrel was level with her face. "Hold still."

She tried to kick me again.

I thumbed off the safety. "Hold fucking still."

She glared at me, probably deciding whether I would shoot or not, and stopped resisting. Her bun had come undone. Her graying hair hung in wild strands around her face.

"Is the chief coming?" I asked. When she didn't reply, I pressed the barrel into her forehead. "The chief. Is he coming or not?"

Jacaruso sneered. "Jerry will call him. He's an obedient puppy."

"But Couttis won't come, or if he does, he'll have reinforcements." I didn't want this to turn into a gun fight.

Frank wrenched her head back. "Where are our wives?"

"Where you'll never find them."

I tightened the grip on my gun. "Where's that?"

"Shoot me," she said, "and you kill the other."

Puzzled by her words, I let the gun dip. It now pointed at her chest. "What other? What are you talking about?"

Jacaruso's laugh was thin and hard and filled with malice. "You have this"—she nudged the egg with her toe—"and you still don't understand. You don't understand!"

We were losing our advantage. She wasn't afraid anymore, which meant she wasn't going to tell us a damn thing.

She had information we needed. I had to convince her we knew as much as she did.

"You mean the proximity lock," I said. "What your mayor, Conrad Hunter, is so keen on retrieving. What people like you and Cyrus Kline and god knows who else are willing to kill for. What Annabel St. Crux hid in the dolls she's been selling to unsuspecting people. That's what you're talking about."

"So you know a little," she said, still sneering. "A small part of something infinite is still nothing."

Something infinite? I recalled my nightmare, the dream where I sailed through dark, endless space with Thumbkin at my side yelling, *"You weren't supposed to see this!"*

What if it had been more than a dream?

I took a step closer. "What about the planet, Officer Jacaruso? A floating rock, waterless and barren, with endless drifts of orange soil. What about that?"

Her face paled. "How—?"

"And the Green Queen?" I said, not knowing where I was going but confident I was on the right track. "What will she do to you when she learns of your failure?"

Jacaruso lost it. She started screaming obscenities and bucked in Frank's grip, twisting and turning in an effort to break free. "Let me go! LET ME GO!"

Frank pulled her against him. "Tell us where our wives are and we'll let you go."

"NO! I CAN'T! THEY'LL KILL ME!"

"Let's take her back to Rock Mills," I said. "Maybe if she's away from this damned town she'll have a change of heart."

"DON'T! PLEASE! I DIDN'T GIVE UP EVERYTHING, COME ALL THIS WAY—"

Jacaruso collapsed, head lolling to one side. Frank had to quickly shift his grip to keep her from falling. Suspecting a trick, I kept the gun trained on her.

Moments later, the officer stirred. She dragged her head up. When her eyes found mine, they were filled with pain. "My babies. You need to save my babies. Don't let them grow up like this. I love them too much. It would break my heart." Her face hardened. "Find the Queen. Find her and kill her."

I lowered the gun. "Officer Jacaruso?"

She nodded. "Marge. The other is called Thyll. It's a part of me now. It whispers to me. It tells me things that frighten me."

My gut tightened. "Who does?"

"No time. It'll regain control soon. Already it's fighting me. Leave while you can."

Frank lifted her a little straighter. "Do you know where they've taken our wives?"

She began to cry. "Kill me. Don't let my babies see what I've become."

"What's going on?" I said. "What are we dealing with?"

"Aliens," she said. "It's an invasion." Then Marge Jacaruso snatched the gun from my hand, pointed it at her temple, and pulled the trigger. The shot sounded like the world cracking. The bullet tore through her skull, blowing the front half wide open. Blood and brain matter splashed my eyes, my nose, my mouth. Frank cried out and released her. Jacaruso crumpled, lifeless, to the floor.

Shaking, vomit burning the back of my throat, I wiped the gore from my face.

"Jesus, fuck," Frank whispered.

"We need to leave." Brain and bits of bone covered my hands. I wiped them on my pants. "Before the chief gets here."

"What about the girls?"

"Later, once we've learned more. If we're caught—"

Two men stepped into the room. One was Chief Couttis. The other was Officer Sytniak. They had their guns trained on us.

"Move," said Chief Couttis, his face grim, "and I'll kill you both myself."

Chapter Fifteen

"Chief Couttis," I said. "We can explain—"

"Shut up!" Gordon Couttis trembled with fury. Except for his gun hand. It remained rock-steady. "Marge Jacaruso was a good officer, a good woman. I've known her and Henry for years. Shit, Henry and I are both members of the Rotary. I even helped them put up Christmas lights last year, when Henry broke his arm after a Hi-Lo hit him at the plant." He licked his lips. "How am I supposed to tell him she's dead? And her kids? They'll be devastated."

Frank slowly raised his hands. "Chief, I understand how this looks, but we didn't kill Officer Jacaruso. She shot herself."

"Bullshit," Couttis said. "One of you did it. I'll run every test CSU can think of until I figure out who. Until then, you're both under arrest. Ted, if you'll do the honors."

Frank bristled. "We're not holding the gun. You didn't see us shoot. You don't have probable cause. You can't arrest us."

"Watch me," Couttis said. "Ted."

Office Sytniak stepped forward. As he drew a pair of handcuffs from his belt, his foot kicked the proximity lock lying on the floor and sent it tumbling. He froze, a look of surprise on his face.

Chief Couttis saw the egg and picked it up. "What's this thing?"

"You don't have to pretend," I told him. "We know what it is."

"And what would that be, young man?"

"A proximity lock. It's the one your mayor was so gung-ho on recovering when he broke into my house."

Couttis gave me a genuinely puzzled look. "Funny, I don't remember you mentioning this earlier, and Connie never said a word about it. Proximity lock, huh?" He held the egg out to Sytniak. "You ever see one of these before?"

Sytniak gave his boss a sad smile. "Yes, I have," he said, and turned his gun on Couttis.

"Jesus, Ted!" Couttis raised a hand to push away the weapon. "Watch where you're pointing that thing."

"Sorry, Gordon." Sytniak pulled the trigger. Gordon Couttis's head exploded into a grotesque mass of pink and red confetti. The impact jerked his body back, his arms flailing as if they still had life, until he slammed against the wall and fell.

Sytniak turned, his gun swinging in a wide arc toward us, but Frank had already drawn his weapon. He leveled it at Sytniak.

"Drop your weapon," Frank yelled. I could barely hear him over the ringing in my ears.

The cop-turned-cop-killer never slowed.

Frank had no choice but to fire.

The first round slammed into Sytniak's chest, punching him backward. He took the second high on the shoulder.

Sytniak jerked his gun up. Frank's third round caught him just under the chin. Sytniak's hand flew to his throat. He coughed, blood spraying from his mouth, and his eyes glazed over. He sank to the floor and came to his eternal rest beside the boss he had just brutally murdered.

Eyes wide, I stood there, my ears ringing, my heart slamming against my ribcage. I raked my hands through my hair. Three people had died. In the span of a few minutes, three lives were irrevocably lost, all police officers. My mind had trouble processing it.

The egg rested in Gordon Couttis's hand. I picked it up. Once again, blood coated the metal. I tried cleaning it off with my finger but I had as much blood on me—blood and bone and tissue. Disgusted, I slipped the egg into my pocket.

Frank tapped me on the shoulder to get my attention.

"We have to go," he shouted. His face was pale. "Before more cops arrive."

I nodded wearily and followed him out. I'd had enough of killing. Except, our wives were still missing. We needed to find them, and we needed to rescue them.

Coated with gore, we climbed into the Charger. The bitter, coppery scent of blood quickly filled the confined space, and underneath it, starting to form: the sweet stench of decaying flesh.

The smell turned my stomach. I leaned out the door and vomited.

Frank waited patiently behind the wheel. When I was done, he pulled out of the parking lot. He kept the flashers off. He took his time, obeying all traffic lights, and soon we were on the road out of Emersville.

* * *

Returning to Frank's house was out of the question. Looking as we did, we would end up frightening his kids more than they already were. I didn't want to return to my house, either. The Emersville goon squad had already paid it a visit, and with three of their own now dead, it wouldn't be long before I received another courtesy call.

Frank overruled me. "We need to clean up. Your house is the only place I can think of where we won't draw attention to ourselves. You don't have clothes that'll fit me, so I'll ask a patrol car to run by my house, check on the kids, and pick up jeans and a shirt."

Walking up to my house, I remembered the front door had been damaged and couldn't be firmly closed, let alone locked.

"Shove something in front of it," Frank said. "If anyone but a Rock Mills officer knocks, give a shout." He handed me his Sig. "Use this if you have to."

As Frank trudged toward the bathroom, I pushed a heavy vanity in front of the door. It may not stop a determined intruder, but it would give me enough time to defend myself.

Frank returned minutes later wearing a towel around his waist.

"Your turn," he said. "Make it quick."

I was cleaned and dressed in less than ten minutes. I thought I'd heard voices while in the shower, and when I found Frank in the foyer, he was wearing jeans and a sweatshirt. His police friend had come and gone.

"How are your ears?" he said.

"Better. At least the ringing stopped. Everything good at your house?"

"The kids are awake but seem okay. Come on, we have things to discuss."

No shit, I thought, and followed him into the living room.

"You're the expert on human behavior," he said, practically collapsing into a chair. "Tell me, what did we witness back there?"

"I don't know. I've been trying to piece it together since we left."

"Let's tackle it one person at a time. Start with Jacaruso."

I nodded. "Suicide, obviously, but her behavior was inconsistent. All business at first, then flying into a rage because of the egg. At the end she seemed more normal. Sad and desperate, but normal."

"What's your take on the alien invasion?"

"Normally, I would have called it a classic paranoid delusion, a symptom of an underlying major depressive disorder. It can lead to irrational thinking and profound hopelessness. In a perfect world, it would explain her suicide better than little green men."

"We're not dealing with a perfect world."

"No, we are definitely not."

"You mentioned a dead planet, one with orange soil."

I told him about my dream. "At the time, I dismissed it as an aftereffect of the accident with the Malibu. Now I'm not so sure. Jacaruso certainly reacted to it."

Frank paused. "She acted as if someone was inside her. She even had a name for it."

"Thyll."

"Yeah, Thyll. Sounds like the name of a person."

Or a thing, I wanted to add but didn't.

Frank massaged his temples. "I don't believe I'm saying this, but could this Thumbkin have been inside your head at the time of the dream? Could it somehow have made you to see the planet?"

I recalled Thumbkin's admonition—*you weren't supposed to see this!*—and said, "I think it was the other way around. I think I was in hers."

Frank let out a low whistle. "This is some far out shit."

"It gets worse." I leaned forward in my chair. "Doug Belle. Like Jacaruso, he complained of someone in his head talking to him, telling him things he didn't like. Out in the marsh, I had the impression I was talking with someone else, someone much older than Doug. And like Jacaruso, when the other presence went away, Doug killed himself." I lifted my eyes to Frank's, saw the doubt, and plunged ahead anyway. "He mentioned a leader, a Green Queen who wants our world."

"You expect me to believe bug-eyed monsters are taking control of people and plotting to overthrow civilization?"

"I know. I'm having a hard time believing it myself."

"Putting aside the H. G. Wells crap for a moment, we still need to find the girls."

"I think they're intertwined—the technology, the conspiracy, our wives. To deal with one, you have to deal with them all."

"The proximity lock," Frank said. "Jacaruso and Sytniak recognized it, but Couttis looked puzzled, like he'd never seen one before."

"Maybe Sytniak killed him because he wasn't supposed to have seen it."

Frank grunted. "The conspiracy goes only so far."

"Then there's Conrad Hunter." I touched the bruise Emersville's mayor had raised on my cheek. "He seems to be part of it."

"It makes no sense. Why have the mayor in the know but not the police chief? It'd be easier if both were working together. You'd have better control of information. Inquiries would have layers of protection. The last thing you'd want is the police chief looking into the mayor about some irregularities. If you want to hide something, you do it from the top down, not the bottom up."

"An imperfect conspiracy," I said.

"Exactly."

I thought for a moment. "Jacaruso was part of it. So was Sytniak. Hunter's involved. I think we can include Anabelle St. Crux, the woman who sold the dolls."

"Dolls that contain proximity locks."

I withdrew the egg from my pocket. The blood coating it had dried to a hard crust. I ran my thumb over the tiny hole its side. It looked like a jeering mouth.

"We only know a name," I said. "Proximity lock. It contained enough energy to shock Doug Belle, but it doesn't have a visible power source. Except for the blood, it looks harmless, an Easter ornament. Something to hang off the branch of a tree."

Frank settled back into his chair. He looked weary—a polar bear left too long in the heat. "What do we do next?"

"The technology is real. Whether it's alien or terrestrial is in doubt."

"You want Steve to examine the egg?" he said, referring to my brother.

I shook my head. "I want to leave him out of it for now. His tests might do more damage than good. Besides, I don't think we have time for an analysis. We don't know what's happening with Toni and Kerry. Wait too long and we may never see them again."

"All right, you got a better idea?"

"Yes," I said. "We get a second opinion."

* * *

After a brief power nap, something neither of us wanted but couldn't afford to go without, we drove to Culver and pulled into the weed-choked parking lot of Womblic Auto Repairs.

"You sure about this?" Frank said as we approached the store entrance.

"I'm not sure about anything." The mechanic was the only space buff I knew, and I hoped to find some real-world answers to our extraterrestrial questions.

I pulled the door open and we stepped into the lobby. A small bell sat on the counter. Frank smacked it with the palm of his hand.

The door to the garage opened. Ricky Womblic poked his head out. He was dressed in mechanic blues. A grease-stained bandanna held back his long hair. His eyes widened when he saw us.

"Hey, wait a minute. I fixed the truck's gate."

"I'm sure you did," Frank said. "We're here on another matter."

"What matter?" the mechanic said.

"Can we talk in your office?" I asked, stepping up to the counter.

"I'm in the middle of replacing tie rods on a stubborn bitch of a Buick. I don't have time for chit-chat."

"Please," I said. "It's important."

"So are old man Starkey's tie rods," Womblic said. He pulled a rag from his back pocket and wiped his hands. "How long is this going to take?"

"It depends," said Frank. "How big is space?"

* * *

Womblic sat in his chair and stared at us with undisguised

anger.

"Aliens. People taken over by beings from another planet. Our world in peril." He glanced at the photographs tacked to his wall—planets, nebulae, entire galaxies—and shook his head. "I can't believe you came all this way to make fun of me."

"No one's making fun of you." I sat in a chair opposite Womblic. The smell of motor oil and gasoline rolled off him in waves. "We're here because we respect you. We want your opinion."

Frank leaned against the door, arms crossed over his chest. "This isn't a joke. Our wives are missing."

"Well, if the joke's not on me, it's certainly on you," Womblic said. "The idea of aliens visiting Earth is a myth. It can't happen. Someone's messing with you big time."

"There's been talk of alien encounters for decades." I'd done a quick internet search on the subject and had gotten hundreds of thousands of hits.

"That's because people don't understand the tremendous distances involved in space travel," Womblic said. "It would take thousands and thousands of years to get from one star to another. No rational civilization would send a ship full of its own kind, only to have them arrive at their destination dead. It would serve no purpose."

I thought of malevolent dolls that could move and mysterious proximity locks. "What if their technology was vastly superior to ours?"

Womblic shook his head. "Even if they could travel at half the speed of light, we're still talking centuries."

"Suppose they could travel at the speed of light," Frank said. "Or even faster. Would it be possible then?"

"Faster-than-light travel is another myth," Womblic said. "The faster an object moves, the heavier it gets, which then requires more and more energy to accelerate it. It works for a while, but as you approach the speed of light, an object's mass approaches infinity. I don't care how advanced a civilization's technology is, there's no power that can propel something that massive. Like it or not, the universe is stuck with slower-than-light travel."

"What about nearby stars?" Frank said. "There have to be a few of them. Maybe they came from there?"

"Detective, the nearest star system to ours is Alpha Centauri. It has three stars—A, B, and the more distant Proxima. Alpha Centauri B has an Earth-sized planet, but its surface is molten rock. No chance of life. But for the sake of argument, let's say the planet has intelligent life." Womblic looked at Frank. "The Alpha Centauri system is four and a half light years from us. Using some kind of fancy constant acceleration drive to approach light speed, the ship would still take about a decade to get here. They would need ten years' worth of fuel and food. Waste disposal and medical care for everyone on board. Then there are the dangers of space itself. Lethal levels of radiation, dust particles or small rocks impacting with the spacecraft. At those speeds, anything with mass would penetrate the hull and exit the other side. Everyone would die from explosive decompression. If that's not bad enough, what about the psychological implications of a one-way trip, because if they were traveling near light speed, they would age far slower than the beings they left behind. Everyone they knew would be dead before they returned. There would be no point in coming home."

Womblic sighed, a wistful mixture of hope and regret. "All of it makes for an impossible journey, and that's looking at our closest neighbors, who we know have barren, lifeless planets. As much as I wish it weren't true, we will never meet a being from another world."

Frank pointed to a photo of the space shuttle *Atlantis* tacked to Womblic's wall. "With our current technology, how long would it take us to get from here to this Alpha Centauri?"

"Using that as a model," Ricky Womblic said, "roughly one hundred and sixty-five thousand years."

I let Womblic's words sink in. A voyage to our nearest stellar neighbor would take longer than the entire span of human history. Go farther out, and the numbers became more daunting. I was beginning to doubt our hypothesis about aliens.

"Thanks for your time, Mr. Womblic," Frank said. He'd obviously come to the same conclusion. "You've been very helpful."

I started to rise. Womblic stopped me. "What makes you think aliens are involved? It's not the first explanation a rational person turns to."

"It wasn't our first," I said. "We came to it reluctantly."

Womblic licked his lips. "You said the townsfolk are behaving oddly."

"That's an understatement," Frank said. "Downright crazy would be more accurate."

"And you haven't seen evidence of an alien presence?" Womblic asked. "No bodies or spacecraft or such?"

I shook my head. "Only creepy dolls moving on their own and this." I pulled out the metal egg and showed it to him. "It's called a proximity lock."

"May I?" Womblic stretched out his hand, and I dropped the egg into it.

Womblic examined the proximity lock. He turned it over, testing its weight. He set it on his desk and spun it like a top. He held it close to his eye and peered through the latticework (which, for some reason, gave me a serious case of the willies). He found a pair of pliers and tried to pry open the hole blown into its side. When it didn't work, he handed the egg back to me.

"Strange," he said. "What's the red stuff?"

"Blood," I said. "Any idea what the thing is?"

"No clue, but I can tell you the metal is unusual."

Frank swung his big shoulders around to confront Womblic. "Unusual in what way?"

"It's almost parchment-thin yet has surprising strength. I'm no metallurgist, but I doubt we have something like it on earth. Have you had it analyzed?"

"We've considered it," I said, "but the thought of putting something unknown into a high-powered machine makes us nervous. It's already knocked out one child." I tried not to think of Doug Belle, lying in cold storage with his eyes and mouth glued shut. "Bombarding it with energy could be disastrous."

Womblic picked up a pencil and began doodling on a scrap of paper. He drew ovals, much like the metal egg, making a chain of them.

"Why do you call it a proximity lock?" he asked as he scratched out oval upon oval upon oval.

"We don't," Frank said from the doorway. "It's what the congregation of the Holy Church of Spielberg call the thing."

"So," Womblic said absently, "it's supposed to keep something locked in place."

"It could also function as a GPS," I said.

Frank snorted. "Yeah, and it makes French fries while you wait for E.T. to phone home. Let's beat feet, Paco. We got people to find."

I watched Womblic draw. His ovals, linked together, looked like a tunnel; a structure you would travel through. That reminded me of something Doug—or whatever was inside him—had said. "One of the so-called aliens said something about going through space rather than across. What do you think he meant?"

My wanna-be astronomer-turned-garage-monkey looked up from his doodling. "Say again?"

"Going *through* rather than *across*. He seemed to think it was some kind of brilliant feat, an act of unparalleled genius, but to me they sound the same."

Womblic glanced at his doodles: rings of graphite forming a tunnel across the page. Using his finger, he traced a path through them, from beginning to end, his grease-stained nail never leaving the center. "That must be it," he said, a smile spreading across his face. When he looked up, his eyes were bright. "Son of a bitch, that must be it."

I leaned forward. "What, Mr. Womblic? It must be what?"

Frank wandered over to join us. "Yeah, spill the beans."

"The distances are too vast if you travel across space the conventional way," Womblic said excitedly. "Think about an airplane flying across the globe. To get from here to Australia, it will always take a certain amount of time to travel the circumference of the planet."

"We got that part," Frank said. "Get to the space stuff."

Womblic picked up the paper on which he'd doodled his tunnel. "While there are large bodies out in space, like we said earlier, the big problem is the distance, but distance becomes irrelevant if you can fold space." He folded the paper in half and punched a hole through it with his pencil. "You can go incredible distances in an instant."

"You're talking about a wormhole," I said, my pulse quickening. "A tunnel through space."

"Yes," Womblic said. "It must be how they got here."

Frank snatched the paper from Womblic's hand. He unfolded it, folded it back again, unfolded it, folded it back. He looked like a kid trying to make a paper bird fly. "This is bullshit. Space is empty. There's nothing to manipulate, to bend." He tossed the paper on Womblic's desk. "You'll need to come up with something better."

If Frank's condemnation upset Womblic, he didn't show it. The mechanic sat forward in his chair, rubbing his hands together like a child about to play with his favorite toy. "Einstein showed how mass effects space-time. The greater the mass, the greater the bend in space-time, and the bend forces us through space. We follow the contour of space-time, similar to the way a marble rolls in a funnel, except we call it gravity. Generate enough mass—enough gravity—and you could fold space into a tube connecting one part of a galaxy to another. A wormhole. Theoretically, it's possible, but in a practical sense..."

"In a practical sense?" I asked.

Womblic seemed to deflate. "In a practical sense, the amount of mass and energy needed to form and sustain a wormhole would be vast. Black holes might do it, but they're lethal. There's no way to survive one. To artificially open and sustain a wormhole, you'd need energy on a scale I can't fathom. And then there's the question of whether you could survive the trip through a wormhole. There might be tidal forces from the gravity that would rip you apart and spread your atoms throughout space. It's too incredible to contemplate, but it's the only answer I can think of."

"Let's say you're right," Frank said. "Let's say these aliens could create a wormhole and travel to our world. Where are they? Why aren't we seeing armies of them marching across the planet? We wouldn't stand a chance. We'd be dead within a year or two."

"Because they wouldn't stand a chance either," Womblic said.

"Our world," I said. "It would be as alien to them as theirs is to us."

Womblic nodded. "If it wasn't the atmosphere, it'd be the germs or the food or the water or any number of threats. The chances of them having the correct metabolic and immunological makeup to thrive on Earth are very small. They would die before they had time to conquer anything. It's another reason the alien invasion theory falls apart. There are too many negatives."

"So we're back to *homo sapiens*," said Frank. "Everyday humans and their everyday struggles for power and dominance. Someone in Emersville is kidnapping people, for whatever reason, and it's our job to find out who and why. We're back at where we started."

I stood. "I thank you for your time, Mr. Womblic. It may have not been particularly helpful, but it was certainly educational."

Ricky Womblic opened his office door. "When you were a kid, did you ever use a magnifying glass to burn up ants?"

"Once or twice," I said, feeling uncomfortable. "It made me sick to my stomach."

"Then be thankful you're dealing with the earthly," Womblic said. "The detective's comment earlier was correct. If this were an alien invasion, we would be the ants, and they would be the ones holding the magnifying glass."

* * *

We climbed back into the Charger.

"Where to?" I asked.

"The one place where we can find answers," Frank replied. "Emersville."

"They'll be looking for us."

"Don't worry, Paco," Frank said. "I got it covered."

Chapter Sixteen

We returned to Emersville in an undercover sedan Frank borrowed from the Rock Mills Police depot. The car had a Remington short-barreled shotgun clamped to the underside of the dash and a heavy plastic chest in the rear foot well. The chest contained two Kevlar vests and extra clips for Frank's handgun, as well as several stun grenades.

Halfway into town, we passed the red-bricked Emersville Public Library and Frank took the first right.

"Where are you going?" I asked.

"I'd rather not drive through the center of town, so I'm looking for another route to the turnoff."

"We're going back to the lake?"

He caressed the cigarette pack in his shirt pocket. "Kerry drove there for a reason. I intend to find out why."

Frank found the road leading to the lake. As we approached the turnoff, he said, "Watch for cops. They may not recognize this car, but I'm sure our descriptions have been passed around."

I nodded. The air was damp. Storm clouds had rolled in overnight, big thunderheads, dark and ominous. They covered the sky like a vast alien spacecraft hovering over the city, blocking the sun as it prepared to destroy all life on the planet.

I tore my eyes away from the sky to look at Frank. "What do you make of Ricky Womblic's alien theory?"

He scowled. "There are no little green men. He said so himself.

What we're dealing with is strictly human."

"And the wormhole?"

"I don't understand a tenth of what the guy said, but one thing stuck with me—travel from one star to another is impossible." Frank slowed the sedan and we eased into the turnoff. "Wormholes and warp speed are bullshit. They're distractions we don't need right now."

"What if Jacaruso was telling the truth? What if we're dealing with an alien race come to take over our world?"

"Womblic said it couldn't happen."

"What if he's wrong? What if it's not impossible?"

Frank grunted. "Then we're royally screwed."

The sedan rolled onto the beach. Tire tracks looped wildly across the sand like Chinese lettering. Beyond the shoreline, the lake was calm. Wisps of mist rose from the surface, as if the water were exuding memories of summers past. In it, I imagined fishermen catching perch and bluegill, children swimming, teenagers water-skiing. Happiness and laughter and smiles and—

—and something more sinister: drownings, boating accidents, bloated bodies with lidless, staring eyes and corpse-skin sloughing away at the slightest touch. Ugly memories. Terrible memories.

I turned away from them. My life was already dark enough.

Frank jammed the gearshift into park, unlocked the chest in the back seat, and handed me a Kevlar vest. After grabbing one for himself, he jerked the Remington free and climbed out of the car. I joined him.

"What's that smell?" he asked.

"Methane. I'd keep the stun grenades in your pocket for now."

Frank rubbed at his eyes. Fatigue was quickly becoming a concern. "Put on the vest and head south," he said. "I'll go north. Call if you see anything."

"Does your phone work?"

"I'm good." He handed me his Sig, along with two extra clips. "Each one holds ten rounds. You've got thirty. It should be enough." He paused. "If you aim at someone, be prepared to shoot. This isn't a game."

I hefted the gun. It was big and ugly, with hard rubber grips. Everything about it spoke to killing.

I stuffed it into the waistband of my pants. "Jacaruso thought I meant business."

Frank chambered a round into his shotgun. "You're lucky she didn't call your bluff. At least, I hope you were bluffing. I was standing right behind her. Your shot would have killed us both." He thumbed off the safety. "Be ready. Remember, the only successful gunfight is the one you walk away from."

He left without saying another word, pushing through the tall grasses growing along the shoreline until he disappeared.

I listened to the sounds of his passage until they too disappeared and I began walking south. The uneven ground made travel difficult. Thickets blocked my way. Long nettles, wickedly sharp and always seeming to angle toward me, pricked my skin until red welts covered my face and hands.

I reached a clearing, another slender stretch of beach. This one didn't have an access road. I stopped and looked back. The woods were quiet, still. No squirrels or chipmunks. No blue jays. No sparrows. No deer.

Only fingers of mist creeping in from the lake.

Where were the animals? With winter coming, they should be racing back and forth in search of food.

I wiped the sweat from my eyes and pushed on. The path became treacherous. Deadfalls appeared more frequently, overgrown bushes turned me aside. At one point, I had to circle back and find another way.

My mind kept replaying what Frank had said: Kerry had come to the lake for a reason. Find out why, and we might find our wives.

Water is the beginning and the end.

I had climbed what felt like my hundredth deadfall, a massive pine whose flesh had turned spongy with decay, when I heard a faint rustling, like a small animal scampering over dead leaves, followed by another coming from a different direction.

"Hello?" I said. "Is anybody there?"

More rustling, movement I could hear but not see.

"Frank?"

Something scurried across the path, low and fast.

Icy fingers gripped my insides.

"I've got a gun," I said. "I'll use it if I need to."

A twig snapped. I spun, the bulky semiautomatic thrust out in front of me.

The forest grinned back, mocking me.

What's the matter, Doc? Having a little hallucination *problem?*

"Who's out there?" I shouted.

The rustling intensified, multiplied. Branches swayed. Leaves twitched.

"WHO'S OUT THERE?"

I heard gunfire, far in the distance. A single shot, then another. Not a handgun. Something larger, something with more punch.

Like a shotgun.

Frank.

My mouth went dry. I vaulted over the deadfall and sprinted back along the trail.

The mist now covered the ground completely, concealing everything beneath it. I ignored the dangers and raced ahead.

A branch as thick as my leg loomed before me. Ducking, I scurried underneath, but by foot caught on something and I fell. Air exploded from my lungs, and my bruised ribs howled in agony. Somehow, I managed to keep hold of the handgun.

A third gunshot sounded in the distance.

I scrambled to my feet, and that's when I saw them.

Dolls.

Cloth ones like Thumbkin, only there were many. Filthy yarn for hair. Lusterless, button eyes. Stitched mouths warped into snarls.

They emerged from the mist—an army of demonic toys. Three blocked the path. I kicked one away. The others attacked, jumping onto me. Soft hands groped at my clothes. I cried out in surprise as sharp needles pierced the skin on my arms.

The fine metal threads we'd found inside Thumbkin. I finally understood their purpose.

More needles dug into my ankles, calves, thighs. Dolls clung to me like blood-thirsty leeches.

I brushed two off with my hand. More took their place. I scraped my body against a tree and dislodged several. Twice as many fell from above. I bit back a scream as they drove wires into my body. More streamed out of the forest, their numbers seemingly endless.

More gunshots, louder this time, almost next to me. Frightened, I searched for the source and realized it was me—I had pulled the trigger on the Sig and fired the shots. One round had hit a doll, an overstuffed Cabbage-Patch-looking thing with bloody cheeks, and blew it apart. The others had missed. I shook off my terror, aimed, and fired. Out of sheer luck I hit four, but there were so many.

I needed a plan. I'd passed a clearing earlier. It had to be nearby. If I had room to maneuver, I might be able to get away.

I charged ahead, knocking dolls away with my feet. More moved to block my escape. I emptied the Sig's clip into them. A few seconds to switch clips and I was back in business. Dolls disintegrated under the impact of the .40 caliber rounds.

A cloth hand reached around from behind my head, blood-soaked filaments sticking out like deadly claws, and swiped at my face. Needles gouged my cheek. I grabbed the little bastard and threw it.

Three more disintegrated before my second clip ran dry.

Slamming the last clip into the handgun, I focused my efforts on the ones in front of me. They died in bloodless explosions of cotton and fabric. It didn't take long to run out of rounds.

Tossing the gun, I bolted forward—

—and almost fell into the clearing.

Panting, I searched the area. Sand, tall grasses, and the lake. More dolls swarmed the path in front of me, cutting off my escape. I had no other choice.

I stumbled into the mist-shrouded water, my legs pumping until the water reached my waist, and dove.

Dolls didn't breathe—I couldn't drown them—but maybe they couldn't function in water. Maybe their mysterious power source would short out or something?

My aching legs propelled me through the murk. The tiny creatures I hadn't dislodged clung tightly to me.

I tried diving deeper, but I wasn't a strong swimmer. My lungs began to burn. Desperate, I rolled like an alligator, praying the rush of water would dislodge my assailants. A few might have let go; I couldn't tell.

The effort took its toll. My lungs cramped and my vision dimmed. I wouldn't last much longer. With a series of kicks, I swam upward until I broke the surface and pulled air into my lungs.

I shook the water from my eyes, then lifted one arm and the other, checked my legs and abdomen, reached around to feel my back.

The dolls were gone.

I took a moment to catch my breath. I was treading water in the deep part of the lake. I needed to reach the shore. The trouble was, I felt as if I had already run a marathon.

Pushing with my arms, I turned until I faced the shore. My stomach clenched.

Dolls covered the thin stretch of beach, dozens of them, row upon row, staring at me with hatred in their soulless eyes. I searched for a way to escape, saw more beaches to the north, but doubted I could swim there. My limbs felt like they were filled with sand.

I drifted toward shore. The dolls edged closer to the water. They looked eager, almost hungry. No doubt they would pounce once I reached land.

My breath came in short, shallow gasps. The muscles between my ribs began to ache. Time was running out. If I could get close enough to shore to stand while keeping my head above water, I could rest my arms and legs.

I kicked, my legs slicing through the water and propelling me forward. After several yards, I stopped and tried to feel the ground with my toes. No such luck. The water was still too deep.

The dolls pushed closer. Several stood waist-deep in water. One, a creepy rabbit with floppy ears and crazed red-glass eyes, hopped in glee.

I estimated the distance. About fifteen yards of lake separated us.

A shiver rippled through my body, forcing my teeth to clatter. My fingers and toes no longer felt heavy. Cold lake water had pulled the heat from them, and they now felt numb. If I didn't get away, I would start suffering from hypothermia as well as exhaustion.

I focused on the beach. I would have to risk the dolls. Gathering my energy, drawing from whatever meager reserves I had left, I swam for shore. Water splashed wildly as I hit ground and began running. Determined to survive, I let out a scream, a bellow so fierce I thought my vocal cords would rupture.

When I reached the shoreline, the dolls attacked. As one they jumped, sailing through the air, their metal claws extended. I managed to block the ones going for my face. Others latched onto my legs, my arms, my chest. None could penetrate the Kevlar vest, and my clothes afforded me some protection; at least they couldn't rake at my skin.

Then I heard my name called, and Frank charged out of the

woods, the Remington clenched in his fists. He looked like hell. His clothes were shredded. Blood seeped from cuts on the backs of his hands and around his neck. A flap of skin hung from a gash on his forehead. His lower lip had swollen to twice its normal size.

The worst injury, the one that made me want to cry out, was his left eye.

It was gone.

It had been gouged out, presumably by one of the dolls, leaving behind a bloody socket that wept pink-tinged fluid.

The injuries didn't stop him. He swung his weapon in a tight arc, firing again and again. Dolls exploded, one after the other, their wretched bodies practically vaporized by the assault rifle.

Emboldened by Frank's courage, I yanked dolls off me and threw them like clay pigeons. Frank shot them out of the air. He had collected an arm full of trophies at shooting contests, and even with one eye, they made for easy prey.

Despite his accuracy, despite being able to channel his rage through the Remington, there were more dolls than ammo, and he quickly ran out of shells.

I hurried over to him. He dropped the now useless shotgun. His remaining eye locked onto me.

"We're deep into the shit this time, Paco."

"What about the stun grenades? We could try and ignite the methane."

"If the gunshots didn't ignite it, I doubt a grenade will." He coughed up flecks of blood. "Besides, I'd prefer a solution where we didn't die in a massive explosion."

We must have killed a dozen dolls. More than a dozen remained. They gathered in a pack and advanced.

"Head back to the car," I told him. "Call for help. I'll do what I can here."

He grabbed my shoulder for support. "Already did. Sent out an 'officer down' and the location."

I should have known. "Any chance you were heard?"

The dolls had crossed the distance and were ready to attack.

Frank snorted. "Saddle up, Paco. Time to fight for our lives."

We turned to face our attackers. They were small, but they were many. No matter. We planned to put up a hell of a battle.

The lead doll, a clown with hair the color of decayed seaweed and rusted bells on its costume, leapt at me, its tiny mouth gaping open.

There was a gunshot. The doll exploded with a loud bang and the stench of burning ozone.

I looked behind us. A man emerged from the woods. It was Kent Couttis, son of Emersville's recently murdered chief of police, his service revolver aimed at us.

He wore his patrolman's uniform, with the same too-large shirt, same pants with the cuffs at flood level. His mouth was a thin, angry slash across his face.

"That'll be enough," he said. "You go on back."

I wanted to ask him what he meant, where we were supposed to go, when Frank turned me around.

The dolls were retreating. They melted back into the forest like wraiths.

Only the three of us remained.

"What a timely rescue," I said to Couttis, not bothering to hide my anger. "How did you find us?"

"I heard the call on the police band. When I arrived, I saw the tracks and followed them. I could have let them kill you—I probably should have—but I didn't." Couttis holstered his weapon. "A little gratitude would be nice."

My fists clenched. "What are those things, and how is it you can control them?"

Couttis acted as if he hadn't heard me. He turned to Frank and said, "I've got a first aid kit in my cruiser. Let's get you patched up, then your friend can take you to a hospital."

Frank's cheeks had gone pale. He swayed a little, like a dying oak caught in a stiff breeze. I grabbed him. It took all my strength to keep him upright.

"You've lost a lot of blood," I said. "This asshole is right about one thing. You need a doctor."

Couttis gestured behind him. "The cruiser's that way."

I began leading Frank toward the beach. "We don't want your help."

"Who said you had a choice?"

* * *

Frank's condition steadily worsened. He tripped over roots. He grabbed branches to steady himself. He breathed so heavily I worried he would rupture a lung. I helped as much as I could, but I couldn't carry him. Eventually, I had to ask Kent Couttis for help. Watching him touch Frank turned my stomach.

Overhead, the clouds thickened and rain began to fall in a steady drizzle, making the ground slick. We had to work twice as hard to help Frank. By the time we arrived at the beach, we were practically dragging him.

Rain-soaked and shivering, we halted next to Couttis's cruiser. Frank leaned heavily against the vehicle's door, his hand covering his bloody eye socket while Couttis pulled a first-aid kit from the trunk. I noticed the patrolman had parked behind Frank's undercover, blocking the access road and trapping us here. Also, only one car had responded to Frank's broadcast.

"You the only one on the road today?" I asked Couttis as he placed a bandage on Frank's face.

"No," Couttis said, his tone still sharp with anger. "We rolled three cars this shift."

"Yet you were the only one to respond to an officer down alert?"

"I called off the other cars." Couttis took a roll of gauze and began wrapping it around Frank's head. His touch was gentler than I would have expected. "I know the area, Doctor. I know what's out here, what dangers exist and what don't. Having other officers present..." He shrugged. "It would only complicate matters."

My face grew hot. "I suppose you called off the ambulance, too."

"There," Couttis told Frank after securing the gauze into place with tape. "That should hold you until we get you into town." He turned to regard me. His eyes were unforgiving. "I did. This was something I needed to handle on my own."

"You'd rather let someone die than have your friends discover your sick little secret?"

"It's more complicated than that."

"Murder seems pretty straight-forward to me."

"Don't lecture me on murder," Couttis said. "You know what I saw earlier? Three cops dead, one of them my father, the others family in a way you would never understand. They were dear to me, and now they're gone. You and your friend were involved. I just don't know how."

Couttis's anger meant nothing to me. He was the enemy; he could control the dolls. For all I knew, he was the one who took our wives. I helped Frank into the car. He slumped against the door, his eye shut. Blood had already seeped through the bandage, more than I liked to see. He needed medical care pronto.

I turned to confront Couttis. The adrenaline dump from the dolls' attack had faded, leaving me exhausted and oh so very pissed. I used the anger to energize me. I stepped up to Couttis and poked a finger in his chest, cop be damned.

"We had nothing to do with your father's death," I said. "Sytniak killed him. He pulled his gun and shot him. Then he tried to kill us. It's like he went crazy."

"You're lying," Couttis said evenly. "Ted Sytniak was my friend and a dedicated police officer. He would never have killed my father."

"He would," I said, "if your father saw something he wasn't supposed to."

Couttis hesitated. "What do you mean?"

I took the proximity lock from my pocket and held it up so Couttis could see it. The metal egg was black with dried blood. "He saw *this!*"

Couttis's eyes widened. For a moment, he seemed to stop breathing, then his chin dropped. His hands fell loosely to his sides. He took an uncertain step back, the soles of his boots scraping the muddy ground. He said something, but his voice was too low for me to hear.

I asked him to repeat what he'd said.

"It's my fault," Couttis said. "My father died because of me."

I put away the egg. "How is it Emersville's Chief of Police doesn't know about a proximity lock, when everyone else here seems to?"

Couttis countered with his own question. "What happened to Marge Jacaruso?"

"She said she'd become something loathsome and shot herself. Then your dad and Sytniak arrived. We killed Sytniak defending ourselves." I left out the part about the alien invasion. Better to keep him in the dark about what we knew. "Cops killing cops. Helluva police force you have. Where did you get your cadets, a mental hospital?"

Couttis's eyes narrowed. Almost leisurely, he drew his gun and leveled it at me. "Get in the car."

"What if I don't? Will you summon your legion of demon dolls to finish the job?"

"You and the detective are a long way from Rock Mills. He has no jurisdiction here, no official capacity, and you're not a cop. You have no reason to be here, which means you came here on your own." He cocked his head to the side. "Does anyone know you're here? No? Well, that's unfortunate. There's no one to rescue you, no one to find your body. You're completely alone." He raised the gun until the barrel pointed at my head. *"Now get in the fucking car!"*

I was out of options. I opened the cruiser's door and climbed inside. Couttis moved around to the other door and did the same. He started the car, all the while keeping the gun trained on me.

"Where are you taking us?" I asked.

Couttis looked into the rearview mirror. "Detective, are you awake?"

Frank stirred. "Yeah, I'm here."

"I can take you to a hospital," Couttis said. "Doctors will treat your wound and you'll eventually go home." He paused. "That is, if you want to remain monocular. There are other options."

Frank's head turned until he could see Couttis. "My eye is gone. It's back there"—he gestured out the window—"torn out by one of those goddamned dolls."

Couttis nodded. "True."

"But you're saying I don't have to stay like this." Frank pawed at the gauze covering his face. "I don't have to wear a pirate patch for the rest of my life?"

"Also true," Couttis said.

Frank's voice almost broke. "Impossible. I can't grow another eye."

"No, you can't," Couttis said. "But I know someone who might be able to do it for you."

* * *

Officer Kent Couttis and I sat in the too clean dining lobby of *Black and Brewed*. He sipped from a cup of strong, black coffee. I couldn't stomach any of the liquid. My gut burned as it was.

"I still think we should have taken Frank to a hospital," I said.

Couttis shrugged, a gesture I found increasingly annoying. "He's in better hands here than anywhere else."

"You'd better be right."

"Your threats mean nothing to me."

From the cool look he gave me, I had to agree. "Where did they take him?"

"To a room beneath the store."

When we'd arrived, *Black and Brewed* had been filled with the usual suspects. At a gesture from Couttis, Cyrus Kline and his gang of hipster hangers-on escorted Frank to the rear of the store. The rest sat calmly, drinking their drinks and murmuring to one another as if nothing out of the ordinary had happened. Their reaction reminded me of the old Doors song, the one about being a stranger among the strange.

"May I see the egg?" Couttis asked.

"Don't you mean the proximity lock?"

"The *egg*," he said.

Reluctantly, I set it on the table. Several customers looked our way. Until now, they had ignored us.

Couttis picked it up and ran his thumb over its gory surface. The gesture seemed oddly endearing. After a moment, he said, "You called it a proximity lock. Where did you hear the name?"

I thought back to the home invasion, the Dementors, and the guy who beat me up. "From your glorious mayor, Conrad Hunter."

"Connie told you?"

"Actually," I said, "it was one of his buddies-in-crime. Hunter was too busy kicking the shit out me to converse."

Couttis hesitated. "Would it help if I told you Hunter was working on his own? No one wanted to see you or your wife hurt."

My gut tightened. "So Toni is hurt?"

"No," Couttis said. "The same can be said for the detective's wife. They're too valuable. No one would risk causing their deaths."

Jacaruso, or whatever had been inside her, had said the same thing: Toni and Kerry were valuable. I plucked the egg from Couttis's hand. "Valuable in what way? And what does a proximity lock have to do with them?"

Couttis settled back in his chair, arms crossed over his chest, his coffee momentarily forgotten. "Those aren't easy questions to answer. I'm not sure it's wise to even attempt one." He pursed his lips. "Are you familiar with the legend of Pandora?"

"She opened a box and allowed evil to escape into the world."

"Are you familiar with the other part of the legend?"

"Why don't you educate me?"

"When she opened the lid, Pandora realized what she had done and quickly closed it. When she did, she unfortunately trapped forever the one thing the world needed most."

"What?"

"Hope." He gave a dry chuckle. "Only hope was left in the jar. Whether it was hope for humanity or hope against the evils she had released, no one knows, but a world without hope is a cold, bitter world." His eyes threaded into mine. "Pandora's Box is a parable—it never existed—but there's a reason why cautionary tales like this have endured for thousands of years: they ring true on a primitive level. As a species we know there are mysteries in the world that, once we open them to our lives, we let evil in. Do you want to let evil into your world, Doctor Jordan? Are you prepared for the consequences of your actions?"

I searched Couttis's face for some indication he was jacking with me, that he was being overdramatic in an effort to scare me off. His expression, however, hadn't changed—the set of his jaw, as inflexible as granite, conveyed the truth as he saw it. Here was a man who believed in himself, possibly to a degree others might find fanatical. The thought didn't reassure me.

"You talk about letting evil into the world," I said. "How asking questions would unleash unspeakable horrors on an unsuspecting civilization. I think those horrors already exist, in this town, and I think you're involved." I gestured to the people sipping coffee. "I think you're all involved. Something dangerous is going on. Just because I want to understand it doesn't mean I'm creating it. I think it's the opposite—I think my questions frighten you. The fact I may discover your secret terrifies you to the core." I leaned forward. "You're attempting an end-around and it failed. Tell me what the egg is or I take it public. I'm sure there are plenty of scientists out there who would love to examine it."

Couttis smiled coldly. "If what you say is true, if I'm indeed afraid of being discovered, what makes you think you'd make it out of here with the proximity lock in your possession?"

I heard a noise behind me. Several of the *Black and Brewed*'s patrons had gathered in a tight circle, hemming me in. Their closeness felt restrictive, as if they held me fast without actually touching me. I turned back to Couttis.

"First you warn me, now you threaten me. I've seen five-year-olds handle schoolyard bullies with more finesse." I stood. "I'm going to find Frank. You and your posse can stop me if you want, but I don't think you will. You brought me here for a reason. Since we arrived, you've been testing me. By now you should understand I won't back down. People I love are hurt or missing. Someone in this town is responsible. I plan to find out who. Now, if you'll excuse me."

I started for the back of the store. Couttis put his hand on my arm.

"Sit down, Doctor." When I didn't comply, he pointed to my chair. "Sit, please. You're right, I did bring you here with a purpose in mind. Let me address it first, then we can see to your friend."

I sank into the chair. "What about my wife, and Frank's?"

Couttis motioned for the others to return to their seats. When we were reasonably alone, he said, "I assure you, I do not have them."

I caught a tone in his voice, something he'd probably heard dozens of times from suspects who were not quite telling the truth. "You know who does."

Couttis nodded. "I'm pretty sure I do, though there's nothing we can do at the moment to help them. Address the matter at hand, deal with the other stuff later."

"The 'other stuff' involves the woman I love."

"The longer we argue, the longer it will take to reunite you with her."

He was right. He had information I needed, and I had to cooperate to get it.

"We'll play it your way," I said. "Why did you bring Frank here instead of a hospital?"

Couttis opened two packs of sugar and dumped them into his coffee. "The doctors would have treated his wound and released him, but not before contacting the authorities. I told you at the lake, involving others is a complication I'd rather avoid. Also, he would have emerged from this with only one eye. I feel partly responsible for his injury. I wanted to make it up to him."

I bit back a retort about his being only *partly* responsible. Instead, I said, "By lying to him and saying he could get another eye?"

"I never said it was a lie."

"I'm also here for a reason. What is it?"

Couttis finished his coffee and went to the counter to refill the mug. It was his fourth since he'd arrived.

"Survival puts you in an awkward place," he said after he'd returned to his seat. "At first you love it. *Hey, look at me! I'm alive!* It's the most incredible, mind-numbing high in the world. Then the high wears off, and your shiny new life begins to dull. You see it more clearly. It becomes real. You look back at what you'd done to get here, at the people you'd inevitably hurt in the process, people dear to you, people you love, and your stomach turns. Survival becomes a massive weight bearing down on you, warping you until you find yourself committing acts you would not normally do, atrocities you have fought against your entire life." He looked away. "What's the point in living if you've become something you despise?"

I watched a small muscle near Couttis's left eye twitch, and sweat broke out along his brow. He was a man under extreme duress and, true or not, what he'd said affected him deeply.

"None of this makes sense," I said. "You're a general leading an army of maniacal dolls that move and act through a technology I don't understand." *Or exists on this world.* Jacaruso's claim of an alien invasion clashed with Womblic's irrefutable facts about interstellar travel. One had to be correct, and the evidence leaned heavily toward the impossible. "You talk about guilt, but to me, you look more like the aggressor than the victim."

Couttis tapped the table with his finger. "What if I could show you what I mean, right here, right now? Would you do it?"

His words caught me off guard. He wanted to show me proof— but proof of what? The possibilities were too numerous to count, too frightful to contemplate.

Couttis must have noticed my expression. "What I'm offering," he said, "is a peek inside Pandora's Box. My only request is, before you look, you tell me what you know. What I'm offering is dangerous. I need to know where I should start, how quickly I can proceed."

I hesitated. Part of what Couttis had said was true: parables like Pandora's Box had lasted for this long because they hold a certain amount of truth, and if I were to accept his offer, I might allow evil into the world.

I think those horrors already exist...

My arms rested on the table top, my fingers twisting my wedding band in fretful circles. I looked down at the plain, gold band, my mind drifting back to the day Toni had placed it on my finger. The day my life had become fuller than I could have hoped. The day I had understood love as a person should.

"It began last week," I said, and told Couttis about Doug Belle, the shock he had received from Thumbkin, how that event led to the discovery of the proximity lock, and how everything progressed from there. I told him about Jacaruso's claim the earth was being invaded by aliens, and how the knowledge had driven her to suicide. I told him about Doug Belle's crisis and my discussion with what I felt was an entity possessing him, and how, like Jacaruso, the entity had pushed him to suicide. I even told him about Ricky Womblic and our discussion about intergalactic travel.

I left nothing out. When I was done, I felt drained, as if I had purged a deadly poison from my system by simply speaking of it.

Couttis watched me as I spoke. When I got to Doug Belle's suicide, I thought I saw pain or regret flicker behind his eyes. Otherwise, I could have been talking to a mannequin.

"I appreciate your honesty," Couttis said when I'd finished. "I know that couldn't have been easy."

"Nothing about your town or your people has been easy."

The corners of Couttis's mouth drew down to fine points. "You know nothing of easy or hard." Couttis stood. "Come with me."

We approached a white painted door behind the service. Couttis opened it. On the other side was a room filled with bags of coffee beans, large grinders, and brew pots the size of industrial dough mixers.

"Where are we going?"

Couttis didn't hesitate. "Into another world."

* * *

I followed Couttis to the back of the room, where he stopped in front of another door, metal with a sturdy lock and a deadbolt. He drew a key ring from his pocket and unlocked them. We were now standing in a room barely large enough for both of us to fit comfortably. A lone bulb threw light down from the ceiling. Three walls were painted harsh orange, much like the surface of the dead planet I had seen in my dream. The fourth appeared to be made of stainless steel: shiny metal covered the wall from top to bottom and side to side. Set into the surface, about chest high, was a glass pad, dark and unadorned, not unlike a computer tablet. Couttis placed his hand on it. The glass began to emit a pale green light. Several seconds later, it changed to blue and Couttis removed his hand.

"I hope you appreciate what I'm about to do," he said. "Bringing you here goes against every precaution we've set up."

I heard a faint hum, like generators running in the distance, and the floor began to vibrate. The vibration grew, not in volume but in intensity, until it made my teeth ache.

I was about to ask Couttis what we were waiting for when a seam formed in the stainless steel wall. It started from the bottom and progressed upward in a line so thin it was as if someone had cut into the metal with a razor. When it reached the top, a brighter light began to shine from somewhere behind it.

The sides of the wall slid aside, revealing a small room made of the same metal as the door. A thick rubber pad covered the floor.

"An elevator?" I asked Couttis.

Couttis ignored my question and stepped inside. The light made his skin look sallow. He gestured for me to enter. I hesitated.

"You wanted answers," he said. "This is the only way you'll get them."

"I'm supposed to trust you?"

"Trust is irrelevant. You want answers. I'm willing to give them. This is your Pandora's Box, and I represent the lid. Look if you want, leave if you don't." His expression hardened. "What I won't do is beg. I've already lowered myself as far as I'm willing to go. Make your choice, because I'm running out of patience."

Pandora's Box. A "gift" filled with the evils of the world, terrors that would plague men until the end of time, and the only thing left trapped inside?

Hope.

I brought my galloping heart under control. "Frank's down there, isn't he?"

Couttis nodded.

A thought occurred to me. Despite everything I knew, everything I'd been told was impossible, all the signs pointed to one thing. "What's your name?" I asked the man standing before me.

"I'm in no mood for games," Couttis said.

"Neither am I. Tell me your name."

The officer gave an exasperated sigh. "Kent Couttis."

"Yes, but what's your other name." Before she shot herself, Jacaruso had said someone named Thyll was inside her, controlling her. "What's the name of the entity sharing Couttis's body? Tell me *its* name?"

Couttis's eyes narrowed. For a moment, I saw danger in them. Then his mood changed, and he chuckled. There was little humor in it.

"You've got some balls, Doctor." He straightened. "My name is too hard for you to pronounce, so Systh will do. Now, will you please get in?"

* * *

There were no buttons in the elevator. Light shone diffusely from the metal, as if the material were irradiated or hot enough to glow. The doors slid shut.

My stomach lurched as the elevator descended. I disliked the weightless feeling you get from elevators and carnival rides. It always made me feel like my guts were about to come spilling out of my mouth.

The sensation changed. The elevator seemed to not quite lurch as shift. Not in direction—we were still falling—but in aspect, as if we were traveling slightly off center. It caused more unpleasant fluttering in my stomach.

The sensation persisted. I glanced at my watch. We had been descending for almost a minute.

The elevator slowed to a halt and the doors opened. Cool air rushed in to greet me.

We stepped into a hallway made of the same weird, light-emitting metal as the elevator. The same rubber matting covered the floor. The hallway went on for perhaps fifty feet and branched to the right.

Behind us, the doors slid shut and the seam disappeared.

I looked at Couttis. "Where are we?"

"Don't you mean, 'how far down are we?'"

"I felt the shift. We didn't go straight down. We might be near the coffee shop, but we're not directly beneath it."

"Interesting." Couttis started down the hallway. "You're right. We're not beneath the *Black and Brewed*."

I rushed to keep up. "Okay, where are we?"

Couttis turned at the intersection. "We're several hundred feet beneath the lake where you and your wife spent most of last night."

I stopped in my tracks, not simply because of what he had said, but also because of what I saw.

The hallway was short, perhaps a dozen feet, and ended in a cavern so expansive I couldn't see the walls or ceiling. What light there was came from giant, cylindrical pillars of metal positioned around the central space. Beneath them, clustered together like prisoners, were people, hundreds of them, each laying on a cot and bound to it with heavy leather straps. Their eyes were shut, their mouths closed. Not one struggled against his restraints.

In fact, they all appeared to be asleep.

There were others in the room, people who wandered among the bound, checking on the straps and taking pulses. One sleeper became restless and was rewarded with an injection of a clear fluid into her vein. She immediately fell back into somnolent bliss.

Couttis stepped into the cavern and gestured with his hand. The metal pillars flared, revealing hundreds of additional cots, each one inhabited by a sleeping, presumably drugged body.

My mouth went dry. "What are you doing to these people?"

"This way," Couttis said, and headed toward a large, canopied area much like a tent. Bulky machines ringed the area beneath the canopy. Couttis led me to a narrow gap between what looked like a government supercomputer and an oversized fax machine.

Inside we found a handful of cots. All but two were empty. Annabelle St. Crux occupied one. The proprietress of *Lost Desires* rested on her side, a blanket drawn to her chin. Her eyes were open, but they had a glassy, unfocused look. One pupil appeared larger than the other.

My gaze drifted to the other cot.

It was Frank. His good eye was closed. A greenish mass like a diseased jellyfish covered his empty socket; tendrils of its slimy flesh pierced his skin. Careful to avoid the intravenous line dripping clear fluid into his arm, I laid a hand on his shoulder. "Hey, buddy."

"He won't answer." Couttis stepped over to a machine and peered at the strange symbols scrolling across the display. "We have him sedated. It'll be safer that way."

"Safer?"

Couttis, seemingly satisfied with what he saw, turned to face me. "The healing process is delicate. If disrupted, things could go south quickly, often with horrible results. It could possibly kill him. Best he remains motionless for a while longer."

I pointed to the jellyfish. "What's that?"

"Have you heard of three-dimensional printing?" Couttis asked. "It's fairly new here."

Already on edge, his words unnerved me further. *It's fairly new here.*

When I didn't answer, Couttis said, "It's an organic 3-D printer. Those tendrils are taking tissue samples and analyzing your friend's genetic sequence. It will use the information to fashion an eye from undifferentiated stem cells. The process is relatively quick but requires the patient remain still. By tomorrow morning, Mr. Swinicki will have a new, fully functioning eye."

"Mother of God," I whispered.

Couttis snorted. "There are no gods, only nature. The laws of physics rule the universe, not unseen, all-powerful beings."

A shadow passed between us. Cyrus Kline walked in carrying a tray of food. He handed me a sandwich and a bottle of water and set the tray on a narrow table. The hipster, his long hair now free of the knit cap, checked on Annabelle St. Crux. He clicked on a penlight and flashed it at her pupils.

"What's the word?" Couttis asked him.

"Not good." Kline sighed. "One pupil is fixed and dilated. Respirations are even but shallow. Her pulse is strong, but she's been unresponsive for days. The damage is too severe."

I set the food and water back on the tray. "It's not a brain tumor, is it?"

Kline fixed attention on me. Gone was the vague hipster attitude, the nonchalant defiance he had shown to Toni and me. They had been wiped away like chalk on a blackboard and replaced with the hard lines of resentment.

"Stroke," Kline said. "It had progressed for hours before we got to her. Now the damage is beyond our ability to heal." His hands curled into fists. "We're too limited here. The technology isn't sufficient."

Wandering over to the tray, Couttis picked up an apple and began eating. "She knew the risks coming into this," he told Kline around a mouthful of fruit. "Pretending otherwise is a waste of our time. You know what we have to do next."

Kline paled. "Don't ask me to do it. It would hurt too much."

"I'm not asking anything." Couttis finished the apple and dropped the core. It bounced off the dirt floor and rolled under a machine. "The decision's not up to me."

"We could set her up for another host," Kline said, his eyes suddenly full of hope. "Maybe a younger one who's—"

"Enough!" Couttis took a step toward Kline, but the other man stopped him with a hand to the chest.

"Don't yell at me," Kline said flatly. "You're the one risking everything. And for what? *Him*?"

There was no mistaking who Kline meant.

"Let's stop playing games," I said. Something had been niggling at the back of my brain since I entered the elevator. I'd finally realized what it was. "You know damn well he doesn't intend to let me leave. I knew too much before, and now I've seen too much. He brought me down here to neutralize me. I'm no longer a threat." I looked at Couttis. "I'll never see the sun again, will I?"

Couttis held my gaze for a few seconds, then looked away.

"No, I don't suppose you will."

* * *

I wanted to run. I wanted to grab the nearest piece of hardware and beat Couttis and Kline senseless. I wanted to rescue Frank and our wives. I wanted to scream. I wanted a lot of things, but in the end, I realized I could do nothing. The only way out of this place required a palm print, and even as furious as I felt, I simply couldn't lop off someone's hand and use it to enact our escape.

"Let's go sit down," Couttis said with unexpected kindness. "Cyrus, go check on the others. The doctor and I have important things to discuss."

Kline looked like he was going to say something, but a gesture from Couttis quieted him. Lips pressed into a thin line, he spun on his heels and left.

"Follow me," Couttis said.

Minutes later, we were sitting at a table near the far end of the cavern. Couttis had brought the food. My sandwich and the water bottle remained untouched. I didn't have an appetite.

I'll never see the sun again, will I?

No, I don't suppose you will.

"You said you needed me," I told Couttis. "That I'm here for a reason. Now you're telling me I can't leave. Did the game suddenly change, or are you so messed up you don't know what you want?"

"This is difficult for me. The choices I've made, the position I've put myself in." Couttis ran a finger over the table's surface. He seemed to be tracing out words, but I couldn't tell for sure. "We're more alike than you think. What you said in the coffee shop, about the difference between victims and aggressors, mirrors my own thinking. My recent thinking," he added, as if correcting himself. "It's a complication I hadn't anticipated or know how to handle. It could mean the end of my life, and the end of my species."

"If I didn't know better, I'd say you've had a change of heart."

Couttis lifted his eyes to meet mine. "It's precisely what I'm saying."

"Does that mean you're ending the invasion?" I said, figuring I might as well call it for what it was.

"Not exactly. I can't reverse what has already happened, but I'm not sure I can allow it to continue as planned. My experiences here," he tapped the side of his head with his finger, "have been compelling. I've changed, and I'm not sure whether I like it or not."

"What the hell are you? How is it you can live inside a human body, a human host, and take over so completely?"

"To understand that," Couttis said, "you need to understand one thing."

"What?"

"I'm both here and not here."

* * *

Couttis led me through a different part of the cavern. As we approached a narrow section, I noticed the walls here were unusually smooth and realized this wasn't a natural excavation. How they had carved such a vast space was another mystery.

As we walked, we passed bodies sleeping on cots. A few had awakened. One of the worker bees (as I had taken to calling them), a woman wearing jeans and a pullover, asked them several questions of the standard "who are you" and "where are you" variety. She followed up with a series of guttural sounds; words, I supposed. If the individuals replied to the sounds, they were escorted out of the cavern. One person, a man of about thirty with thinning hair, panicked and tried to run. He was subdued and restrained, a hypodermic sending him back to sleepy time.

"What's with the Rumpelstiltskin bit?" I asked. "Why do you keep them asleep?"

"It's necessary," Couttis said.

We stepped through an opening and left the cavern. We stood in a hall, much like the other I had seen.

Couttis paused, his expression troubled. "My father, did he say anything before he died?"

"Nothing about you, if that's what you mean."

Couttis gave an angry shake of his head. "I mean about this—the cavern, the people, the *invasion*."

I remembered the puzzled look on Gordon Couttis's face when he saw the egg. He seemed genuinely confused. "I don't believe so. In fact, I think Sytniak killed your father because he saw the proximity lock, because he would naturally look into it. I think he died because he was close to finding out about your plans."

Couttis's eyes darkened. "My plans? You think too highly of me. I have status—I'm not like Annabelle, too inconsequent to warrant a younger conveyance—but I'm far from what you would call executive personnel."

"What does that mean, conveyance?"

"Soon," Couttis said, and proceeded down the hallway.

I had no choice but to follow.

Chapter Seventeen

The hallway took several turns and finally ended at a door. This one wasn't stainless steel. Rather, it was constructed of a hard, blue substance, as if someone had taken a slab of clear summer sky, turned it to stone, and set it into the wall. It did not have a palm-print scanner. As we approached, I felt a bone-numbing chill, similar to what I would experience if I stood too close to an enormous block of dry ice.

"Why are we here?" I asked.

Couttis used his finger to trace a symbol onto the door's surface, the heat of his flesh apparently searing it into the material. Once completed, the slab grew translucent, then transparent, until nothing remained. Or so I thought. The cold hadn't dissipated.

"It's still there," Couttis said, rapping the now invisible material with his knuckles. "You have to retrace the symbol to open it."

Beyond the transparent door lay another cavern. If I thought the previous one was large, this one was enormous. Light pillars lined either side, going back as far as I could see. There were no cots, no people. Only an enormous machine.

It was constructed of the same light-emitting metal I'd seen used throughout the underground complex. It had grotesque shapes rising at odd angles; some thrust into the air like spikes, others twisted and flowed with uncertain purposes. Thick fleshy cables, dark green with red and yellow stripes, emerged from the base and stretched into the distance like enormous tentacles. Bolts the size of truck tires secured the construct to the floor. Darker, lightless metal formed a scaffolding along the machine's length, encapsulating it. Set into the end nearest the door was an opening like a porthole in a cruise ship but three times larger. Through it I could see light. It sparked and crackled like lightning, so bright at times I had to avert my eyes. Even so, the display left a faint, silvery image dancing on my retinas.

My dream of the dead planet—the light resembled the one I had seen flashing and sparking on an alien mountain top.

"There's your answer, your Pandora's Box," Couttis said, his voice filled with pride. "We call it the Conveyance. It's how we get from our world to yours."

"What is it?" I whispered.

Couttis put his mouth near my ear. "It, Doctor, is a wormhole."

* * *

My mind shrank from what I'd seen, from what Couttis had told me. I needed time to regain my mental equilibrium. I insisted we check on Frank.

As Couttis walked us back, I stuffed my hands into my pockets so he wouldn't see them shaking.

"Now that I know your secret," I said, "what do you expect from me? I doubt there's anything I can do that you can't do better."

Couttis kept his head down. "We've been on your planet for nearly a hundred years, building this infrastructure, working on Emersville, gradually developing it as a base of operations. We co-exist with most of the town's citizens. We—" He hesitated. "We've finally completed what we set out to do. Except now we're out of room. We need more space, which means expanding out into the rest of the world."

"You don't want that?"

"In a way, yes," Couttis said. "Though not to the extent others do."

"Let me guess. The Green Queen?"

Couttis gave me a sharp look. "You're remarkably well informed."

"I also know your queen isn't satisfied with a 'co-existence.' She wants more. She wants our world."

"Conquest was not our initial plan," Couttis said.

"What other reason could you possibly have for coming to another planet? You're not stupid. You knew we wouldn't let another race step in and take over."

"We have much to offer your people, ways to improve your lives to an extent you cannot imagine. We had hoped to offer an exchange—technological advances for a peaceful co-existence, a chance to integrate ourselves into your civilization with minimal disruption."

I snorted at the thought of "minimal disruptions" but decided to let it go. "What changed?"

Couttis hesitated. "Remember when I said I was both here and not here? It's because of the wormhole. It connects our part of the universe to yours. Travel is almost instantaneous. Except there's a problem—your world is poison to us. The air, the food, the bacteria and viruses, the intensity of your sunlight, they would have killed us."

"*War of the Worlds*," I said. "H. G. Wells covered this long before you got here. Get to the point."

"We needed an alternative. This is where the proximity locks come into play. They're the means by which we can safely travel to your world."

My mind raced to put the pieces together. "You're here and not here—your body is back on your home planet, but your *mind* is here." I suddenly had it. "That's what proximity locks are. They hold your minds, your thought patterns."

"Until we can transfer them into human brains," Couttis said. "We call ourselves the Conveyed. Not only did we solve the hostile environment problem, we ended up using far less energy. We weren't transporting millions of tons of physical artifacts. We were sending brainwave patterns, and those have no mass."

"But this cavern, the equipment. Someone had to construct it."

"In the beginning," Couttis said, "we sent nanobots through the wormhole, semi-sentient beings so small they could survive the journey. They performed the initial work. We transitioned to slightly larger robots once the cavern was finished. We experienced numerous failures but kept trying, and we eventually succeeded. That's when we started employing the proximity locks, and sent our minds to this alien world. It was an act of desperation that turned into the greatest achievement in our long history."

His words reminded me of something Doug Belle, or more correctly, the being inside of him had said.

It was our greatest accomplishment. Some said it cemented our genius. Ask the Stranded...I doubt they'd be so charitable.

"Who are the Stranded?" I asked.

Couttis blanched. "How do you know about them?"

"I'm remarkably well-informed, remember?"

Couttis opened his mouth to reply, but closed it when a worker bee walked past, looking askance at us. Couttis waited until the man was out of earshot before continuing. "Our sun is close to going nova. When it does, our world and our civilization, with its long history of triumphs, will be gone. In an effort to save some scrap of ourselves, we decided to abandon our planet. Unfortunately, we found it necessary to limit how many would make the trip. Our population had reached over one hundred billion. Earth's population has yet to reach a tenth of that. There were simply more of us than you, so most of our kind had to stay behind. They were, to give a name to them, the Stranded."

"You condemned them to stay behind and die?"

"A painful decision but a necessary one," he said, "though many are still alive, scraping out a meager existence deep underground and safe from our sun's now lethal radiation. We left behind family and friends we had known for centuries. The selection process resulted in riots. Many died who could have made the journey. It was a dark blot on our shining moment."

"What do they have to do with what's going on now?"

"A small faction of the Conveyed felt we had been too harsh to our people, that we should have brought more of us to Earth. The rest, myself included, argued to stick with our original plan. We can't save our world, and condemning another civilization into extinction for the sake of saving ours went against every moral tenet we held." He looked around the cavern, at what they had created, and sighed. "The bitter feelings remained. Now, decades later, we face the prospect of expanding our influence, and the question of the Stranded has resurfaced. There is a push to convey more of our kind, to bring more of the Stranded to Earth."

"How many?"

"As many as will be left on your world."

"What do you mean, as many as will be left?"

Couttis rubbed at a spot on his temple. I had the feeling it was a gesture the real Kent Couttis would have made.

"We left an overpopulated and polluted planet," he said. "Earth is on the same trajectory. Do the math, Doctor. At the pace humanity is reproducing, you will experience the same problems as our planet within six hundred years. There will be too many of you, and you will be close to depleting your planet's resources. The same faction who wants to bring over more of the Stranded feels we are abandoning one disaster for another, and it needs to be stopped."

I suddenly found it hard to breathe. "Stopped how?"

"The new plan," Couttis said, "is to release a virus, one we are working on modifying. It will infect every human on the planet, but it will remain dormant until it detects a trigger. At that point, it will become virulent."

"And the trigger?"

"Aging," he said. "The virus bonds to the mitochondria inside human cells. When someone reaches a certain age, those mitochondria start releasing a small peptide. The peptide is the trigger."

"What happens when the virus is triggered?"

"The body will begin to age far faster than normal. Within weeks, it will fail and the person will die. They intend to solve your overpopulation problem with, as you humans like to say, extreme prejudice."

"You can't be serious. Killing everyone who gets older?" He was describing a global holocaust, death on an unprecedented scale. "What kind of monsters are you?"

Couttis stiffened. "I'm not the monster. I don't want this to happen."

"But what about your human hosts? They'll age, and you'll end up killing yourselves as well."

"That won't be a problem," Couttis said. "We'll simply convey ourselves into younger hosts before the virus is triggered. That's why we're focusing on children, on creating a broader population of youth we can use." He suddenly looked uncomfortable. "We've never conveyed a mind into a human fetus, which would be our ideal method of staying with a host for as long as possible. If we can successfully accomplish that, there would be no stopping this horror from happening."

A sound came from inside the tent where Frank and Annabelle St. Crux were held. I heard a groan, then voices arguing, then shouting and the crash of metal. A man ran out of the tent, his nose dripping blood. He saw Couttis and stopped.

"The man in there was due for his sedative," he said, holding up a syringe. "He woke up. He wouldn't cooperate."

Frank staggered from the tent. "What the fuck were you trying to put into me?"

I stepped forward. "Frank."

"Paco?" His voice was scratchy. "What the hell?"

The other man used the opportunity to run. Couttis let him go.

"Frank," I repeated. My friend, for the first time since I'd known him, looked frail. I helped him back inside the tent. "We owe Ricky Womblic an apology."

"The grease-monkey? What for?"

"For not believing him."

* * *

"This is bullshit," Frank said. He sat on the cot, the jellyfish-thing still attached to his face. There was no sign of Annabelle St. Crux. "I can't fucking believe it."

"Detective Swinicki," Couttis said. "Please calm down. The healing process isn't complete."

"You wanna see what I think of your E.T. crap?" Frank grabbed the creature attached to his face and worked his thick fingers under it.

Couttis jumped forward. "NO!"

Frank tugged at the jellyfish. Like a suction cup, it pulled his skin, and the thin tendrils were stretched thinner. He tugged harder until the jellyfish suddenly popped free. He threw it at Couttis. It hit the man in the chest and fell to the ground.

I stared at Frank's face. His wounded socket had healed—sort of. New skin replaced most of the ragged edges where his eye had been ripped out. It flowed into the socket until it disappeared behind his new "eye." The alien orb was smaller than a human eye, milky white and perched atop a stalk, with thin red lines like sickly pinworms crawling across the surface. It lacked a pupil, and there wasn't a proper eyelid, only a fold of pale flesh hanging from his brow. Beneath the eye, a patch of his cheek had turned an ugly, purple color. It looked like no bruise I had ever seen.

"You fool!" Couttis picked up the jellyfish-thing. Its vibrant, sea-green color was already fading. "I try to help you and this is how you repay me? *YOU DAMNED FOOL!*"

Frank eased his bulk off the cot. He looked alarmingly thin; his clothes hung like veils from his frame. He grabbed Couttis by the shirt.

"Listen, pal," he rasped. "You want to murder most everyone on the planet so you can take over. Forgive me if I'm not fawning over your efforts to 'help' me." He shoved the officer away. "You're a freak, even if you look human."

I took hold of Frank's arm. "He doesn't want that to happen. He's asking for our help."

Frank glared at Couttis. "He's a space alien. What could he possibly need from us?"

"The doctor's correct," Couttis said, smoothing his shirt. "I need your help." He approached an aluminum case, opened it, and withdrew our stun grenades. He dropped them into Frank's hand. "A sign of good faith. I wouldn't do this if I didn't need your cooperation."

Frank pocketed the grenades. "Fuck you, asshole. You started this, you finish it. We're not here to clean up your mess."

Couttis's face went crimson. He took an angry step toward Frank.

Footsteps could suddenly be heard echoing in the cavern, growing louder and accompanied by low, angry voices. A body sailed into the medical tent and landed on the floor. My eyes widened when I saw who it was.

Cyrus Kline, his clothes torn, his tanned, hipster face marred by blood, his eyes closed.

A man strolled into the tent. He wore jeans and a tight, black sweater. A series of angry scrapes marred the skin on his cheek and chin. A skull earring gleamed from his left lobe.

Conrad Hunter, Emersville's mayor.

Couttis and Hunter seemed to size one another up, their eyes searching, their expressions tight. On the ground, Cyrus Kline groaned. His lanky body shifted, and he rolled onto his back. Bruises covered the other side of his face. He had received a hell of a beating. When he saw Hunter, his expression darkened.

"You had no right to attack me." The hipster spat blood; a small tooth joined in for good measure. "I'm the one who warned you about Systh, about what he was doing."

Quick as a betrayal, Conrad Hunter kicked Kline in the ribs. More blood flew from between his lips.

"I not only had the right," Hunter said. "I had the authority."

"Whose authority?" Couttis said, his young face a mask of fury.

"Mine," said a third voice, young and thin. A girl walked into the tent. She looked to be about four, with a pudgy face and long, chestnut hair pulled back into a ponytail. Either her mother was color-blind or a madwoman, because the girl wore an odd mash-up of green and orange cloth loosely assembled into a kind of dress. She glared at Kline with an anger I had never seen in a child her age.

Tears filled Kline's eyes. His lower lip quivered. The poor man looked like a beaten puppy as he pleaded with the girl. "But I helped you!"

Hunter jabbed a finger at him. "You also conspired with Systh to bring two unconveyed humans down here. You didn't try to stop him. You used—"

"Enough," the girl said, cutting Hunter off. "I swear your voice is as grating as his."

To my surprise the mayor nodded, albeit abruptly, and stepped back.

"Pussy," Frank said to Hunter. "I don't let my kids order me around."

I placed a hand on Frank's shoulder. To the girl, I said, "Hello. You must be the Green Queen. I've heard a lot about you."

The girl lifted her gaze to me. She had cold eyes, stark eyes, like the eyes of the maniacal dolls that had attacked Frank and me. I saw neither empathy nor compassion in them, only arrogance and utter, profound contempt.

"The puppy deigns to speak." She cocked her head to one side. Her innocent, little girl voice hardened to black diamonds. "Do it again and I will see your tongue is removed."

Couttis held up a cautioning hand. "Doctor, please. Don't say another word."

Frank drew a breath. I squeezed his shoulder before he could say anything and nodded at Couttis.

The officer turned his attention to the girl. "We've already had this discussion. I know how you feel, but we can't go ahead with your plan. It's an abomination, and it makes me ashamed." His voice softened. "Please, Kyly, reconsider going back to the original plan. There's no need—"

Conrad Hunter strode forward and struck Couttis across the face. The blow snapped the younger man's head back.

"Address her with the proper respect," Hunter said, his face even redder than Couttis's. "You more than anyone should be setting the example."

Blood trickled from the corner of Couttis's mouth. He wiped at it with the back of his hand. Then he laughed, his shoulders trembling with broken mirth. "Always the pet on a chain, eh Sarth. Tell me, when did you become her ally, her spy? Are you smitten with her, or are you simply hoping for a younger conveyance?" His eyes moved from Hunter to the girl and back to Hunter. "I believe it's the former. You desire her, yet you know you cannot have her." Couttis stood a little straighter. "Touch me again and I'll kill you. Your mind will be lost forever. You will have made the trip for nothing."

On the ground, Cyrus Kline's face grew pale. Blood dribbled from his lips as he scooted away from the two men. The Green Queen remained calm, almost bored, her head tilted up as she took in the exchange.

I sensed Frank shift next to me. Out of the corner of my eye, I saw him slip a hand into his pocket.

The stun grenades.

I swallowed hard. Time to play Eagle Scout and be prepared for anything.

Conrad Hunter tensed, his muscles bunching dangerously. He had two inches and at least thirty pounds on Couttis, yet the officer seemed unconcerned: he stood calmly, his hand nowhere near his gun.

When Hunter seemed about ready to strike, the girl said, "Enough. Sarth, step back."

Hunter shook his head. "He can't be allowed to—"

"He is *Parthol*, and of a caste higher than yours," the girl said. "Unless I give you leave, you may not strike him again."

Hunter hesitated, his body trembling. I could almost see him weighing his options. Then the mayor reluctantly moved to the other side of the tent, murder etched into the creases around his eyes and at the corners of his downturned mouth.

The girl stepped up to Couttis.

"We may be related," she said, her voice too young for her words, "but do not think our relationship gives you immunity. My tolerance for mutiny is limited. Essentially, it's zero." She snatched Couttis's gun from its holster and aimed it at Cyrus Kline. The hipster issued a terrified scream and tried to scramble away. Without taking her eyes off Couttis, the Green Queen pulled the trigger, again and again, emptying the revolver into the hipster's body. Kline jerked, his blood splattering everything. Droplets hit the Queen's pale cheek. She ignored them. Holding the weapon out to Couttis, she said, "You will do as I say."

Couttis reluctantly took the gun and holstered it. "We were never like this, Kyly. *You* were never like this. I don't know why you changed, or when you did, but our sires would not approve. With this plan you demean us all, and in the process, our entire history. Better we'd died on our world than become that which we loathed for so long."

More footsteps. People rushed into the tent, their faces pale. "We heard gunshots," one exclaimed, a man in his early twenties with acne-scarred cheeks and wispy fuzz on his chin. Another rushed to Hunter's side.

Taking advantage of the distraction, Frank withdrew a stun grenade from his pocket and whispered, "Time to rock and roll."

Frank tossed the grenade at the girl. I barely had enough time to close my eyes and clap my hands over my ears before it went off.

Chapter Eighteen

People were screaming.

Light as bright as the sun flared inside the tent, momentarily blinding those unfortunate enough to have their eyes open. The explosion, over a hundred and fifty decibels loud, rendered hearing difficult and often caused brief episodes of disorientation. This time was no different.

Moments later I opened my eyes. Smoke filled the air. I searched for the others.

The newly arrived worker bees staggered as if hit by a cyclone. Couttis stood hunched over Kline's dead body, retching. Hunter rubbed his eyes, his jaw pulled wide as he tried to shake off the effects of the grenade. The Green Queen lay motionless on the floor, eyes closed, blood seeping from her ears, burns discoloring her right hand and arm. Her mind might have been old, but her body was still that of a four-year-old.

Someone fell heavily into me. I barely had time to catch Frank before he collapsed. This close, I could see his alien eye weeping a milky fluid.

He grabbed my shoulders. "Hurry, the effects won't last long."

Nodding, I hoisted Frank by the armpits and we stumbled out of the tent.

The cavern was eerily quiet after so much commotion. No one raced toward us. No alarm sounded. Emersville's missing residents continued to sleep peacefully, no doubt assisted by narcotics.

"Over here," I said, hauling Frank toward the back of the cavern. We passed cot after cot. Frank, his face a mask of anger, said, "What the hell is this?"

"In each person," I said, "a human and an alien share a brain. Both personalities exist as one. Obviously the alien mind is stronger, but maybe not always." We passed a boy of around ten. He twitched under his blanket, his face pinched into a frown. "There are hundreds of them down here."

"Some should be waking up. God knows we made enough noise."

"Drugged. All of them."

"I don't get it," Frank said. "Why go through the hassle?"

I thought of the coffee shop above us, and how popular it was. "Sleep," I said in wonder. "What if their hold weakens during a deep sleep? Delta waves are strongest when we're dreaming. Maybe they disrupt the aliens' ability to maintain control of humans. It would make sleeping dangerous, but the human body absolutely requires rest." I warmed to the subject. It possessed a logic I could understand. "This would explain the drugging—it allows the people to get the necessary rest, and the aliens don't risk losing their control."

Frank pushed to keep up. "Give it to me in plain English, will you?"

"Sleep deprivation," I said. "Go without sleep long enough and you become psychotic. If the aliens risk losing control during sleep, you would want to drug the people to keep them under control." I thought back to the man who had woken in a panic, and how the worker bee had put him back under by injecting something into him. "That has to be the answer. Their weakness is sleep."

"Fucking wonderful."

Another thought struck me. "Gordon Couttis had epilepsy. I bet that's why he was never part of the conspiracy. His condition likely prevented him from being possessed."

We entered the hallway leading to the wormhole. I'd abandoned the idea of using the elevator to *Black and Brewed*, believing it wouldn't respond to my touch, and I didn't see another passage out of the cavern.

Someone shouted behind us. Another person took up the call, and another. Some very angry people were about to give chase.

I pushed Frank along the hallway toward a door about fifty feet away. Like the others in this complex, it had a screen embedded in the flawless, impenetrable metal. Couttis and I had gone through it earlier.

Frank finally shook off the effects of the grenade and stood on his own. Sweat coated his face. He glanced over his shoulder at the sound of footfalls. "We're running out of time, Paco."

I approached the door and placed my hand on the screen. The surface felt warm, but that was it. No shock, no other unpleasant reaction. Nothing.

The door remained shut.

I looked at Frank. "We need one of those guys to open it."

"Couttis?" Frank said.

"Sure, but he's back in the cavern."

With an angry shout, Conrad Hunter charged into the hallway, followed by two worker bees.

"You have your gun?" I asked Frank.

He shook his head. "They must have taken it while I was unconscious. Not that it would have done any good. I ran out of rounds shooting the dolls." He reached into his pocket. "I still have two grenades."

"Save them in case we run into a mob," I said. "I say we go old school. You up for a fight?"

Frank's grin stretched nearly to his ears. "I thought you'd never ask."

Hunter charged at us, his expression a mixture of fury and wounded pride.

Frank advanced until the two collided near the intersection. Hunter threw a left. The swing was powerful but poorly aimed. Frank took the blow on his shoulder, letting the force spin him, and hammered Hunter with a right hook. The other man grunted. Frank was a strong man, despite his wounds. Hunter was about to find out how strong.

The two worker bees focused their attention on me. As they approached, one reached into his lab coat and withdrew a syringe. The other did the same.

Neither was as burly as Hunter, though the one on the right had a slighter build. He looked more like a nerdy professor than a fighter. The guy on the left posed a greater threat. He held his syringe with the ease of a seasoned knife fighter. As he advanced, his eyes scanned my body, presumably looking for an opening.

I had taken self-defense classes as a teenager. Nothing sophisticated—a few basic blocks and kicks, along with some release techniques. That was almost twenty years ago, and they hadn't covered syringe attacks.

The more experienced-looking bee shot ahead of his partner. When he was within striking distance, I snapped my rear foot forward. Not expecting a kick, the man couldn't block my leg fast enough, and the toe of my shoe connected with his solar plexus. Breath exploded out from between his teeth and he doubled over. Despite the blow, he managed to bring the syringe around and stab at my leg. His aim was reckless, and the needle skittered harmlessly off the hard surface of my tibia. I jerked my leg back, too amped up to feel any pain, and threw a punch at nerdy bee. He let out a panicked shriek and danced back.

In the middle of the hallway, Frank and Hunter grappled with one another. Hunter was bleeding from a cut above his eye and had added to the collection of scrapes on his face. Frank, his hands drooping more than I liked, panted like a man who had run a marathon. He was tiring, while Hunter looked like Rocky Balboa in the second round of a ten round fight.

Frank needed my help or this would end badly.

As my opponents regrouped, I thought of Toni and how she had cried in the shower when she realized she wasn't pregnant. I thought of how badly she wanted to be a mother, how badly she *needed* to be a mother. I thought of the joy she would feel when a human life was finally growing inside her, and the horror she would experience if an alien presence invaded its brain and took away what made her precious little baby so special.

I thought of what she would lose—what the world would all lose—if the aliens succeeded. Rage built up inside me. I let it grow until it was all I could feel.

The guy I'd kicked started to straighten. I grabbed him by the back of the head, my fingers twinning into his hair.

"Not today, asshole," I said, and brought my knee up into his face. The man didn't make a sound—he simply fell, blood flowing freely from his nose and upper lip. I'd hopefully taken the fight out of him.

I felt a stabbing pain and turned.

Nerdy bee had stuck a syringe into my arm. Eyes wild, sweat slicking his hair, he hesitated, his thumb hovering over the plunger.

I took advantage of his hesitation and punched him in the throat. The delicate cartilage of his airway ruptured with a sickening crunch. His hands flew to his neck, clawing for air that would not come. His eyes bulged, his face purpled. With his lips moving but no words coming out, he crumpled to the floor. He would not be getting up.

I jerked the syringe out of my arm, the barrel still filled with fluid.

Mere feet away, Conrad Hunter pounded at Frank with blow after blow. Frank countered with a massive, two-fisted chop to the side of Hunter's head. The bloodied mayor staggered.

Stepping up, I stuck the syringe in the meaty part of Hunter's shoulder and emptied the contents into him. Seconds later he was unconscious. Some awful part of me wished he would die.

Prior to visiting Emersville, I had never done anything remotely life-threatening to another human being. Now I had killed someone—two, if Hunter died. I dropped the syringe, nauseated at what I had become.

Wheezing, his face marred by cuts and bruises, Frank checked Hunter for a pulse.

"Alive," he said. "At least we have that going for us."

"He tried to kill you."

"No." Frank's unblinking, alien eye seemed to contradict my shock. "The thing inside him did. We have no idea what the real Conrad Hunter is like. He might be a loving husband and father. At least he'll have a chance to be fully human again. If he can be fully human again." He rubbed his shoulder. "I owe you, Paco."

"Pay me back by getting us out of here."

"Where do we go now?"

I dragged nerdy bee's lifeless body to the door and placed his hand on the scanner.

The door remained shut. No surprise. Nothing in this place was ever easy.

"It probably uses some kind of recognition program," Frank said. "You need an authorized fingerprint or palm pattern or something to open it."

I gestured to Hunter. "I bet he has the proper clearance."

We dragged Hunter to the door and pressed his hand against the scanner. At first nothing happened, then a seam formed down the middle and the two halves slid apart.

Beyond was the long hallway leading to the Conveyance. I stepped inside.

"Hold on," Frank said, pulling Hunter into the hallway, followed by the dead worker bee. When I asked about the third guy, the one with the broken nose, Frank said, "Leave him. The trail of blood would show where we went."

"Where else would we have gone?"

Frank ran a finger over the cellophane-wrapped cigarette pack sticking out of his shirt pocket. I was surprised he'd managed to keep hold of it. "It might buy us a few minutes. They might wonder why we left him behind."

I didn't agree with his thinking but, lacking a better plan, I stepped away from the door. Frank joined me. The door stayed open.

"Any idea how it closes?" he asked.

I looked at the bodies slumped inside the doorway. "Maybe it has some kind of sensor, some way of preventing it from closing on someone." I grabbed Hunter's arm and pulled him down the hallway. Frank did the same with nerdy bee.

When we were about ten feet from the door, the two halves came together without a sound.

I released Hunter's arm. Frank did the same with his guy. The mayor was still breathing. Hopefully it would be hours before he woke.

The hallway extended for another sixty or so feet before branching left and right. I remembered the left passage led to the Conveyance. Doorways lined the walls, most of them closed. One was open. We approached it and looked inside. Stacks of cardboard containers lined the walls. I searched several for markings or letterings.

"Nothing," I said. "No shipping labels. No company logo. No customs stamps."

Frank lifted one. "Whatever's in it isn't heavy." He tore at the packing tape and opened the flaps.

What I saw made my heart race.

Proximity locks. The carton was filled with them, maybe three dozen, all nestled in a framework of silver metal much like an egg crate. Each lock had a thin wire connecting it to a device that might have been a battery.

I stared at the remaining boxes. If they all contained proximity locks, there would be thousands of them.

"It's the heart of their invasion," Frank said, rubbing at the area under his alien eye. The oddly bruised skin had grown and now covered half his cheek. I peered at the discoloration. It looked almost scaly. I touched it with my finger. "Does that hurt?"

"No." Frank gave me a worried look. "Brad, what's going on?"

"It's your skin." I described how his cheek had changed. I also realized he hadn't seen his eye yet. Instead of trusting my words, I pulled out my phone, snapped a picture, and showed it to him. "The bruised area is growing, and that's your new eye."

He touched the skin under his eye. "What's happening to me?"

"We'll figure it out later." I put the phone back into my pocket. "First, we need to find a way out."

Back in the hallway I counted the doors. There were too many. "We can't keep dragging Hunter around to use his hand. We need a better alternative."

Beside me, Frank muttered something under his breath. His face had gone pale, and his human eye was looking a little wild. He reached up and took the cigarette pack from his pocket. His fingers shook as he tore open the cellophane, shook one out, and jammed it into his mouth.

"Don't suppose you got a light?" he asked.

"You want to smoke? Have you lost your—"

"Do you or do you not have a *goddamn light!*"

I shook my head. "You know I don't."

"Just as well." He took the cigarette from his mouth and dropped it to the floor. "Stupid time to start back up."

"Pull it together," I said. "Those doors, we need to see what's behind them." I paused. "If Hunter was the one who took our wives, he might've brought them here."

"Wouldn't Couttis have mentioned that?"

"Hell if I know." I grabbed Hunter, hauled him to the next door, and used his hand to open it. Beyond lay a room, roughly twenty by ten, with walls that glowed faintly. Bunk beds were set against one wall, a table and chairs against the other. There was no one in the room.

We opened the next door and found what appeared to be a lab. I recognized an autoclave, centrifuges, banks of refrigerators. Pipettes and jars of chemicals. Rows of sealed test tubes. At the far end, an attractive woman with red hair stared at a computer monitor. She looked up when we entered, a frown marring on her pretty features.

"This area is off limits," she said. "You'll have to leave." Then she noticed Frank's eye and froze. A cell phone sat atop some notebooks. She went for it.

Frank bull-rushed her, covering the distance in seconds, too fast for a man his size. The woman, her eyes wide, opened her mouth to scream.

Frank grabbed her, spun her around, and pushed her face into the wall. He jerked her hands behind her back, and the scream never made it past her lips.

"Fight me, make any noise at all, and I'll break your arms," he said to her.

"You've escaped," she said, her tone dismayingly calm. "Unfortunate, but not a disaster. It's not like you can report to anyone." She smiled. "Besides, you'll be dead before the hour is out."

Frank wrenched the woman's arms upward until she winced. "Manners," he told her. To me, he said, "Looks like we found a research lab. Wanna bet on what's in those refrigerators?"

I opened one. Clear rectangular bottles filled with fluid lined the shelves. There were strange markings like glyphs written on each one. I couldn't read them, but I had a good idea what they said.

"I think we've found the virus."

Frank grinned. "Sweet. How do we destroy them?"

The woman began shouting. "No! NO! You can't!"

"Shut up," Frank said, pressing her more firmly into the wall. "We can, and we will."

I looked at the banks of refrigerators. There were over a dozen. There was no time to destroy them individually.

"We need something big," I said, my eyes scanning the room. "A fire, or an explosion. Something that would destroy the entire lab."

"What do you know about chemicals?" he asked me. "There are jars all over the place. Maybe the stun grenades can set them off?"

"I don't know nearly enough." I had taken chemistry in college and barely squeaked by with a C-. "We need to find something we know will work, and we need it fast."

"Let's go, then." Frank spun the woman around. Her hair hung in wild strands. She glared at him, her green eyes burning with hatred.

"You're coming with us," he told her. "We need a hand with the doors."

* * *

Frank dragged the woman into the hallway and forced her hand onto the nearest pad. The door slid open.

We found another room filled with boxes. At least forty of them, each one presumably containing proximity locks.

We moved on, dragging the protesting scientist with us. The hallway ended at another intersection. One way led back toward the wormhole machine. I went down the other.

Here we found a short corridor with three doors, one on either side and the third at the end.

Frank grabbed the woman by the hair and jerked her head back. "What's behind those doors?"

She winced in pain. "Supplies. Spare equipment. It's another storage area."

"Our wives," he said. "Where are they?"

"I don't know," she said. Frank yanked her head back until her neck bowed. "Honestly, don't know!"

Behind us, the sounds of pursuit could now be heard. They must have found the bloodied bee. Several voices yelled. One might have been Couttis's.

"Pick one," I told Frank.

Dragging the woman to the right-hand door, he said, "Open it." When the woman refused, he grabbed her wrist. This time she fought him. She kicked and bit and tried to break free.

"Let me go!" she yelled. Then, in a louder voice, "Down here! We're down here!"

I exchanged a curious look with Frank. "She doesn't want us to go in there."

Frank nodded. "Which makes it the most interesting place is this cesspool." He forced the woman's hand to the door. At the last moment, she made a fist.

"Open your hand."

"Help!" She was screaming at the top of her lungs. "Down here! Help!"

"Open your goddamn hand!"

"Fuck you!"

Panting from the effort of restraining her, Frank said, "That's not ladylike, which excuses this." He punched her in the forehead. The woman crumpled. He pried open her hand and pressed it to the pad.

The door opened.

* * *

Toni and Kerry lay on cots similar to the ones we saw in the other room. Their eyes were closed, and bright blue blankets covered them to their waists. Their shirts were pulled up, exposing their torsos. Small, sticky pads like EKG leads were stuck to their skin between their belly buttons and the waistband of their pants. Thin wires connected the pads to proximity locks sitting on a table next to them. Two women, two locks.

It was the next step Couttis spoke of: the attempt to convey an alien mind into a fetus.

In addition to her lock, Toni had an IV pumping a cloudy, yellowish fluid into her.

Frank grabbed Kerry by the shoulders. "Honey, wake up."

I rushed over to Toni. Her face looked pale, the skin beneath her eyes muddied by dark circles. I shook her.

"Toni," I said. "Wake up, it's me."

Neither woman responded. I lifted Toni's eyelids and checked her pupils. "I think they've been drugged."

Out in the hallway, the scientist groaned. She was starting to come around.

Worse, the echo of footfalls was growing louder.

We were almost out of time.

Panicked, I pulled the IV from Toni's arm, grabbed the wires attached to her stomach and yanked them free. Frank did the same with Kerry's wires, then kicked the table. The proximity locks flew across the tiny room.

"Fucking bastards," Frank said. The dark, scaly skin now covered half his face. Streaks of green stretched down from his alien eye like the colorings on a snake. "What were they doing to them?"

"The locks act like a repository, holding the alien minds." I pulled Toni to a sitting position. "They were transferring those minds into the babies." I began gently slapping Toni's face. "Come on, Toni. Open your eyes."

Frank threw me a puzzled look. "But Toni isn't pregnant."

"Remember the test she asked us to buy?" We had stopped at a drug store to pick up a pregnancy test. I couldn't recall what had happened to it. Probably left in the car. "I think she's finally going to be a mom."

"After all this time? Isn't that stretching coincidence?"

"Not if the soap we bought acted as an aphrodisiac and a fertility drug." I returned my attention to Toni. "Wake up, dammit!"

Toni began to stir. Her eyes fluttered, but they didn't open.

Frank lifted Kerry until she sat upright. He rubbed her arms, slapped her wrists.

Kerry's eyes opened slightly.

"Frank?" she said, her voice muddled by whatever drug she had been given.

"I'm here, honey," he said. "I'm here."

Beside me, Toni finally opened her eyes. She lifted a hand to touch my cheek. "Brad?"

I allowed myself a quick, relieved smile, and pulled her to her feet. "We have to leave."

She nodded. "I know." Her hand drifted to her belly. "I'm pregnant, Brad. We're going to have a baby." Tears filled her eyes. "Do you know what they've done? What they're doing? It's *evil!*"

"Later," I said. "First we need to make it out of here alive."

"The IV," she said weakly. "The garbage they were pumping into me. They said it would make the baby grow faster. The girl, the one wearing the green and orange, she said my baby was going to be special. A gift of some sort."

I grabbed her hand. "Let's go."

Before we could move, Kerry screamed.

* * *

"Frank! Oh Jesus, what happened to you?"

Kerry backed away from her husband, her face bloodless. Next to her, Frank was hunched over, his arms wrapped around his gut. His lips had pulled back into a snarl, revealing teeth that were too long and too narrow and too many. The purpled, alien flesh now covered his entire face. His hair fell in sad tufts from a head that seemed to be elongating.

"Oh fuck, it hurts," he said.

Toni released my hand. "What's happening to him?"

"He's changing," came a voice from the hallway. "I warned him, but he wouldn't listen."

We turned. Kent Couttis stood there, still looking boyish in his too large uniform, but the stranger behind his eyes revealed more: an ancient, alien intelligence—part empathetic, part furious. Beside him was the scientist Frank had knocked out, an angry red spot on her forehead. And in front of them, the little girl in the madly colored clothes.

The Green Queen.

The stun grenade had wounded her. Blisters marred the skin of her right hand and cheek, and part of her dress had been singed. But her gaze was clear, and it was terrible.

"Kill the men," she said in her eerie, kindergarten voice. "Leave the women alive." She smiled. "For now."

Couttis drew his gun. It was a revolver, and I could see new bullets in the chamber. "I'm sorry," he said. "I had hoped for a better ending."

I stepped forward, hands raised. "You spoke of Pandora's Box. You said by coming down here, it would be like looking inside and witnessing the evils of the world." I nodded to the gun. "This is your Pandora moment. If you kill us, you'll not only have brought evil into this world, you'll have condoned it. You'll have fled one dying planet only to destroy another. It's not what you wanted, you told me as much."

I locked eyes with Couttis. "If you're an honorable man, if you're from an honorable *race*, you'll let us go. There's no need to do what this girl says. This is a different world, with a different future. Change the path of your life. Make it what you want, not what's being forced on you."

I lowered my hands and stepped back.

Couttis didn't immediately respond. His eyes had lost their focus. He was looking at me, but I could tell he wasn't seeing me. His attention had turned elsewhere.

I imagined the dialogue going on in his head, the back-and-forth between alien and human: one pleading for mercy, the other struggling to understand its place on this small, strange, wonderful planet.

The seconds passed.

"I told you to kill them," the Queen said, sounding like an impertinent child.

Her words worked. Couttis's head snapped up. His eyes regained their focus. He was seeing me again.

I couldn't tell from his expression what decision he had made.

"The laws of nature are the same throughout the universe," Couttis said, and holstered his gun. "So are the laws of morality. We came here with one intent: to save our race, and not to exterminate another. I refuse to live like that. Better I die than become something evil."

I drew in a relieved breath. Maybe we would make it out of this alive.

But then a figure stepped up behind Couttis.

Conrad Hunter, his bloodied face warped into a look of pure malice. He snatched the policeman's revolver and jammed the barrel against Couttis's temple.

"May I?" he asked the Green Queen.

The little girl with the old, cold eyes looked up. She seemed to regard Couttis for a moment, then shifted her attention to Hunter. "He's become a disappointment, much like his father, and his father before him. Do as you wish. His status can no longer protect him."

Couttis paled. He didn't speak, didn't try to defend himself or his decision. He simply nodded in understanding.

Hunter licked his lips. "Now I will be *Parthol*," he said, and pulled the trigger.

With the barrel so close to Couttis's head, the round made a small hole going in, and only a slightly larger one coming out. But with it came brain matter and fragments of bone and pellets of blood. The gory mess splattered the wall, the ceiling, and the red-haired scientist. She gagged and turned away.

As Couttis's dead body buckled, I thought I saw a faint smile cross his face. Perhaps he was thinking, *at last, I've become who I was meant to be.*

Stepping over the man he had murdered, Conrad Hunter raised the gun. There was a rustle of movement as Toni came forward, interposing her body between me and Hunter.

"If you want to kill him, you'll have to kill me first." Her hands went to her belly. "And the child I carry inside me."

Conrad Hunter shifted his aim. The gun now pointed at Toni's head. "Gladly, bitch."

"No!" The Green Queen stepped into the room, her clothes swirling like a tempest about her tiny body. "You will not harm her. What she carries is precious to me." At some unseen signal, five worker bees filed into the room. One was the man whose nose I had broken. "Take the women," she told them. Pointing to Toni, she added, "This one is to be restrained until I say otherwise. Kill the other two."

"No." Red-faced, Kerry advanced on the Queen. "You made promises. You promised to take care of my family, including my husband. You promised my daughter would do great things. You promised my boys would live a privileged life. You promised a better world." Her voice cracked. "I gave up everything for you, and you will hold to your word."

"You knew about this?" It was Frank. His transformation had accelerated. His body had thinned and elongated. The scales making up his skin seemed to have fused into some kind of insect-like armor. Instead of fingers, his hands ended in black-tipped claws. He had turned into a nightmare. "You knew what they were doing and you helped?" he said, his voice rasping like a saw drawn across a log. "How could you?"

Kerry rounded on her husband. Rage had contorted her features. Gone was the gentle soul who would fuss over everyone but herself, the mother who would lay down her life for a child, the friend I had known for so many years. In her place stood a fiend, someone I didn't recognize. In some ways, she had changed as much as Frank.

"I wanted another child, a little girl, but you said we couldn't afford one, like money was all that mattered." She drew herself up straighter. "Then we came to Emersville, and I was offered a chance to have a daughter. She would be special, would change life on this god-forsaken planet for the better." She pointed to the Queen. "She promised to take care of us. We would have enough money for you to retire. Money to send the boys to college. Our lives would have been set." She looked at Frank, at his transformation, and whispered, "What choice did I have?"

"That's why you were at the lake," I said. "You knew they lived under the water, but you didn't know how to reach them. You dove in it trying to find them. You thought they had Frank, and you came to ask for his release."

"Of course," she said angrily. "He's my husband. I love him. I had to try."

"I can't believe it," Toni said. "You turned against your race for a baby?"

Kerry whirled to confront Toni. "You're no better than me," she said. "You did the same."

"Not knowingly," Toni said. "*Never* knowingly."

Conrad Hunter trained his gun on Frank. "Enough of this pathetic family drama," he said, and pulled the trigger.

"NO!" Kerry jumped in front of Frank. The bullet punched a hole in her chest. Blood immediately soaked her shirt.

Frank grabbed his wife. "*KERRY!*"

Gasping for breath, Kerry touched the boney ridge that had formed on Frank's forehead. "I'm sorry," she said, then her eyes closed, and her head slumped back.

Kerry Swinicki, along with the unborn child in whom she had placed so much hope, left this world for another, perhaps better, existence. I prayed the daughter she had never known would find her way to her mother's side. Love and madness were often intertwined, and I would not condemn my one-time friend to an eternity of the latter.

The gunshot's echo faded. Frank's eyes snapped to Hunter. A growl escaped from his throat. Dropping his wife, he launched himself at her killer.

Hunter fired, again and again. The rounds bounced harmlessly off Frank's newly armored hide.

Landing on Hunter like a fury released by the gods, Frank's claws sank into Hunter's chest, his teeth bit into the man's neck. Hunter let loose a gurgled cry and dropped the gun.

"She was my wife!" Frank roared, his voice barely recognizable. *"She was my wife!"*

Frank's alien muscles flexed, ripping Conrad Hunter's chest open until his still-beating heart could be seen. Frank tore at Hunter's flesh, his claws digging at the man, until Hunter's heart stuttered, then skipped and jerked, and finally fell still.

Frank dropped the corpse and turned to the Queen.

The little girl finally showed fear. She attempted to flee, to dart past the worker bees, but Frank snatched her by the hair. Shrieking, the Queen kicked and thrashed. Mouth parted in what might have been a smile if he'd still had lips, Frank calmly tore her head from her body. Gouts of blood flew from her exposed neck. He tossed the decapitated head across the room, turned to the red-haired scientist, and quickly disposed of her.

The worker bees fled in terror. He moved to follow.

"Frank," I said. "Stop."

He paused. Beneath his clothes I could see ridges, much like the one on his brow, rising up along his spine and the back edges of his elongated limbs. When his gaze fixed on me, I couldn't help but shudder.

"Leave," he said in his guttural voice. He reached down and casually ripped the hand from Hunter's body and tossed it to me. "Go now. Use the hand. Take the elevator."

Holding the hand made my skin crawl. "What about you?"

His human eye blinked. "I will not leave this place."

"The virus?"

He nodded, and his alien smile seemed to widen. "Savior of the human race."

My heart sank. He was going to sacrifice himself. "How?"

"Proximity locks," he said, his voice little more than a rasp. He seemed to be having trouble breathing. "Destroy them. Release the energy. Maybe enough to destroy the lab."

I recalled my reluctance to have the egg's metal analyzed, fearing an energy release that would be disastrous. I thought back to all the machines I had seen down here.

My heart started to race.

* * *

Frank and I stood at the door to the Conveyance. We had gathered more than two dozen boxes of proximity locks, enough to hopefully implode the cavern, the lab, and everything else in here.

I traced the symbol Couttis had used on the door, understanding now why he had let me see it. The sky-blue material faded, exposing the wormhole machine.

Frank, his body hunched, his breathing labored, struggled

forward. His transformation was almost complete. He was now more alien-reptile than man. I hoped he had enough human left to finish the job.

"Go," he said. "Toni. Escape."

I'd sent Toni back to the cavern with the hand. If I didn't return, she was to find the elevator and leave. She fought me on it, but in the end, I played the mother card. She had another life to consider.

"Come back," she'd said tearfully. "Don't make me do this alone."

Then she'd turned and left.

"Frank—" I said but stopped. The rest of my words remained stuck in my throat. He was my best friend, and I would never see him again.

Frank shook his head. "No. Save mankind." He made a hitching noise, as if he was choking on the air. "Hero." He tried to laugh. "Finally got my point!"

It took me a moment to remember the craps game from years ago, how we had gotten thrown out of the casino because an inebriated Frank had insisted on getting his *fushin point*.

"Yes," I said, my voice breaking. "You did."

Frank bumped the door with his head. With his body twisted, he had to stand on all fours. "Open."

"Are you sure—?"

"Open!"

"All right," I said, and traced the symbol again. The door's unearthly chill disappeared, only to be replaced by a searing heat. Energy from the wormhole, I assumed. "There you go." I put a hand on his shoulder. "We're below the lake. Remember the methane? It should help finish the job."

Frank nodded, then turned his attention to the Conveyance—the wormhole machine. I thought I saw a hint of awe in his alien face. "Leave," he rasped. "Hurry." He cocked his head. "Take care of boys. Love them."

"Jesus, Frank," I whispered, tears filling my eyes "How am I supposed to do this? I can't leave you behind."

"Toni. Baby." He prodded me with his head. "Go."

"But—"

"Go," he said again, and a single tear rolled down from his still-human eye. "Go, please."

I saw what he had become, and what small part of him still

remained, and my strength failed. He was right. I needed to look after my family, and his.

"Okay. I'll go, but know this: your boys will one day understand. I will tell them about you, and the sacrifice you made." I paused. "Try to give Toni and me enough time to get away from Emersville."

"Yes," he said. It was more a hiss than a word. "Go."

I wiped at my eyes. How did you say goodbye to a person who meant so much to you? I guess the easiest way was best. "Goodbye, my friend. I love you."

I quickly turned to go. I made it several steps before I heard his voice for the last time.

"Paco."

I turned.

He held the opened cigarette pack between two clawed fingers. He tossed it to me and gestured for me to go.

Good Christ. It was more than I could handle. Weeping for my friend, I ran.

Behind me came the scrape of boxes being dragged across a floor.

* * *

Toni and I raced out of Emersville.

There'd been no way to save the people in the cavern. Most were drugged and couldn't be woken. Besides, I suspected they had more than one scientist among them, someone who could recreate the virus. Harsh as it sounded, it was better to let them die.

"How far away do we need to be?" Toni asked, her hand absently rubbing her belly. Her mother's instincts had already taken over.

"No idea," I said. The speedometer slipped into triple digits. Thank god the road was straight. "We just keep going."

After a few moments of silence, Toni let out a sob. "I can't believe this."

"What?"

"I'm showing. I have a baby bump," she said. "I can feel her. She's moving."

I did the math. "That's not possible."

"The IV. Whatever they were giving me was supposed to accelerate her growth."

"How far along do you think you are?"

"I don't know, end of the first trimester?" She paused. "I'm scared. What if the drug did more than make her grow faster? Can they understand human physiology well enough to accomplish it without horrible side-effects?"

"Let's hope not."

More silence, then Toni said, "There's bound to be aliens who survived. People out of town or something. They could start this all over again"

"Without their base, I don't know what more they could do."

"And the—"

There was a loud pop, and the car lurched toward the embankment. I jerked the wheel around, hoping to straighten it before it fell into the ditch. Another tire blew. I slammed on the brakes. The car skidded to a stop inches from a fall that would have caused it to roll. I killed the engine.

Toni was gripping the shoulder harness. "What the hell happened?"

"The tires blew. I didn't see anything on the road, nothing that would have cut them."

A scraping sound came from underneath the car. It slowly travelled up the driver's side. More scraping came from the passenger side.

A doll climbed into view, grinning evilly from the other side of the window. A second doll emerged opposite Toni. Their metal claws were extended, scraps of rubber clinging to them.

More dolls converged on the car from every angle. Soon it was covered.

"What do we do?" Toni said, panic in her voice.

I locked the doors. "Stay inside. I don't think they can get—"

The dolls began clawing at the car, their weirdly elastic-yet-indestructible wire nails peeling away threads of metal and glass. If there had been two or three, I wouldn't have been too worried, but there were so many. Layers of the car came off like hard cheese in a grater. At this rate, it wouldn't take long for them to tear it apart.

"Drive away," Toni urged. "Start the car and drive away."

I cranked the engine but it wouldn't turn over. I kept twisting the key while I swore and cursed and kicked the floorboard. Nothing worked.

"They must have done something to the starter," I said.

Toni put her hand protectively on her stomach. "I won't lose my baby. I'll tear each one apart before I let them hurt her."

The car was slowly but methodically being torn apart. I searched the dash for a cigarette lighter. Maybe if I could burn something, make a fire large enough to catch the dolls on fire.

The rear window shattered. Dolls began pulling away chunks of glass. Two dropped into the back seat. More pushed their way into the car.

"Get out," I told Toni as I prepared to fight, not that I had much of a chance against so many. "Run, find your way back to Rock Mills."

Toni shook her head. "I won't—"

"Leave!" One of the dolls leaped at me, its claws digging into my face. I grabbed it and threw it at the others. "Save our daughter!"

"Brad—!"

"*Go, goddammit!*"

Crying, Toni nodded and reached for her door handle.

The ground suddenly rumbled. From the direction of Emersville, the sky lit up a bright, brilliant blue.

Seconds later, the car surged forward, pushed by some invisible force.

Shock wave, I thought. Frank's done it.

Another wave hit the car. The back end lifted off the ground.

I grabbed the steering wheel. "Hang on!"

A third wave hit, and the 4Runner flipped. Toni screamed. I held tight to the steering wheel. The car tumbled off the side of the road, rolling, jarring us, and came to a stop when it hit a tree.

Toni and I hung upside down, suspended by our safety harnesses. I could hear her breathing heavily.

The dolls emitted a high-pitched shriek that hurt my ears and fell limp. Smoke rose from several. The bitter stench of ozone filled the air.

"Toni, honey. Are you all right?"

"I don't know," she said. "The door, it's jammed up against me. I can't move my arm."

I fumbled for the harness release, found it, and dropped heavily to the roof. I barely acknowledged the pain. I found Toni's harness release and let her down slowly. Soon we were standing on the road.

Smoke could be seen rising from the distance.

"The dolls," Toni said, her voice shaking.

"Whatever Frank did must have destroyed them." Either the locks or the alien minds residing within them.

I pulled out my cell. We barely had a signal. I reported our accident. We were told to stay put, that an ambulance would be there as quickly as possible.

I hung up with the dispatcher. "Let's find a place for you to sit. This may take a while."

We found a patch of grass beneath a large oak. We had been sitting for perhaps a dozen minutes when Toni stiffened. "Brad, something's wrong."

I froze. "What?"

"I'm bleeding."

I scrambled around to face her. "Why didn't you tell me you were hurt? How bad is it?"

"That's just it," she said, and began to cry. "I think I'm miscarrying."

The End

REVELATION

A Forever Man Novel

Brian
W. Matthews

CPSIA information can be obtained at www.ICGtesting.com
Printed in the USA
BVOW08s1322170616

452476BV00001B/21/P